Ever Wonderful

D1446788

Ever Wonderful

KIM LOUISE

ARABESQUE®

If you purchased this book without a cover you should be aware that this book is stolen property. It was reported as "unsold and destroyed" to the publisher, and neither the author nor the publisher has received any payment for this "stripped book."

EVER WONDERFUL

An Arabesque novel

ISBN-13: 978-0-373-83030-5
ISBN-10: 0-373-83030-0

Copyright © 2007 by Kim Louise Whiteside

All rights reserved. The reproduction, transmission or utilization of this work in whole or in part in any form by any electronic, mechanical or other means, now known or hereafter invented, including xerography, photocopying and recording, or in any information storage or retrieval system, is forbidden without written permission. For permission please contact Kimani Press, Editorial Office, 233 Broadway, New York, NY 10279 U.S.A.

This is a work of fiction. Names, characters, places and incidents are either the product of the author's imagination or are used fictitiously, and any resemblance to actual persons, living or dead, business establishments, events or locales is entirely coincidental.

® and TM are trademarks. Trademarks indicated with ® are registered in the United States Patent and Trademark Office, the Canadian Trade Marks Office and/or other countries.

www.kimanipress.com

Printed in U.S.A.

To The 1 Plus 1

Acknowledgment

So many people to thank, so few memory cells! Well, here goes... Thank you to Tammy and Jerry for making me feel right at home and answering every question I had about the ways of ranching. Thank you to Connie Crow and Kurt Bolish for sharing their life experiences with me. Thank you to Heartland Writers group—the HWG brainstorming group and my HWG critique group for helping me with the nuances of life in western Nebraska. Thanks to Victoria Alexander for helping me with plot points. I have to give a great big shout-out to Niobia Bryant, Melanie Schuster and Lisa Harrison-Jackson. I want to be like you all when I grow up.

Thank you to all the Exodusters and homesteaders who came to Nebraska during the great migration and left such a fascinating legacy.

And finally, thank you to my creator. I love you and I'm listening.

Chapter 1

Ariana MacLeod sprinted across the grass to where Tony Jara struggled against gale-force winds to seal the shutters of her ranch home.

"Got 'em!" he said. The wind turned down the volume of his voice and although he stood right beside her and shouted, he sounded half a mile away.

"It's not the house I'm worried about, it's them!" Ariana shouted pointing to her cattle. From her home's vantage point at the rise of a Nebraska bluff, she could see nearly all four corners of her three-thousand-acre ranch. The sight was typically peaceful, serene, pride-inducing. But the sudden violent windstorm had her hundred head of cattle huddling, looking for shelter and trying the barbed-wire fence.

"Are you sure you locked all the gates?" she asked Tony.

He slid a nail sideways and hammered it down against the shutter. "Yeah! They're locked up good."

"What about the s-south point?" she shouted over a gust that stole her breath and made her gasp.

"It'll be fine!"

"So you fixed it?"

Tony jogged over to where one shutter had come loose and swung wildly. He slid the nail down. Hammered it into place.

Ariana stepped up beside him. "Tony!"

"I didn't get to it, but—"

Before he had a chance to tell her, "It's not that bad," Ariana was off—furious at the way life often dealt her a fit whenever she thought her world had calmed down.

Just when she believed her ranch was ready to sell—lock, block and livestock—fate turned Tony into a half-handed hand, and Mother Nature sent her a windstorm.

Ariana sucked air, but it barely did her any good. No sooner had she pulled air into her lungs than the wind snatched it out, or blew so fast and so strong she couldn't pull enough air in. Still she ran. Toward the range, past the silo, past the feed troughs.

Her cattle grew from rusty red dots on the horizon to red Angus, a couple thousand pounds each with individual markings she knew by heart.

Barely able to breathe, she ran around to the most vulnerable part of the fence—the part where her prize Angus loved to crash through. The darn thing hadn't injured itself badly, but Ariana's fence had been in bad shape ever since. Tony had promised to fix it every day since it first happened.

That had been two weeks ago.

"Get back!" Ariana shouted to the frightened and disoriented cattle, but the wind caught her order and flung it aside like a thin leaf.

Tony ran up beside her. He brought a hammer and his bag of nails. Ariana snatched the hammer and they went to work.

"I'm sorry!" he said. "I should have taken care of this last week!"

"Yes, you should have!" Ariana said, but she didn't think he heard. The wind had invited its cousins thunder and lightning to the party.

"It's a dry storm!" she shouted anyway, hoping he heard.

Dry storms were the worst. The animals understood rainstorms. Rain made sense. Rain was normal. Natural. But dry storms typically meant that something somewhere was way out of whack. And typically, sooner rather than later, Ariana would find out what.

"But the rain is coming!" Tony said, pulling a long white slat into place and holding it.

Ariana took a nail, bent over and hammered it down. "I know!" she said and tested her handiwork. It wasn't the best, but under the circumstances, it would have to do.

She and Tony worked quickly. He positioned the broken and displaced slats; Ariana hammered them together.

By the time they heard the great crash, she'd thought her herd would be safe.

The sound came from the southern edge of the pen. Even over the gusts as strong as Samson, the crash was tremendous. Tony started and frowned. "What the hell?"

Neither of them waited for an answer. They rushed

over to the south end. No sooner had they gotten there than they both stopped short.

The great willow, the largest tree on the Sugar Trail Ranch, had fallen over. The upper branches had crashed into the south corner of the fence. Ariana's breath snagged in her throat when she saw the dark figure struggling in the undergrowth.

"Uncle Jesse!" she screamed and took off toward the calamity.

The wind whipped around her waist, grabbed it like a strong arm. Nearly lifted her off the ground. She fought, flung herself free and ran on.

Wet air pummeled her face and arms. Dirt and debris struck her skin and stung her eyes. She squinted and ran on.

Ariana's voice echoed in the storm around her. She made the words *slow down* and *watch out* barely audible in the torrent.

Her herd, all hundred head, had huddled together against the back fence. Her heart pounded against her chest like an anvil. She knew their thousands of pounds could easily push out the wood or crush it. Frantic, arms flailing, she willed her sprinting feet to slow to where the old willow had fought the wind and lost and crashed down upon the south end of the fence.

"Uncle Jesse!" she shouted as if the Angus could hear her, understand her, come to her when she called.

Her vision swept the pen quickly, methodically. Even in the gale, her eyes were sharp, cataloging tag numbers, markings and body shape. One glance and she knew.

"Uncle Jesse's gone," she said to Tony, finally.

The ranch hand stood at her side, gasping. Finally, he bent, grabbed his knees and sucked air.

"I'll go!" he said.

Ariana was already pulling branches from the debris of her fence. She stopped to steady herself, fatigue finally catching up with her. "No. See if you can clean this up. I'll go get Uncle Jesse!"

Tony shook his head. "The storm's too bad!"

"That's why I need you here. Try to keep them from runnin'.

"Besides," she added, starting to run toward the road, "Uncle Jesse don't like you!"

Before she realized it, Ariana was running faster than she knew she could. She wondered if the Fates could be so cruel. To let her get so close and then take away everything that she'd hung her entire future on. Her mother had told her time and again, "Never put all your eggs in one basket." Well, Ariana hadn't been one to listen too closely to anyone, including her mother. Uncle Jesse was the key to her future. And Selena's future. She was so close to that future, her mind had seen it in perfect and minute detail. A normal life. Not one that smelled like manure or buzzed with the flies and gnats so constant in her world.

Wanting to be prepared for anything, Ariana grabbed a rope from the barn and her shotgun. She jumped on her horse Sirocco and rode out toward the edge of her ranch.

Her soul had touched her new future. Her spirit had felt it—heard it like a song. Her being had smelled the new air of it. But if something had happened to Uncle Jesse, well, she wouldn't allow herself to think about that.

"Jesse's just wandering…again. That's all. Spooked

by the gusts," she bragged to the wind. Not somewhere hurt, injured or just plain confused by the storm. Ariana was determined to find the Angus, bring it back and secure her future.

Chapter 2

Brax Ambrose squinted at the phone in the passenger seat of his F-350. He'd turned the ringer off, but that didn't stop the damn thing from lighting up and vibrating every time a call came in.

He turned away, focused on the fog-saturated road and the debris he'd been avoiding for the last half hour. Instead of driving past the storm zone, he'd come into the thick of it. The blowing trash had doubled, the fallen branches had tripled in size and his phone was still buzzing.

Freakin' *Honey*. It had to be her. No one else had the nerve to call him while he was on—damn, it even pained him to think about it—vacation.

Before the light on his caller ID screen flashed for the last time, Brax snatched the phone from the seat and answered it.

"Fort Calhoun," he said.

"What? That's eight hours away. You can't be eight hours away. You said you'd be here by three and it's almost two!"

"Cheer up. I'm just outside of Sidney coming up on Kimball."

"Don't play with me."

Funny. He didn't think he was playing. He wanted to see if she was really serious about wanting him there. If her reaction to his comment had been neutral, he might have taken that as a sign that, as usual, Honey's *emergency* wasn't really an emergency at all. That would have been just the excuse he needed to drive down to Arizona and see the sweet-smiling cashier he'd met at the Interstate 40 truck stop once.

Since he and his years-long companion, Hazel, had split, Brax kept his mind away from women. At least until he could figure out why Hazel had really kicked him out.

"Are you there?" Honey's voice called across satellite pulses and cellular energy.

"I'm always there for you, Honey," Brax crooned.

"Don't be sarcastic!" she responded.

Brax held the phone away from his ear, then dialed down the volume. "Look, I'll be there in less than an hour. I promise, as soon as I set foot inside your house, we'll—hold on!" he shouted, dropping the phone. He grabbed the steering wheel with both hands and yanked it to the left, just as a large branch rolled off the side of the highway and out into the road.

Anyone watching would have thought Brax was the star of *The Fast and the Furious 4, 5* and *6*. The truck swerved and slid toward the opposite lane on the two-lane highway. The closest oncoming car was about a mile off, but Brax moved with quicksilver speed to correct the careening truck and get himself back in the right lane. His cell phone tumbled to the floor along with an Earth, Wind, and Fire CD and an empty coffee cup.

None of that stopped Honey. Her voice blared up at him even from beneath the passenger seat. "Brax!"

With his heart slamming against his chest, he reached down and picked up the phone.

"I'll see you when I get there," he said. Instead of giving her time to reply, he turned his phone off and snapped it closed.

The road was much more difficult to navigate now. Some kind of terrible storm hit this area like an Ali right cross. Brax turned off the music—right in the middle of "Serpentine Fire"—and turned on the radio, searching for a local news station.

He and the other drivers on the road took turns avoiding obstacles, sometimes straddling the center lane to maneuver around blown tires, two-by-fours and branches split away from trees.

He finally found a radio station and the tail end of a discussion about a severe windstorm that had hit the area just the night before. According to the broadcast, barns had been toppled, old trees blown over and windows crashed into.

Mother Nature had turned the world upside down and shaken it. Dumped out all the loose change out of her pockets.

Brax hoped against hope that there was no part of the road that was just plain impassable. Not only would it be a rotten start to his *vacation*, but Honey would be so out of sorts, he didn't think she'd be able to rein her emotions in.

It was a curse, he thought, passing by a dilapidated barn. He and Honey had this thing about their emotions being strong, running deep and at times making them crazy. Over the years, he'd gotten real good at keeping the lid of his emotions airtight. But Honey was the exact opposite. Her emotions shot out of her pores, twisted up her face, widened her eyes or raised her voice. She could hide nothing. He, on the other hand, could hide everything. Thinking about Hazel, he realized that maybe he hid his emotions too well.

Another five miles and both the debris and fog started to clear. Large branches were replaced by twigs, shrubs and the occasional street sign, like the one that read Cheyenne 46 Miles.

Brax breathed a bit easier knowing the end of his trip was close. Funny, on the road, driving trucks for fifteen years, he had experienced a different kind of tired. One that came with the exhilaration of making money, running his own business and taking care of that business. So he'd thought that driving from his home in Savannah to Cheyenne, Wyoming, would be a piece of cake. He'd learned quickly that it wasn't. There was no load to drop and none to pick up. Just his sister and all the drama that came with her.

He hoped that one day she'd learn to take her heart off her sleeve and not take everything so personally.

But if she did that, she wouldn't be his sister. The one he loved. The woman he would help and protect no matter what. He just wished that she didn't need help so often or so frantically.

And he wished—

A flash of blue up ahead caught his eye. A woman clad in denim rode a black horse toward the highway. She was shouting something. One arm waving toward the sky, her hair flying in long golden-brown waves behind her head.

If she didn't slow down, she'd run right out into the road just as—

The crash came so fast, Brax didn't have time to react or recover. It felt as though he'd hit a brick wall. He wondered if he had until a brilliant pain sliced through his shoulder. Brax wanted to hold on to the steering wheel. He really, really wanted to. But the pain forced him to let go and his truck slid past the *brick wall* and came to rest on the side of the road.

Brax didn't know how much time had passed. Not much, he guessed. There was no ambulance and no passersby pulled over to offer help. Despite the wooziness in his head, he released his seat belt and felt the rush of blood return to his shoulder like a hundred tiny feet sprinting through his veins.

"Aggh!" he said as the pain in his shoulder stabbed him again and again.

He opened his door and stepped out of the truck to assess the damage and find out what he'd hit.

"Uncle Jesse!" a female voice called. Brax turned to see the woman in blue jump down from her horse and run past him. She stopped and knelt by the large bloody body of the largest cow Brax had ever seen. The woman knelt nearly draping herself over the animal's crumpled body.

"Oh, God. Oh, please." She rocked with anguish for a few seconds. Brax regained his senses and started over to help.

"Hey," he said.

The woman didn't move at first. Then she lifted herself from where she'd ridden down to the animal lying in a pool of blood. "Please tell me you have a cell phone!"

"Yes," Brax said, staring at the strange sight. He trotted back to his truck, located his phone and turned it on.

The woman reached out for the phone, hands shaking, covered with the animal's blood.

She pulled back her hands. Tried to steady them. "I can't dial it. Can you?"

"Yes," Brax said, noticing the twinge in his gut. The pain in the woman's eyes looked as though it were a human being dying on the side of the road instead of the animal.

She gave him a number and went back to soothing and consoling the beast. Her blouse was soaked through with blood.

"Hello?" the voice on the line said.

Brax had no idea who he was calling. "I got this number from a woman. There's been an accident. I was driving on Interstate 40 and hit a cow. A woman asked me to call this number."

"Tell him it's Uncle Jesse," the woman said.

Brax took a deep breath, watched for cars. "She says to tell you it's Uncle Jesse."

There was a long pause and then, "Oh, my Lord. Where are you?" the man asked.

Brax looked around for a mile marker. "Mile marker 49," he said.

"Tell Ariana I'll be right there," the man said and hung up.

Brax walked over to where the woman knelt over the bull. The animal's breath was labored. Bright fear widened its eyes. It snorted and raised its head.

"Hold still," the woman said.

Brax didn't know why, but he pressed against the animal's shoulders and together they somehow kept it from moving, jumping up or making its injuries worse.

"Yours?" Brax asked, at a loss for words but feeling a need to take the woman's mind off the fact that if the blood pooling quickly beneath the animal's head was any indication, it was dying, and fast.

"Yes," she said. "Since birth."

Could something this big be a family pet? Brax wondered.

Brax had driven though enough cattle country to know that the massive beast beneath his hands was a red Angus. One of the best breeds in the country. Brax admonished himself silently for the split second that he imagined Uncle Jesse as a twenty-ounce porterhouse.

And then it dawned on him. He'd hit several thousand dollars' worth of merchandise. It could have taken a serious chunk out of someone's livelihood.

Sadly, he realized that the worst thing that could happen was for the animal to live. He'd have a miserable, mangled and painful existence to be sure. Brax wouldn't wish that on anyone—not even an animal.

The woman, Ariana, looked up. It took him a moment to see them...rolling slow, wet tracks down her face. Her nut-brown eyes grew dark with pain, and Brax felt her pain stab his heart.

The woman dragged herself up and the animal reared its head to follow. Brax held the thing still, surprised at the warmth and power of the Angus despite the fact that parts of its body lay twisted and cut open.

When Ariana returned with a shotgun in her hand, Brax's body filled with the sense of acute danger. In her state, he could take her gun and all if it came to that. He'd knock her out, take the gun and wait for the cops. Then she raised the shotgun and realization closed down like a cold fist in his gut.

Brax stood up and stepped back. The animal struggled then, trying to get up, get away from the misery. But it was too mangled, too weak and had lost too much blood.

The highway was strangely empty. The wind picked up a bit, blowing the leaves on a nearby maple and bending the sunflowers on the grassland around them. A perfect Friday afternoon, except for the smell of blood and death riding the air.

She put the animal down with just one shot between the eyes. Brax would never forget the way her aim never faltered, the way the animal's head hit the pavement with a slick thud or the way Ariana whispered, "Good-bye," just before she squeezed the trigger.

He knew that no matter what happened to him the rest of his life, he'd never be free of the haunting look in her eyes afterward or the feel of her body against his as she shook gently and cried while he held her.

Chapter 3

By the time Brax pulled into the driveway on West Seventh Avenue in Cheyenne, Honey was on the front porch, waiting. The expression on her face bordered on murderous. For a hard second, he longed for the days before he knew he had a sister and a brother. Ten years of foster care and only-childhood. He'd moved around. Nothing stuck. And for sure, he didn't have sibling troubles.

Brax stepped out of his crunched truck, surprised that it still ran. He put one long, tired leg in front of the other, his shoulder smarting. He loved his sister, but she had issues.

"Well?" she said, the word stabbing the air like a blade. "You sure took your time about getting here."

He didn't say a word. Just waited to see how long it would take her to notice that his shirt and the top of his jeans were splattered with cow blood or to acknowledge that the front end of his truck was bashed and clobbered.

"That's just like you. Any excuse not to come see about—what the hell happened to you?"

"I had an accident."

She glanced from him to the front of his truck. Part of Uncle Jesse's flank still claimed the front of his bumper.

"Good God, Brax. What the hell did you hit?"

"Angus."

"Oh, damn."

He sat on her front stairs. "Tell me about it."

She ran a hand through her rust-red hair. "Why don't you tell *me* about it?"

Tired from his trip, but still filled with adrenaline, he recounted his story.

"Good thing she shot him," Honey said. Her voice held no emotion and very little compassion.

Brax stared at his sister. He was born first, but he was only older by ten months. Technically, they were the same age, but since he'd found out that he had a sister, he'd looked upon her as his younger sister. He lifted her chin and stared into her eyes. "Just because something—or someone—is down doesn't always mean that they're out."

Brax glanced around Honey's high-end neighborhood. These folks certainly weren't down. Close-knit, newly built houses with lawns that looked like they'd had a coiffing instead of a mowing.

He glanced back at his sister, who sat on the stair tight-lipped. He expected a fight or at least a challenge. He got neither. Instead his little sister surprised him and said, "Come on, let's get you cleaned up. Then we'll see about your truck, and then I'll call my lawyer."

"Hold up," he said, standing. "What's the lawyer for?"

"You hit someone's property."

"That's what insurance is for. But Ariana should be calling her lawyer. *Her* insurance company. I don't want to sue, I just want Big Bertha fixed."

"Big Bertha. Uncle Jesse. You two are cut from the same skein. She pretty?"

"Don't," Brax said. "That's how I got started with Hazel."

Brax walked into Honey's house, remembering how he hadn't paid that much attention to Hazel until he'd mentioned to his sister that he was consulting an accountant about his business plan. And then came the questions. "Are you sure she knows what she's doing? Who else has she represented?" When Brax mentioned that she was a sister, there was only one thing Honey wanted to know. "Is she cute?"

From that moment on, he couldn't shake that question from his mind, until he saw her. And then he'd decided that, yes, she was cute. And not only that, but smart, funny, intelligent and good-hearted. Just the sort of woman he could get comfortable with. At least for a while.

That *while* had lasted ten years.

The dramatic change from neat, clutter-free porch to untidy, messy, straight-up junky house jarred him from his memories back into the present. He thought he'd left the sight of strewn debris behind him.

He was wrong. Very wrong.

Honey came back from the bathroom with a set of towels and a bar of soap. She'd maneuvered around the mess like a pro. Like she saw it and didn't see it at the same time.

She looked up at him with eyes liquid with pain and pleading for help.

Suddenly, he realized that his sister was really serious this time. She really had experienced an emotional crack.

"I'm sorry I'm late," he said.

As soon as the words left his mouth, tears rolled quickly down the front of her face.

He took a deep breath. Brax wasn't the most touchy-feely man on the planet, but his sister needed to be held. He opened his arms, wrapped her inside them, blood and all. She sobbed softly.

He held tighter, getting blood all over her designer originals. "I'm here now. Tell me everything."

Ariana flung the wooden chair against the kitchen wall, missing Tony by half an inch. He jumped away just as the wooden pieces went flying.

"This is not helping," he said, brushing giant splinters off his left arm.

"I just can't believe it."

Anger choked off the rest of her words. She wanted to curse the universe, fate and the man who'd single-handedly set her future back by at least a year.

"How can you not see a cow that weighs two thousand pounds?" she asked. She was pacing now, wearing out the already-worn kitchen linoleum.

"Ariana—"

She slapped her palm against her forehead—the sound sharp in the early morning air. "An Angus, Tony. Big as a barn. And what about the signs? They're all over. "Cow crossing. Cow *crossing!*"

The anguish and disappointment welled up inside

her—over the lump in her throat and straight into her brain to make her already-existing headache worse.

Tony had finished picking up most of the chair mess. "He obviously couldn't stop. Otherwise, he would have. Right? He could have totaled his car or been killed."

"Well, he and his car are fine. Me, on the other hand," she said, sitting in one of the two remaining and intact kitchen chairs, "I'm screwed."

Brax paced his sister's large, three-bedroom home with guilt riding his soul. His *baby* sister was really hurting this time, really in personal pain, and he didn't know how to help her.

He picked up a blue blouse from the couch, a red one with long, flowing sleeves from the high-backed chair and knew that Honey's life right now was just as messed up as her living room. Just as out of order and messy.

Damn, I hate cleaning, he said to himself, then slowly, methodically began the task of at least getting her clothes in a pile next to the washing machine. He'd consider actually washing them tomorrow.

While his sister slept, he considered what she'd told him. It seemed he wasn't the only Ambrose unlucky in the love department. Cliff, Honey's on-again, off-again love machine for the past five years, had finally had enough of her mood swings and decided that it took more than chemistry to make a good relationship. Brax and his sister had fallen into the same basket. The one with all their eggs in it. Neither of them had a plan B or had ever imagined that they'd need it. While Brax had used his pain and frustration to build a trucking business, his sister seemed to be floundering in her own self-pity.

Brax followed a trail of towels to the bathroom, picking them up like bread crumbs.

Housework! He despised it. When he and Hazel split, he'd hired a housekeeper as soon as he'd moved. Kuri. She was wonderful. And Japanese. Didn't speak a lick of English, but knew how to spit-shine a toilet. Brax recoiled as the piles of clothes, towels and other fabric items he didn't even recognize multiplied like rabbits. She must use everything once and then toss it.

Yep, he figured, picking up the fifth pair of red socks, his sister was right on the line between creative and crazy. He'd come just in time to make sure she didn't tip over into the wrong side.

When he walked into her kitchen and saw a mountain range of dirty dishes, he wondered if he might be too late.

He closed his eyes and prayed that this was the last time he would ever do dishes, even though all he was really doing was loading the dishwasher. If he had to pay a thousand dollars per office visit, he'd make sure that his sister got the help she needed to get her out of the funk she was in. And if he had to raise Kuri's pay by a thousand dollars, he'd make sure that she'd keep right on keeping his house.

I love my sister, he thought, *but damn, I'm never doing this again.*

Brax took a break and tried to watch the game. His mind wouldn't let go of the image of the woman on her horse. If he hadn't wanted to console Ariana so badly, he might have been attracted to her. Might have wanted to see what she looked like beneath the tight jeans and snakeskin boots. Might have wanted to untie her hair, set it free in all that wind. Stick his hand in the thickness of it and grab hold.

But he wasn't attracted. Mildly fascinated maybe. And what he wanted from her, he wanted soon—information on how quickly her insurance company would make the repairs on his truck. He needed to be ready to leave at a moment's notice. He'd left his brother, Collin, in charge of the company, and although Collin claimed to care and be business-savvy, Brax knew better. He knew his brother had only come into the business because he thought it was easy money. To Collin, *working* with his brother meant collecting a paycheck for just showing up. Only Brax had other plans. He'd left a to-do list a mile long, every item on it designed to teach him something about the business. Enough to provide his wayward brother with some badly needed marketable skills. Talk about a rolling stone. Collin had no idea what he wanted to do with his life—although every six to eight months, he declared in large capital letters that he'd finally found his calling. He'd look into his newfound passion for a few weeks. Then as soon as he discovered that his new *calling* took work, hard work, and wasn't nearly as easy as he'd imagined, he'd back away from it and flounder again until he became smitten by something else.

The Celtics scored a three-pointer from way downtown. Brax took another drink from his beer and cursed the foster care system. It had seemed to make a mess of his siblings' lives. He closed his eyes, thinking how sad it was that they were all adults and not one of them was truly happy. Brax had a fairly new trucking business that was going well, but as for grinning with happiness, he was far from that. All he could say at this point in his life was that he wasn't unhappy.

Brax closed his eyes, tuned out the game and the thoughts of discontent. His mind was heavy—and not just because he was tired from a long night of driving and the accident.

His life was weighing on him—pressing down. He couldn't get a grip on it. He was free again. A bachelor. He could come and go as he pleased. No attachments. No accountability. He could date—several women if he wanted. Buy a truckload of Trojans and go crazy. He could pour his all into his business and work seventy-hour weeks if the desire struck him.

But the thought of those things came without the smallest spark of excitement. Just a yawn, a turn of his head and troubled sleep.

When the phone rang, Brax bucked up like he'd been thrown from an angry steer.

He cleared his throat, checked the time and reached over beside him to pick up the receiver, thinking that it better not be that bastard Cliff calling to start trouble. Brax brought the receiver to his ear, thinking of several ways to handle his sister's *business*.

"Hello?"

"Hello. This is Stuart Willows, arbiter of Shoresville. I'm calling for Brax Ambrose."

That was quick. "This is Brax."

"Mr. Ambrose—"

"Brax."

"All right. Brax. I'm calling with regard to the accident you had yesterday."

"Yes."

"You told Ariana MacLeod that you're with State Farm Insurance."

"That's correct."

"Do you know if your policy has comprehensive farmer's liability?"

The muscles in Brax's hands tensed. Balled them into fists. "I'm not sure. Why?"

"We'll need to verify a method of payment if you're not covered."

"Why would I pay for my own repairs?" Brax asked, irritation deepening his voice.

There was silence on the other end, then a shuffling of papers, and then, "Mr. Brax, you're liable for the Angus you hit. Uh…Uncle Jesse was a prize-winning—"

"I know all that," Brax said. Anger tightened his throat. His pulse roared in his veins. He'd made the mistake of giving Ariana one of Honey's business cards in case she needed to reach him. All morning she'd choked his sister's fax machine with information about Uncle Jesse. It was too much. He'd stopped reading after the cover letter.

"Well, what you may not know is that when you hit a free-range animal, not only are you liable for the value of the animal, but in some cases the residual profit the animal would have garnered, so for Uncle Jesse—"

You have—

"—that comes to—"

—got to be—

"—five thousand, six hundred—"

—kidding me!

"—fifty-six dollars and eighty-three cents."

"Holy sh—"

"Who's that? Cliff?" Honey's groggy voice snuck up behind him. She'd come downstairs. He hadn't even noticed.

"No," Brax answered.

"Yes," the arbiter said.

Brax choked back a barrage of expletives. "I wasn't talking to you."

"Well, you should be, Mr. Brax. This is very serious. You've taken away a significant piece of my client's livelihood."

"You can't tell me that cow is worth six grand."

"Not just a cow, Mr. Brax. A red Angus."

"You want dinner?" Honey asked.

Brax waved her off. He couldn't think about eating now. And if she had any intention of serving beef, he was likely to hurl it against the wall.

Brax hadn't been driving trucks for fifteen years without learning a few things, like the fact that ranchers and farmers had to keep their animals locked up good. And when they didn't and they were in an accident, it was the rancher's fault. Plain and simple. To hell with the Cattle Crossing signs. Ranchers had fences for a reason. And obviously Rancher Ariana had been slippin'. Well, he'd be damned if he'd pay for her neglect.

Brax decided upon another approach. "Give me all your information," he said.

He took down Mr. Willow's information to relay to his insurance company. They ended their conversation on a civil note, but there was no way *he* was paying six thousand dollars. And with his business just starting, no way could he afford this kind of expense. He'd poured all his money into getting his trucking business in the black. Dipping into his reserves right now could wipe him out. He couldn't risk it.

"I'll put some steaks on!" his sister called from the kitchen.

Brax's stomach clenched up. For a meat-and-potatoes man, this incident was enough to make a brother turn to tofu.

Brax turned his frustrations from the call to his sister's home. It wasn't the best cleanup job, but it would do. At least the clothes were off the floor and furniture, the dishes collected and ready for the washer and books, magazines and mail stacked in rows ready to sort. The only mess he didn't mess with was the items off her home-based business...Web-order sex toys. There were boxes from floor to ceiling in every room with gadgets, creams and condoms. Most things he recognized, but there were a few devices so strange he couldn't imagine what they were for.

When she'd first told him about her business, he'd thought she was a little loose in the head. Then she told him how much she made in a month and he had a quick change of attitude.

Honey needs a housekeeper, he thought, sitting down for the first real moment since he'd arrived. He wiped a thin film of sweat from the back of his neck and the tops of his arms. *Guess there's a reason they call it chores.* Brax couldn't remember the last time he'd done anything close to housework. It must have been during his bachelor days. And he hadn't been a single man in many a year. Before Hazel, there was Tracy. Before Tracy, there was Cynthia. Before her, there was—damn. Brax realized that it really had been some years since he was a single man.

He got himself a beer from the fridge, turned on the sports channel and propped his bare feet on his sister's ottoman. There was always some woman. Waiting or showing just enough interest for him to pursue. Eventually, he found himself in the comfortable relationship with a woman who wanted nothing more than to take care of him and be taken care of. For a man on the road, that arrangement worked well. He'd pay the bills. His woman would keep house. And when he came home, they'd made wild, damn-I've-missed-you love. And the whole thing would start again.

Only Hazel eventually wanted more.

She wanted a husband. She wanted children. She wanted a family. Brax took a slow draw from the long-neck bottle, thinking about how much he didn't want those things. He'd known since he'd graduated from college and watched his close friends pair off and marry that marriage just wasn't in his blood. Companionship. Loyalty. And all the sex you could handle. Yes. But being tied to anything—anyone—permanently turned his stomach sour as if he'd swallowed a gallon of milk three weeks past its expiration date.

No sooner had that thought entered his head than another nudged it right out.

Ariana MacLeod.

Even distraught and covered with blood, she was one feisty, hot, long drink of woman. As the image of her flared up in his mind, Brax ran the fat part of the bottle across his forehead to cool himself. His skin tingled where the glass touched him as if the memory made it sizzle.

Chapter 4

Brax drove toward Shoresville, Nebraska, while tension tightened like a fist inside his head. He couldn't believe it. Couldn't freakin' believe it!

No insurance.

He had no auto insurance on his truck. Against his much better judgment, he'd let his brother, Collin, hire his neophyte girlfriend, Shyla, as an office assistant for their trucking company. When it was time to renew insurance for the business trucks, Brax asked the woman to renew the policy for his personal truck, as well. Luckily, she'd gotten the business part taken care of. But Brax believed that between scheduling the important things like her nail appointments, pedicure appointments and hair appointments, renewing his auto insurance had faded like cheap perfume.

Idiot! he chided himself. He should have taken care

of it. But his brother was *in love,* and they were both trying to give the woman a chance when what she really needed was a trip back to the brain factory.

As soon as he'd discovered the oversight, he'd called his lawyer. Their first conversation gave Brax hope.

"What are my options here, Jack?"

"Well, a driver should have a reasonable expectation to a thoroughfare without private obstruction."

"Man, in English! I'm too edgy for legalese."

"Even in cow country, you should be able to drive down the street without it turning into a cattle obstacle course. Ranchers have to keep their animals in check."

Brax let go of his frustration. Just a little.

"There are exceptions to every rule. Let me do some checking and call you back."

Brax had hung up hopeful. Until Jack Mathis called back in less than an hour.

"I may have spoken too soon."

Brax had stopped pacing and cleared off the couch where boxes of super ribbed condoms, motion lotion and something called a Joy Stick from his sister's Web-order business had taken over the area.

"What is it?" he asked.

"That part of Nebraska is free-range. Cows are like pedestrians. They can come and go as they please. Ranchers have to post signs to that effect, but it's pretty much up to the driver to avoid a collision. And if you do hit a free-range animal...to put it in *English*...that's your ass."

The remainder of Brax's frustration came out in an explosion of expletives.

He blew out a long hot breath and tried to think

clearly. "You said there are exceptions to every rule. What about an exception to that one? I mean, it was foggy. There'd been a storm. If there had been signs, the storm took them out, because I damn sure didn't see any."

He was up again. Walking, stepping as best he could between edible undies and something that looked like you stuck it up—

"Unless you hit a bull."

"What?" he said, hope daring to rise up inside him.

"A bull. Ranchers have to keep their bulls corralled. Something about their temperament and controlling breeding stock. You said a cow. Did you hit a bull?"

"Yes," Brax said. "And his name was Uncle Jesse."

Brax borrowed his sister's Porsche, insisted that she show him her insurance papers and kept them on the passenger seat beside him as he drove into Shoresville. Along Highway 30, he checked the roadside for Free Range signs. So far, he'd only seen one and it was knocked down—obviously from the storm. He was being ridiculously thorough, but he didn't care. Once he learned a lesson, it stuck. He wasn't one for repeating mistakes.

With cornfields behind him, cattle to his right, open prairie to his left and an empty two-lane road ahead of him, he planned his strategy. He'd go in and play his two aces. No signs and a loose bull. Jack had faxed him the ordinance information and Brax had taken a picture of the downed Free Range sign he'd passed on the way in. If everything went quickly, his insurance wouldn't even come up. Just how long would it take before an adjuster came out to assess the damage to his truck? Heck, his shoulder still smarted from the accident. He might even throw in a request for physical therapy.

Ariana's life—the beautiful, serene, citified one she'd planned—was crumbling to pieces faster than she could repair it. Uncle Jesse was dead, she was late for her appointment and if that weren't enough to upset her world, the man who'd hit Uncle Jesse had the nerve to threaten a countersuit when he was clearly in the wrong.

Ariana tried to focus but she was too busy thinking about what was in store for her. A look over her shoulder and she saw a brand-new Porsche parked in the driveway. The Wyoming license plate told her it belonged to Brax's sister.

The arbiter's car was in the lot, as well. Ariana imagined that city hall hadn't seen this much action since Curtis Derkins caught his wife in bed with the postmaster and decided to spray-paint the word *fornicator* on his white pickup. Well, after this afternoon, she suspected Kimball county would have plenty to talk about when word got around that Ari MacLeod cussed out the man who hit Uncle Jesse.

Just thinking about his carelessness made her want to break another chair. She stepped inside, taking a deep breath, and prepared for battle.

Ariana smiled, feeling a strange sense of anger and calm. She was angry because this whole business of fighting or protesting his fault was just plain stupid. Brax Ambrose was in the wrong and he would pay. Willows would see to that. Knowing that she was absolutely and completely in the right brought her calm. She would take the money from the settlement, make major repairs on her property instead of the minor ones she'd planned and hopefully she could still get her asking price.

Ariana entered the building. It looked the same as the day she'd first walked into it with her mother. Ariana must have been seven or eight years old. She remembered thinking that the place looked like a giant schoolroom with the wooden floors, chairs and desks, and the large flag flying from the tall pole just outside the front door. Every time she'd come into the building since, she'd half expected to see children running at the sound of the dismissal bell with books and backpacks in hand.

But there never was any of that. Just a long hallway, exposed painted radiators and creaky floors. She followed the creaks to the meeting room and stepped inside.

She noted thickly painted iron grates and old, overly waxed wooden floors. The building smelled like dust and layers of cheap floor wax years thick.

Ariana's boots struck the gleaming floor like hammers.

She walked into the room noting the time, 1:57. Already an hour behind, she didn't have time for this foolishness and didn't see the need for a face-to-face, but Willows insisted. Said that there were "extenuating circumstances" that were better negotiated in person. He wouldn't go into detail, but she could only imagine that instead of using his insurance company, Brax must have wanted to pay her himself. And that meant installments. Well, she didn't have any room in her schedule for "arrangements." Her ranch had to be ready for sale by fall. That gave her just three months to get everything in—

Order was the word her brain searched for and it

came to her mind, after the words *whoa, Nelly, hot damn, sweet Lord* and *mmm, hmm.* She stopped short at the sight of the man taking up all the extra space in the small, confined meeting room. Willows pummeled into her.

"Sorry," he said, grabbing her so that she didn't fall.

"My fault," she said, remembering why she'd come. It certainly wasn't to ogle a man who was too good-looking for words, she didn't care how much the sight of him made her pulse quicken. He had a white T-shirt on that fit him like skin and showed off every ripple and contour of every muscle in his chest and upper arms. And if his khaki pants fit him any more snugly at the thighs, the reinforced seams would burst. The man was tall, thick and solid as a tree. His body belonged to a football player or heavyweight boxer. His face belonged to a deep-thinking man, a handsome man with penetrating eyes, a square jaw and a mouth that could stop a stampede.

"Thanks for riding over, Ari. This shouldn't take long," Willows said.

Brax's eyes caught and held Ariana's. She felt warm and flushed as if she'd been surrounded by sunlight. She pushed a stray hair back from her face and yearned for ice water. Her anger and calm vanished. In its place came a hot rush of curiosity and apprehension at the sight of the man standing near Willows.

He was the same person she remembered from the other night, but at the same time he wasn't. In the brilliant light of GE rather than the foggy haze of panic, he looked like a man—a decent man. Not an irresponsible maniac like her mind had made him into. He was standing by the window, as if looking out, but his eyes said otherwise. His eyes told her, as he turned and held her gaze, that he was fully aware of everything going on in the room.

The room shrank with each second that ticked with the lock of their eyes. The man took up so much space and exuded so much confidence, Ariana fought a gasp and a twinge of nervousness. No, this wasn't the man from the other night at all. That man was a careless idiot.

This man was sure of himsclf and for a split second she thought he was sure of her, as well.

"Shall we?" Willows said, gesturing at chairs at the table.

Ariana and Brax sat down at the same time in chairs directly across from each other.

"As you both know, since the accident, Mr. Ambrose has maintained that he's not at fault. What we need to decide today is how the damages for the accident are going to be settled."

"What's to decide?" Ariana asked. "I faxed you a copy of the amount. I brought another copy with me if you need to see it again."

She fished the folded paper out of her back pocket. It clearly listed the full amount due. The value of the Angus, certifications of her worth, notifications of prizes it had won. Ariana had honestly itemized the list. There was no padding. No gouging. Just the worth of the Angus. Its value to the ranch.

Brax blinked like he had sand in his eyes, "What does that say?"

"It says 'prize-winning female.'"

The moment Brax heard the words, anger, disappointment and apprehension grappled for control inside him.

They all won.

His face went to stone as he contemplated taking a substantial sum of money out of his reserves to pay for a prize-winning female cow and for repair to his truck.

The woman, soft-eyed and beautiful though she was, set her jaw and crossed her arms. "Go get Mary."

Willow's eyes widened with alarm. "I don't think that's a good idea."

Brax's caution antennae went up. "Who's Mary?"

The arbiter loosened a blue tie that had seen better days and tossed his pen on a blank notepad. "Mary Shane is the law around here."

"A cop!" Brax said, shifting in his seat, wondering how a dispute over oversize roadkill had gotten so out of hand.

"No. We have a sheriff for that. He means the legal authority," Ariana said.

Brax would have preferred the cop. He'd heard too many long rumors and watched too many B movies on small-town justice. Since Shoresville wasn't even a blip on a Midwest map, he couldn't even imagine what he might be in for. *Shyla is fired,* he said in his mind and prepared to concede defeat. "Look, why don't we—"

"Mary!" Willows yelled. He'd looked back over his shoulder and called out toward the doorway.

"I told you not to bother me!" came a woman's irritated reply.

"Hey, Mary!" Ariana said.

"Mornin', Ari!"

"Can you pop in for a sec?"

Sounds of a chair scooting back, wooden legs against wooden floor traveled through the thin walls. A grunt and then marching sounds. Brax ran a hand down his face.

The woman stomped into the meeting room—all four feet six inches of her. Her smooth dark chocolate skin and hard eyes belied her age, which Brax would put at about fifty. She planted her hands on her hips, and all Brax could think of was a fire hydrant.

"Willows, damn it! Can't you do anything by yourself?"

"Mary, we just need a little clarity, is all," Ariana said, before the man could answer.

"What kind? He hit Uncle Jesse. He pays for Uncle Jesse."

"Mr. Ambrose believes that because there were no free-range signs, Ari's at fault."

"Mr. Ambrose is wrong."

Brax swallowed. The woman still hadn't taken a seat.

"Call your insurance, Mr. Ambrose. They'll—"

"No insurance," he said, deciding to take the high road.

"No insurance!" they all said. But it sounded like a moan of anguish coming from Ariana. She got up. Turned toward the only window in the room. Her face was drawn tight, her eyes full of pain.

"Then you write a check," Mary said.

"I'll pay in installments. We can work out a payment plan."

Ariana whirled around. "Installments won't work. If I don't have Uncle Jesse, I at least have to have Uncle Jesse's value or it will take me until hell freezes six times to sell the Trail."

"I'll put down a large deposit," Brax said, annoyed. The three Shoresvilleans in the room had turned to each other and all but shut him out.

"When were you looking to sell?"

"Now. I wanna be out of there by the time school starts for Selena."

"So, early fall? This is June." Mary counted on her fingers for emphasis. "Three months, will that work?"

"I need cash now. There's still so much that needs to be done on the place. Uncle Jesse was just gonna make all that easier. But now I might have to sell the Trail as is."

Brax felt like a volcano with a lid nailed on. He stood up to get their attention. "Hey," he said. "You want to include me in these three-month plans?"

The fireplug of a woman gazed up at Brax—eyes wide and appreciative. "You're a big dude. Thick, too. And sweet on the eye."

A vein at Brax's temple throbbed impatiently. "I'll need longer than three—"

"Here's your answer, right here," Mary said, grabbing Brax's arms. The woman had a strong grip.

"Do you mind?" he said, looking down on the woman's salt-and-pepper hair and dark eyes that had softened.

"I don't if you don't, honey." Mary smiled, let go and took a seat. "Brax Ambrose, I hereby sentence you to three months of hard duty on the Sugar Trail Ranch."

"You what?" The woman couldn't be serious.

"Unless you want to write a check today." Mary wore a smug smile, and her eyes danced with determination.

"You can't do that."

"It's done, Mr. Ambrose. Ari needs a fixed-up ranch and you owe her about six large. Considering interest and the mark this could make on your driving record, you're makin' out pretty good here."

Now it was Brax's turn to walk to the window. Stare

out into the countryside. Could he leave his brother in charge for three months? Damn, he hadn't thought about interest. Putting in the work would allow him to keep his reserves and only use what he needed to repair his truck.

"Silence is consent around her, Mr. Ambrose."

"No," he said, turning to face his accusers. "My *word* is my consent."

"Ari?" Mary said.

Ariana gave Brax the most thorough once-over he'd ever received. He was being sized up for durability. But there was something else, too. An intensity in those caramel-colored eyes of hers that woke up his libido and made him think of strong whiskey and soft skin.

"Yeah," she said, finally. "With Selena going to Grand Island, I could use the extra hand."

"Willows! Where's my gavel?"

The man, who'd looked on for the last few minutes with apprehension riding his pale features, scrambled through drawers in a file cabinet.

Mary shook her head. "Never mind," she said, then slammed her fist against the wooden table. "This agreement is official and binding. All parties, et cetera, et cetera. And hereby agree to et cetera, et cetera, or until such time as I am in the mood to hear you in my court again."

Mary turned, shook hands with everyone and left the room the same way she entered…stomping.

"You know anything about ranching?" Ariana asked.

"No," Brax admitted. "But I'm good with my hands."

He was big, she'd give him that. Solid. Packed. Not a scrap of fat on him. A delicious brown wall of muscle. She had no doubt he could do the work, even if he wasn't used to it. The piercing determination in his eyes let her know he would not go down easy. She glanced at his hands. They were unscarred, unlike her own.

Well, that was about to change.

"You'll start tomorrow," she said.

"I'll start today. I want to get this over as soon as possible."

She gave him a once-over. Mary was right. Brax was really sweet on the eye. She imagined him in a Stetson, on a horse with the bluffs and sunset as a backdrop. Nah. Too much of his smooth brown face said *city*. The muscles in his arms bulged from iron and not hammers or shovels. Gym work, not a day's work in the sun. "You won't last two weeks," she said, disappointed in the whole situation. No Angus and no money. Her ancestors were punishing her because she wanted to sell the ranch. Well, damn it, she would have a better life than that land could ever give her. She and Selena. Ariana would make sure of it.

"I may be many things, Ariana, but a slacker or a quitter is not, nor has ever been, any part of who I am. Now, you can give me directions to your ranch and I'll meet you there—" he said, moving toward her.

He was going to need a *big* horse, she thought.

"—or we can leave together right now."

Ariana smiled. He was determined. She'd give him that.

"Let's go," she said.

Chapter 5

"Let me tell you about the ranch," Ariana said, as Brax stepped inside her black truck. She'd followed him to his sister's house and waited outside the few short minutes it took for him to throw clothes into a suitcase and come back outside.

He looked at her, trying to stare softly. After so long as a self-employed truck driver, he had no experience with *working* for someone. And not only that, but a woman he found attractive.

She was silky brown-skinned with a cup of warm milk stirred into her complexion for good measure. Her hair was long, wavy, light brown, and her eyes were the most mysterious shade of amber he'd ever seen. He wouldn't mind looking down into them for a nice long stroke of nighttime.

"...so, it's been in the family for four generations.

Her eyes were so round, he knew they belied her age. She looked twenty-five, so that meant she was probably thirty, no more than thirty-five. With those voluptuous lips and angular nose, he wondered who she took after most, her mother or her father.

"Okay, how many are there?"

He blinked at the sudden change in her facial expression. "What?"

"Freckles. How many freckles do I have? You look like you're counting them."

Brax smiled. He could have counted them. Maybe one day he would. "Right now I'd say seventeen. Give or take five or six."

"Oh, a smart-ass," she said, turning her pickup onto the highway.

Brax fastened his seat belt. "Pretty much."

"Well, that makes two of us."

They shared a laugh and she tossed him a friendly smile.

"Look, Ariana…I really didn't see Uncle Jesse until it was too late."

She nodded, kept her eyes on the road.

He decided he'd better keep his eyes on the road. Before he ended up counting other aspects of her body in addition to her freckles.

It had taken Ariana twice as long to get ready that morning. She'd actually run a styling brush through her hair, smoothed out her unruly eyebrows and put on some clothes that were less worn and more snug. And there was no getting around why she did it.

Brax.

He was a mighty handsome man. It had been over a year since she'd taken notice of a man in the way she had him. Most of the men she encountered, neighbors, guys in town, the hired hands, well, she thought of them more like tools than anything else. It was a shame, but it was true. When she looked at their bodies, her mind started to imagine them in relation to tractors, backhoes, augers, fences—things they could drive or fix. But when she'd seen Brax's body, her mind imagined it naked and in close relation to hers. Also naked.

Like her mother and her mother before her, Ariana had come to think about men in terms of what they could repair. And in those rare moments when she could no longer stand the stress and the urgency to be close to someone, Ariana would turn to a friend in town to cool that part of her nature, so she could get on with other things—more important things like raising her sister and taking care of her land.

She hadn't felt randy, needy or sex-empty in quite some time. She'd had way too much going on—repairs, the Angus show, breeding and the eventual sale of the ranch. It usually wasn't until the fall, when things slowed down just a touch, that she'd start to feel pent-up and frustrated. She had a pattern then. She'd ride down to Buckey's, order a beer, play a round of pool with Edny and a few other locals. Then she'd usually end up with Stew, one of the perpetual bachelors of Shoresville. It'd become like a ritual. Everyone in the town knew what it meant when she showed up in the local bar come October. It was just her way. And she liked her way.

Brax was messing things up…already. It was summer and she felt excited just by sitting next to him. And she had a hard time picturing him as just a tool. He wasn't some six-foot pleasure toy she could slide batteries in, use like she wanted, turn off and put away. And that's what really bothered her. Because that's what she found so intriguing about him. That beneath that brooding silence, there seemed to be a man as untamable and unbreakable as her land.

"What about you?" she asked.

"My brother and I own a trucking company. We're doing well except..."

His voice trailed off. He didn't want to come across as an angry man, but the fact that his brother let that little no-brain woman of his *keep the books* ticked him off every time he thought of it. If it hadn't been for her error—

"What?" Ariana asked.

"My brother is twisted over a woman who is, in my opinion, less than deserving."

"In what way?"

"She's an opportunist. If she'd done her job, my insurance would be taking care of you right now instead of—"

"You?" she said, cutting him of. Was that an innuendo? Was she flirting? He had to admit, he'd caught her appraising glances more than twice. She wasn't shy about showing interest. He'd give her that.

"Yes," he said and left it at that. He wasn't about to complicate his task by sleeping with the boss, although her lips and eyes and thighs made it damned tempting.

"So, you own a trucking company. What else?"

He sensed her unease. "I'm not Jeffrey Dahmer. I work hard. I work fast. As soon as my debt is paid, I'm out."

"Fine by me," she said.

Brax chided himself for not liking her response. "Well, what about you? How do I know you're not some crazed spinster? Nebraska Chain Saw Massacre and whatnot?"

She didn't laugh this time, she giggled. Just a light quick sound. Rolling out of her lips and then it was gone, all but the smile. "I suspect my reputation speaks for itself. Folks around here will probably tell you I am part spinster. But I'm also a hard worker. A fast worker, and when you're done, I'll be so glad to sell the Sugar Trail I won't know what to do with myself, except take the longest bath in the world."

Her eyes looked dreamy. Thoughtful. There probably wasn't much time for indulgence and pampering on a ranch. Brax could only imagine work, lots of hard, unending work. After sitting behind a desk for part of the last two years, he was actually looking forward to getting rough with his body again. Drawing his muscles up, sweating. There was a benefit to this fiasco after all. The work would do his body good.

He slid a glance in Ariana's direction and thought, *real* good. "So, ranch life. Is it like all the stereotypes?"

"Well, since I don't know what the stereotypes are, I don't know. But we work hard. That's the truth. We work. Unlike you city folks, we don't have forty-hour weeks. We don't get paid overtime or time and a half. We work until the work is done, and then we get up the next day and do it again. And the work is part of us and we are part of it."

Ariana extended her arm and offered him her hand.

At first, he didn't understand. And then he saw them. A quilt of calluses. He took her hand between both of his and rubbed his fingers across her rough palms. The calluses were deep. Like they'd grown up with her for years. Probably had names, personalities. But there was something else. He could tell that despite the thick, rough layers of skin, she took care of her hands. The calluses were tough, but not rock hard or crusty. She must do something every day to keep them from turning into concrete.

Strange, he felt her hands as if he was trying to read her life. Like a fortune-teller trying to divine the future. Like a blind man reading braille. The uncharacteristic roughness of her hands intrigued him. Women were supposed to be soft and smooth and tender. But this woman was obviously rough and tough and strong. He wondered what the peaks and valleys of her hands would feel like on his skin.

"That's what it's like, Brax," she said. He heard the care in her voice. Saw the passion in her eyes and wondered...why in the world would she want to sell that away?

He looked for other signs that she was as rugged as she appeared. But the fact that her pickup was clean and neat spoke volumes. She was feminine. Somewhere buried beneath her jeans, cowgirl swagger and work-worn hands was a woman—a woman he was looking forward to working hard with under the sun and sky.

"You play poker?" she asked.

"Sometimes."

"Well, that's good, 'cause you sure got the face for it."

Brax grunted. Gave her a sideways glance. He was insulted.

"Not that you are ugly or anything. Far from it. It's just that, well, your face doesn't move much. It's not like it's dead. Just stuck."

Another grunt.

"You could be on ESPN poker tournament with that face is all I'm sayin'. What is it that you do again?"

"Truck driver."

"Not much call for a poker face in that line of work, now, is there? Well, what's that like?"

He crossed his thick arms over his wide chest. "Quiet," he said.

"Hmm."

Ariana waited a beat, then, "You always been a trucker?"

"Always."

"Ever haul cattle?"

"I've managed to avoid that aromatic load."

"Cow stink. There's nothing like it on the planet. Most days, I don't notice it. But every sweet June or so, I get a whiff—a good one. The kind that makes my eyes water and I remember what it's like to be new to this stuff. Just taking it in, you know?"

Brax nodded, but he really didn't know. He had no idea what it was like to be really new to something. His trucking business was like driving, but with more paperwork and longer hours. The only new thing in his life recently was being alone. And he was going to savor that newness every minute that passed.

They continued driving on the dirt road. Ariana passed first one truck, then another and then a car. Each time, she stuck a finger up in the air. The gesture was returned by the other driver. Brax figured it was an acknowledgment, like some truckers did. A nod or a wave. A *we're all in this together* kind of vibe. He liked it. People around here had their own code language. As a trucker, he could appreciate that.

"So, how much farther?"

"Not far," she said. She was so relaxed behind the wheel of her pickup, she looked like she'd been born there.

"Not far in the city means less than an hour."

"Out here, too," she said.

"So then, we're less than fifty minutes away?"

"Chill out, Big Rig. The Sugar Trail ain't goin' nowhere."

By the needle on the speedometer, neither were they. Hell, who drives twenty miles per hour? He didn't drive that in his own driveway.

Despite that, he relaxed a bit. He couldn't help it. The open space, big green hills and blue sky as far as his eye could see wouldn't allow him to stay tense.

They were on one of those off roads. The ones he often saw from the interstate and wondered where they went. He imagined to farms, ranches, small rural communities and backwoods homes. He found the fact that he was finally on one of those mysterious roads fascinating.

For an older truck, it sure rode well. He'd give her that. Good shocks, packed dirt roads and good driving. Even if the ride was long, it wouldn't be excruciating.

"What's left for this afternoon is checking the fence. You can ride, or walk if you're so inclined, the perimeter. Make sure there are no breaks or places where the herd has tried to get out or a coyote or mountain lion has been trying to get in. Look for weather wear or any spot that looks like it might be weakened. Most of us just strap on a tool belt. There's bound to be something somewhere. Fix it as you go if you can. Or just tuck it in your mind. I got two ranch hands. Either Tony or Red can go back and fix it tonight or first thing tomorrow."

Brax knew one thing for sure. He would learn fast and work fast. He was no rancher, he was a trucker. The sooner he got back to his business, the sooner he could put things right in the admin department. The first thing he would make right was *Little Miss Oops I Forgot.* He didn't care what his brother did in his personal life, but in a professional life that involved both of them, Shyla had to go.

Another index finger up. Brax couldn't resist. "Is that the Shoresville signal?"

"It's just somethin' we do 'round here. It's like sayin', 'Hey' or 'Good mornin'' or 'I ain't seen you in a month of Sundays. Why don't you stop by for dinner?'"

"Umm," Brax said, folding his arms.

"You got somethin' against being neighborly?"

"No."

"You don't elaborate much, do you?"

"No," he said, thinking of the many times women referred to him as the strong, silent type.

"Good. I wasn't lookin' forward to no long explanations 'bout why things have to be done the way they do."

Ariana glanced at him. Sized him up quickly, like she was sizing up a questionable situation.

"How's your back?" she asked, avoiding rut lanes.

"It's good."

"How are you with equipment, machinery, tools, fixin' things? Handy? You look handy."

"I can repair most any motor. Built a shed or two in my time. And I do all my own wiring."

"Good. This might not take too long after all. Now, what about dirt? You got a thing for bein' clean? 'Cause in this job, you gotta get *real* friendly with long days, dirt, mud, cut-up hands and funky armpits even with strong deodorant and lye soap. Can you handle that?"

"Piece of cake."

Ariana laughed at that. She laughed hard and hearty like they were out at a bar and someone had just told a raunchy—but extremely funny—joke. She sounded like one of the fellas. He expected her to pull out a cigar, slick it up and start puffing. Unabashed.

"Can't wait to see that piece of cake turn into humble pie," she said.

He didn't say anything. Didn't need to. He had no doubt working on a ranch was hard work. But he was used to hard work. He'd grown up with it. Every foster home he'd been in was different, but the hard work was the same. It was part of him. *Humble pie*. If there was any to be served, he damn sure wouldn't be the one eating it. If everything went his way, he'd be long gone by the time that pie started cooking in the oven.

"You'll need some gloves. Tony'll loan you a pair. You'll have to get some sturdier clothes. You look like a sunscreen kinda guy. You a sunscreen kinda guy?"

Brax turned from hill after rolling hill of cattle. The land was black with them. The smell was an overwhelmingly thick combination of dirt, bovine sweat, bovine waste and animal hormones.

Concern focused his eyes on all those cows.

"Don't worry," she said. "That's Hank Snooden's place. Got 'bout fifteen hundred head. Largest ranch in three counties. My spread's not nearly that big."

Relieved, Brax decided to keep his gaze inside the truck for a minute. With her legs gapped open the way they were, and her jeans as snug as they were, Brax could admire the muscles in her thick thighs. He had no doubt that she worked hard, but she obviously ate well, too. Probably moo-fresh steak every night. Rib-eye and eggs for breakfast. T-bone and salad for lunch. Porterhouse and potatoes for dinner.

Brax half smiled. He'd always liked a thick woman. To him they just seemed sturdier. Less fragile. More independent. The kind of woman who wouldn't need to call him several times a day while he was on the road. Just the kind of woman he'd consider hooking up with…if he were looking.

"So, no sunscreen?"

"I don't burn easily."

"Good. 'Cause I don't think there's a drop of sunscreen on my ranch. We've been working the cattle so long, our skin drinks the sun instead of fightin' with it."

He'd been to the cities on the east end of the state. *Cities* being the operative word. He distinctly remembered tall buildings, five-lane highways and rush-hour traffic. But this end of the state lived up to quite a few stereotypes. Corn, prairie and cattle.

"Where are the people?" he muttered mostly to himself, but loud enough so that she could hear.

"On the range. I guess you noticed, I haven't done my finger wave for several miles."

She waited a beat. Then continued. "Round here the ratio is 'bout ten to one—ten cows to every one person."

"You're sudsin' me," Brax said. But he didn't have

to be convinced. The next ranch did all the talking. In addition to "Where are the people? he wanted to ask, "Where's the land?"

He couldn't see a blade of grass for hooves, flanks and tails. Stomachs that looked like potbellied stoves and big, round, innocent-looking eyes. They were all mooing at once.

"Is it always this noisy?"

"Yes," she said without elaboration. Guess it was her turn for one-word answers.

Well, he could take what he gave. But he wanted to know more. "Even at night?"

"Especially at night. Cows are nocturnal. They don't really get going until about ten-thirty. You oughta hear them then, I tell ya—"

"You're lying," he interrupted.

"Round here we call it fibbing, but yeah. I made that last part up."

She chuckled a bit, and Brax said something completely unexpected. "Are we there yet?"

This time, she laughed. No, *belly*-laughed was more like it.

As Ariana turned from one dirt road on to another, Brax realized that his days at the ranch might be uncomfortable, but if he could hear that laugh once in a while, they would be bearable.

It was a spell, Ariana thought. It had to be some kind of spell. And she knew all about them, with one being cast on the women in her family.

She certainly wouldn't call Brax the most handsome man she'd ever seen. Ariana had seen plenty of good-looking men. Heck, Stew Ridley was the handsomest man in three counties, all the women said.

But this Brax…he was on an altogether different hill. And he reminded her about her mother's "passin'-through" stories.

"You best git you a passin'-through man. That's somebody you know for a certain period of time, and while you got 'em you have the grandest time. Then when that time is over, you let 'em go on they way. If you takes care of yo'self right, you ain't got to worry 'bout love, you ain't got ta worry 'bout no babies, and you sho won't have ta worry 'bout the curse."

Although Ariana's "passin'-through" man lived in town, she'd kept up with her mother's wishes.

And it worked. No curse, no babies and no love.

This Brax seemed like the passin'-through man to end all passin'-through men. Just somethin' 'bout him made her want him to work off his debt in bed with her. Forget tendin' to the ranch. Ariana needed tendin' to in a bad way. And as soon as she saw him smile at her joke, she'd fixed her mind on havin' him before he left for good.

She walked and sat like she'd just stepped down from the saddle. Legs gapped and slightly bowed, the words *cowgirl, rancher woman,* and *bronc wrangler* wrestled in Brax's mind for accuracy. He was starting to get the feeling that he'd just been dropped into a completely different universe. One that didn't bother with time or urgency. It existed on its own terms without apology, explanation. Just like its landowner.

"I'll show you around the house first, get you settled.

Then we can go out to the pasture. The herd should be just about full by now."

Brax nodded and followed her into the ranch house.

"Ari!" came a voice wrinkled with age.

"Yes?" she answered, turning to the man who'd come up behind them.

Brax turned, too, and could barely believe his eyes. The old coot looked like a real-life forty-niner miner. Tall. Thin. No, brittle was more like it. Red Stetson, red suspenders and red pants. His four-inch white beard was so thick, it was almost nappy. If his name was Red, Brax didn't know how he would control his laughter.

"Ida's broke off," he said. His voice was wiped with sandpaper as if he'd smoked a pack a day for fifty years.

"I knew it was time. Tony watchin' her?"

"Ain't seen hide nor hair a' Tony all mornin'. Selena's with her."

Ariana slapped Brax across the shoulder. He winced.

"Guess you'll have ta change later. Come on.

"Brax Ambrose, meet Red Finley," she said.

The two men shook hands quickly as they left the house so fast, Brax didn't get a chance to get his laugh on. And the expressions on their faces told him now was not a good time to laugh.

"Who's Ida?" Brax asked. He wasn't sure, but being "broke off" didn't sound like a good thing.

"A cow. She calving late. We just need to watch and make sure nature takes its course the right way."

Red leaped up on his horse like he was sixteen years old and had just finished off three cups of coffee. He swung his leg up loose and limber and so practiced it was as natural as seeing the man blink. He trotted alongside them as they headed for a barn. Once there, Ariana stopped short. "Ever been on a horse?"

"Yes," Brax said, remembering the time he and his college friends lost their minds for a weekend. They had been celebrating Brax's birthday when someone—he couldn't remember who, hell, it might have been him—suggested that they pile into his friend Race's car and drive. And keep driving.

Fools that they were at that time, they did it, with not thirty dollars among the five of them. When they were too tired to go on, they pulled into a state park observation road and slept off their insanity. When they woke up the next morning, they were hungry and still adventurous. They ended up eating breakfast at the park lodge and spending nearly every penny they had going horseback riding.

That was the first and last time he was on a horse.

"Yeah," he said again, not wanting to seem ineffective and his work hadn't even started. "I can ride."

"Then saddle up," she said and jumped on a large black horse just as swiftly as Red had jumped on his. She pointed to a horse just as large with a white stripe running down the center of his face like a lightning bolt.

"Don't tell me," Brax said, stepping into the stirrup and swinging his leg up, "Lightning," he said.

"Run Amok. And this is Sirocco," Ariana said and trotted her horse off to where Red was barely holding his horse at bay.

"Easy, Three Socks. Easy, boy," Red cooed.

So, the old codger had a softer side. He looked like he could spit tobacco with one-hundred-percent accuracy.

Ariana's horse was all black except for a round spot of white right between his eyes. Red's horse, Three

Socks, was a soft reddish brown much like Run Amok. Instead of a streak of white down his nose, white rings rimmed three of Three Socks's legs.

Brax knew enough to kick Run Amok to get him going. The horse was warm and powerful beneath him. All flank and muscle, moving at a solid trot. Brax worked to keep himself from bouncing wildly or jostling off to the side. The muscles in his legs tensed and corded with the strain. He grunted as they headed toward the pasture.

"Helps if you don't fight it," Red said, leading his horse beside Run Amok.

"Hmm?" Brax asked, wondering what this constant bouncing would do to his backside.

"Don't fight it. You're gonna bounce. So bounce. Just keep your balance in the middle of ol' Amok's back there and you'll be fine. It's up to you to catch the horse's rhythm. Not vice versa."

Brax didn't know anything about a rhythm. He just knew that he wanted off the beast's back and on the ground.

Unlike the steer-blackened hills he'd passed on the way to Ariana's ranch, the pen they rode up on probably held a hundred or so head of cattle, with the exception of the calves, the smallest among them weighing at least a thousand pounds, although Brax pegged the Angus he hit at something like two thousand.

Their ruddy red coats and white faces made the calm intensity of their eyes stand out like big black pearls.

Against his own ego, Brax breathed a thin sigh of relief. Ariana's herd wasn't nearly as large as those they'd passed. The ninety days would be a cakewalk.

That must be Ida, he thought as they came upon a cow that had obviously separated itself from the rest of the herd. She was lying down and her stomach was so distended it looked like a miniature hot-air balloon. Only there was something in this round ball. It was moving and churning and pulsing with life.

The three dismounted. The cow struggled. A low rumbling of discomfort emanated from its throat. She was clearly in distress.

When she struggled to her feet and snorted wildly, Brax started and looked to Ariana and Red, who hadn't moved or said a word since they'd ridden up.

"Is she supposed to stand?" Brax asked.

"Yeah. They stand so the legs can drop. Once those legs get started, it's not long before the rest comes out."

"That gol'darn, Tony!"

"Why? What's a'matter?" Red asked.

Ariana jogged toward the fence. "There's only one leg!"

"Oh, sheista!" Red said.

Brax followed behind the old man, who was quick on Ariana's heels. In four-hundred-dollar Feragamos, Brax had to struggle to catch up. He was tired of asking questions and decided to just keep quiet and watch.

"I'll go find Tony," Red shouted.

"Like he'd get here in the next five minutes. We can't let her suffer."

"But the last time you tried to—"

"This is not the last time," Ariana called back as she entered the pen. She took off her blouse, revealing a gray tank beneath. Brax turned to Red.

"She gonna pull it out?" he asked.

"Nope," Red responded. "You are."

Brax looked Red up and down as if he'd just stripped naked and started dancing on a quarter.

"Don't give me that face. You came here to help out. So help out. Consider this your first job."

Brax was about to tell the man he'd lost his liver-spotted mind when a girl's shriek pierced the crisp quiet.

Brax turned to see a smaller version of Ariana run down the path and straight into the pen. "Let me help!" Mini Ariana cried.

Now it was Red's turn to give Brax a look. "I'm too old and they aren't strong enough."

Damn, Brax thought, and took off his shirt. Unlike Ariana, he wasn't wearing an undershirt and a sizzling June sun pushed against his back like big hot hands.

He stepped inside the pen and moved between Ariana and the Angus. Brax steeled his nerves and clamped his teeth shut, not believing what he was about to do.

"Talk me through," he said.

Chapter 6

False bravado, Ariana thought. Macho fool. Well, if he wanted to christen his first day on the ranch that way, then so be it.

It had been at least three years since Ariana had tried to pull a calf. And at that time, the calf had pretty much pulled her. She was thinner then, and foolhardy. She believed there wasn't a thing on the Sugar Trail that she couldn't do. So when Uncle Jesse got turned around at birth, Ariana had insisted on pulling her out. Her mother tried to convince her to let Tony and Red handle it. But she'd been stubborn and oversure.

Thirty minutes later, caked with wet dirt and gestational fluid and blood, Ariana still hadn't gotten the calf free. The only thing she'd done was distressed the mother and nearly killed the calf. Ariana realized that her mother was willing to sacrifice the young animal to help her daughter learn that she had limitations.

Her mother had always taught her lessons like that. And Ariana only needed to learn one time. In pulling a calf, there are some things only an experienced man can do.

"Selena, go find Tony," she said.

"I wanna pull the calf," her sister threw back.

Ariana saw so much of herself in her eleven-year-old sister. Too much. "Go, I said."

Selena grunted like a mare. "Who are you?" she asked Brax.

"Brax," came his dry response.

The girl stopped. Recognition pulled her young features into a question mark. "You hit Uncle Jesse," she said.

Brax's features hardened. *Yes*, Ariana thought. *Word gets around*. "Selena!"

"I'm going! But I don't see why you'll let the guy that hit Uncle Jesse try and you won't let me!"

"Because I love you!" Ariana shouted after her sister, who'd jumped on Ariana's horse and was galloping off toward the house. Brax gave her an inquisitive look.

"No offence," she said.

"None taken," he responded.

Ida looked like she was going to burst, rip or start running. She thrashed, shook her head and snorted like she had a june bug up her nostrils.

"Okay, we can't wait for Tony," Ariana said, stepping beside Brax.

Brax didn't know where the confidence came from, but he knew he was grateful for it. He was about to slide his arms into a place that was never meant for human arms. Ariana pulled something out of a leather pouch on Three Socks that she called a calf puller. She handed it to Brax. The thing looked like an anemic crossbow.

"Easy, now," he reassured the struggling animal. He held his arm out before him. An instinctive *I come in peace* gesture he knew the animal had no understanding of, but somehow, it made Brax feel infinitely more assured.

"Ida," Ariana said in a voice so sweet and silky smooth, he couldn't believe it came from the same woman he'd ridden to the ranch with. "This man here is gonna help you with your baby. Now, no fussin', no kickin', no getting upset and tryin' to run off. Ya hear? He's just gonna slide in a hand..."

Her stomach, wildly swollen, rolled from the inside. The hot sun and cool wind made a strange and unfamiliar contradiction on his back and chest. The rest of the herd mooed, snorted and moved off, giving the birthing cow plenty of room.

Brax nodded, took a deep breath, and slid his right hand into the opening on the cow where a bony leg poked through.

The cow snorted and shifted. Ariana and Red got into place to hold her down, but kept their hands soft and soothing. Smoothing her fur. Patting.

"Good girl, Ida. Now, he's gonna quickly feel around for the hooves and when he finds them, he's gonna take his other hand, wrap the chain and pull the legs through."

Brax set his jaw and did as she instructed. The soft, strong sensation of wet matted fur over muscle and long bone swallowed his forearm. He realized quickly that blood must taste the same way it smells and no amount of mouthwash would rinse the taste away. He breathed hard, pulling in dry air and pasture smells—pungent animal sweat, so sharp it burned the inside of his nose. Blood so thick with new life every cell had a fragrance.

His hand searched for the other leg. It was hard at first. The calf was slick from birth fluids and startled by his touch. As the calf jerked and resisted, Brax struggled to pull out both feet and get the chain wrapped. At one point, he lost his footing and fell forehead first onto the cow's flank.

Both mama and baby cow jumped. Brax kept his grip on the puller and their sudden motion gave him the leverage he needed. He pulled himself back to a squatting position, pulling the calf's feet with him.

"Good!" Ariana cooed. "Good job, Ida. It won't be long now, girl."

His hand, wrist, arm felt swallowed by a living, undulating tube of flesh and spirit. The urgency of life flowed between his fingers and surrounded his skin. He felt charged by it. Awed.

He didn't know if it was the mother's heartbeat or the calf's that pulsed warmly against the back of his hand. Maybe it was both of them beating together. A shared rhythm.

He sensed the calf's determination to live, to be born and to be free. He recognized the need for freedom. The urge to be loosed and unencumbered. Brax had lived with that desire his entire life.

"I gotcha," he whispered, so quietly he barely heard the words himself.

He was so lost in the feeling he barely heard Red instructing him, or his own thoughts. It was as if not just his arm had gone in, but larger parts of himself and he and the calf struggled together to inch out of the darkness. For a fleeting moment, he'd traded places with the calf.

He leaned back and started to pull. His arms smelled wild and gamey with blood. He stared at the cow's opening where two hooves now replaced one.

"He got it!" Red declared.

Ariana's expression—tight-lipped and close-mouthed—was none too impressed. "Hmmph."

After several minutes of steady pulling, nature took over. All three of them stood back and gave the mother cow room with her chore. She lay all the way down now and the opening widened with the struggling calf.

"Looks good," Red said.

Ariana wiped perspiration from her forehead. "What did Selena say…Usher?"

Red swiped at a bead of sweat and missed. "Yeah, after that singer."

"What if it's a girl?" Brax asked.

"Don't matter," Ariana and Red answered together.

Brax turned his attention back to the calf, on a swift mission now. Five minutes—the head. Another five—shoulders. Five more—an arched back. Then nothing for a while until its front legs scrambled, scampered and pawed at the ground until thc back legs slid out and the poor thing collapsed against the wet dirt.

Both mother and baby panted hard and fast. Soon the mother stood, a little shaky at first, then began licking the baby clean.

"A girl," Red announced.

Brax didn't know how fathers who helped deliver their children felt, but something in him swelled with pride about being present and having a literal hand in the birth of that calf.

Ariana and Red stepped away. Brax followed suit, his right arm covered with small clots of blood and amniotic fluid.

"When people say, *Don't have a cow*, they have *no* idea what they're really talking about," Brax mumbled. "So what happens now? Do you have to…do something?" The only birth process Brax knew anything about was the human one and not having any children, he only had a cursory knowledge of that.

"Now we wait until she's clean, walking. Help her nurse if we need to."

Sounded like they were going to be there for hours. Brax wondered if they were just going to stand and wait or whether they all took seats on the ground. He watched and followed suit as they gathered at the fence and looked on.

The mother tended to her newborn as if the whole world had shut down and been reduced to just the two of them. Brax felt a tiny twinge of revulsion in his gut as the mother's tongue lapped blood, mucus and chunks of who knows what off the young animal. But in minutes it was licked clean. As if on cue, the calf tested her legs less than half an hour out of her mother's womb. The animal seemed fearless as it tried again and again to gain footing. It would prop up its body, falter and fall, and tiny clouds of dirt would puff up around it. Finally, it struggled and stood, quivering a bit and mostly wobbly. This time it didn't fall and began sniffing the underside of its mother's body until finding and latching on to a teat.

The whole thing took all of thirty minutes.

"Welcome to the world, Usher," Ariana said.

The pride and awe on Ariana's face were unmistakable. She must have seen this happen hundreds of times, but her face warmed at the sight as if it were her first time ever witnessing a birth. The sight brought out a softer, more easy Ariana.

This Ariana was someone Brax wouldn't mind getting to know.

"Let's leave them be," Red said. He swung up on his horse a little slower this time and Brax realized there was only one horse left.

Before he could comment, Ariana was already up in the saddle.

"You coming?" she asked.

Brax walked over to where his horse had been waiting patiently beside a scrub bush and some trees. He picked up his shirt, stuck his feet in the stirrup, took hold of the saddle horn and swung up behind Ariana.

They were snug. His front against her back. A wave of contentment moved through him, quickly replaced by unease as he struggled with where to place his arms.

"Don't mind the blood. Just hold on," Ariana said.

Brax took one more look at the calf being licked by its mother's big, pink tongue.

Usher, he thought.

Red had said something about leaving them be. But after this afternoon, Brax's mind was already fixed on checking on the calf at the first possible moment.

"Ha!" Ariana shouted and snapped the reins.

The horse galloped off toward the house and Brax

had to hold on tight not to bounce right off the hindquarters. Real tight.

Hmm, he thought, trying to keep his teeth from clicking together and biting his tongue in half, this assignment might just have its perks.

Her waist was thick. Sturdy. Muscular. It flexed and moved beneath his arms in time with the horse's run. Synchronized power. Made him wonder which one came into this world more wild and untamed, the horse or Ariana. He had a feeling in his gut that before his ninety days were up, he'd have his answer.

Chapter 7

Brax's restless energy kept him from sleeping through the night. After a brief tour of the ranch house, Ariana had let him off the evening chores hook, so he'd taken that time to settle into his room.

He woke up several times during the night, muscles protesting, eyeing the round white clock on the nightstand with the round Day-Glo-green face: 1:00 a.m., 3:27 a.m. Finally, at 4:18, he got up, pulled on his jeans, slid his feet into his work boots and headed outside.

Ordered by the quiet, he walked softly down the short hallway and down the staircase. The stairs took a gentle turn to the left and then he was down and standing by the door.

A light from a post beside the front porch shone in through windows with valances but no other coverings. Anyone with a curious mind and nosy nature could look through every window in the place and see everything.

But he didn't guess there was much chance of that happening. Not in the middle of Nowhere, Nebraska.

He opened the front door thinking that he would walk around for a bit. Cool his restless energy and get calm before the day's work started. The moment he stepped outside, all thoughts of walking vanished.

He was so close to heaven he thought he could hear God planning his day. He couldn't move and believed for a moment that he'd forgotten how his lungs worked.

Maybe someone stole him during one of the moments he'd actually managed to sleep and took him to a brand-new galaxy—a part of the universe where the black and twinkle of the sky was almost even…and close.

How many stars were there? he wondered, then realized he could just stand there and count them.

"That's what everybody thinks," Ariana said, walking up beside him.

"What?" he said, playing along as if she'd actually heard his thoughts.

"Whatever you're thinking, that what all the city folk think when they come out this way."

She sat down on the porch step. Already dressed. Plaid shirt, jeans, boots. Hat in her hand. She crossed one thick leg over the other and hung her hat on her knee. "I don't pay too much attention to it, till I see somebody else lookin' up there like they can't believe it."

Brax took a seat beside her. By the time he added his backside to hers, there wasn't much room left on the step. "How do you forget something like this?"

"When you're raised with it, it just don't faze you much."

Silence fell between them. It seemed to push them apart despite their closeness on the step.

"You drive a truck. When you drive past mountains or come into a city and drive by them tall buildings, do you look up like you never seen 'em or do you just keep goin,' get to your destination and start again?"

Brax thought about her question. Played his routes in his head. Georgia to Wyoming. Georgia to Illinois. He'd certainly seen his share of mountains and skyscrapers.

"Yes," he said. "I look up. Every time."

Ariana turned to him. "Why?"

"I don't know. I don't do photos. My mind is my camera. In case what I see isn't there when I come back."

"Why wouldn't it be there?" she asked.

Brax didn't want to answer that question. Too many foster home memories. Instead he took a picture of the stars with his mind and kept most of the sarcasm out of his voice when he said, "What time does this party get started today?"

Brax went back to his room and hit the alarm before it had a chance to go off. Five a.m. It was still dark. Even the chickens, if Ariana had any, weren't awake. He grabbed a towel from the back of a rocking chair and hoped that the only shower in the house was unoccupied.

After yesterday, he felt pretty good about himself—pretty damned good. After the accident, he thought his shoulder would give him some problems. So far, he was wrong.

For his first order of business, before getting bogged down by chores, he had to check on things back home.

Instead of a bad feeling in his shoulder, Brax had a bad feeling in his gut. He made it to one of the ranch's numerous high hills and pulled out his phone.

He realized that the hardest aspect of working on the ranch would not be the work, it would be being away from his business. With the insurance fiasco, Brax had asked his brother to do a complete audit of all the accounting and account maintenance before he got back. He'd also told him that he wanted Shyla fired. His brother had agreed to his first request. The other, he'd refused. Well, if Miss Inept caused one more inexcusable problem, he'd make his brother pay with his own money and then either his brother or his brother's girlfriend would have to leave the business. He'd thrown down the gauntlet and Collin had picked it up with confidence.

"I'm telling you," Collin said, voice thick with bravado, "Shyla's cool. She just needs a chance."

What Brax thought she needed was a breast reduction and a brain transplant. He'd never met an African-American bimbo before, but Shyla could be the pinup girl for the species.

A lot seemed to be going on back home, but not much had changed.

Brax looked around from where he sat on top of Run Amok. They were headed to the highest hill near the house. In the early morning, Brax hoped he could get reception.

All his life, Brax had been detached from things, from people—his real parents, his brother and sister, a normal home life. Through it all, he'd adapted. He'd become transitory, thriving on the freedom that came from not being tied down and from letting go of what few roots he had. But now, for the first time, Brax wished the connections he had were stronger. With his brother. His sister. With his own life.

"On the range" literally meant he was *on the range*. Brax imagined tending to animals. Mending the fences, fixing equipment and inspecting tools that helped tend to the animals. Making plans to tend the animals and considering all the variables that can throw those plans off like too much rain or not enough. From gas prices and the changing attitudes Americans had on red meat to man-made clothing, Brax's head was full. And to have to spend time away from his chores to make sure all hell hadn't broken lose in Savannah was not his idea of how to run a business and pay off a debt.

But right now it was the only option he had.

"Whoa," Brax said, pulling back on the reins and bringing Run Amok to a halt. He flipped open his phone and prayed for a signal.

Thankfully, he got one. Even if it came with only one bar, he'd take it.

Quickly, he dialed the number. "Good morning. Thank you for calling Big Rig Trucking. This is Shyla. How may I—"

"Shyla, it's Brax. Where's Collin?"

"Hey, Brax. Have you turned into a cowboy yet?"

Shyla's voice cracked and snapped across a badly distorted connection.

"I can't talk now. I need to speak to Collin."

"Oh. Sorry you can't talk. I'll tell Collin you called."

Click.

The barrage of expletives spewed from Brax's mouth

with such force and vehemence, Run Amok turned toward him and whinnied.

"Yeah, me, too," Brax said and dialed the number again.

Before the call went through, Brax's cell phone rang. The caller ID said Big Rig Trucking.

"Collin?"

"Yeah?"

"You finish the audit?"

"Almost. We still have a few files to pull and then—"

"What do we need to fix?" he asked, impatience snapping his words like a whip.

Brax couldn't tell if the sudden silence was his phone going dead or Collin holding back. "Collin, my reception is bad. I'm on a hill."

"The Department of Transportation was here. They had a look at the logs and, well, there were some overtime discrepancies. Uh, let's see. Our number three truck is down. Blown motor. And truck one…we're still looking for it. Other than that—"

Brax didn't wait for the call to drop. He snapped the phone closed and shoved it into his pocket. He was too angry to do anything else.

"Get up!" he shouted to Run Amok, snapping the reins and steering him down toward the bottom of the hill. He gave it a swift kick and the horse took off at a quick trot.

Brax was stuck on a ranch, his own truck was busted and his business was going to hell in a bimbo's pink purse.

He clenched his jaw, realizing he probably shouldn't have hung up on his brother. He'd apologize later, after he figured out a way to salvage his life.

* * *

Ariana admitted to herself, he hadn't done half bad with that calf. He seemed a little too awed by it all, though. A big man like that staring on like he did. But she guessed it was good to know that he could be humbled if even for a moment or two when he thought no one noticed.

Ariana had gotten dressed that morning hoping for two things: one, that Brax had set his alarm, and two, that he hadn't hit the snooze button and gone back to sleep. But the five o'clock giddyup, as Red called it, was the hardest part for hired hands to get used to. Before Tony, hands came to the Sugar Trail with wide eyes and big dreams. They all thought ranching was John Wayne, country songs, pork and beans. Then when real life set in, along with raw hands, blisters, aching backs, endless mounds of fly-covered dung, they lost the taste for ranching and went back to the cities and small towns they came from.

Ariana headed toward the kitchen and decided that come dinnertime, she would call Judge Shane and tell her that she would need a plan B—another way to get reimbursed. Calf delivery or no, Brax would turn out to be like every other man who showed up on her land—the kind who didn't stick around long. And when he left, she wanted to be able to carry on without missing a beat or the money he owed her.

With that thought, she entered the kitchen and stopped short, then played off her surprise as if she'd expected it. But she hadn't expected to see the truck driver sitting there with Tony and Red. The three of them were laughing about something. When she came in, they stopped and looked guilty as hell.

"Don't get shy now," Ariana said, taking a seat across from Brax. She grunted when she sat. She wasn't impressed by Brax getting to the kitchen before she did. She wondered if being a truck driver meant he was an early riser.

The man looked rested and ready for the day. Tony's clothes fit, but just barely. Brax had to be a size or two larger than her Mexican hand. So the shirt and pants looked, well, damned sexy actually.

"We were just talkin' about you, is all," Red said.

Tony set down a plate of eggs, ham and toast in front of her. Ariana inhaled the aroma of butter and grease, thought, *My poor arteries* and dug in.

It got quiet again and Ariana realized what they'd been saying about her before she walked in. So what? She liked to eat. She knew she could put away some food, but there was nothing like the taste of what her hands—or the hands of those she knew—grew. It was care and attention she was savoring. Time and patience. Long hours and love. Every bite was full of all those things.

"Umm," she said and meant it.

Tony and Red laughed. She didn't care. She kept right on eating and kept her eye on that last piece of ham in the skillet, fixing her mouth for it.

She noted, out of the corner of her eye, that Brax hadn't touched his food since she started eating. He just watched her and she couldn't tell if he was repulsed or fascinated.

Either way, she didn't care. She chased a forkful of eggs with a bite of toast. "Don't you like your breakfast?" she asked Brax.

He moved a piece of ham closer to a helping of egg, slid both onto his fork. "Yeah," he said. "It's good."

"Hmm," Ariana said. "Can I get some milk, Tony? And I'll take that last piece of ham if no one wants it."

"Damn," Brax said and reached into his pocket. He fished out a twenty and handed it to Red.

Red held the bill up to the light as if he was checking for signs it was counterfeit. When he seemed satisfied, he pocketed the twenty and patted Brax on the back. "See, you just met her, but I've known her since before she knew herself."

"And ever since I've known you," Ariana countered, "you've been a scam artist."

She couldn't keep the smile from her face. As much as she wanted to, she didn't mind being teased about the things she loved. Ranching, eating…even her kid sister. It didn't bother her one bit. The only thing that really bothered Ariana was knowing that her sister could grow up in the same trap that she'd grown up in. Tied to land and never to love. Ariana was determined that wouldn't happen to Selena, no matter how much their mother would have protested if she had still been alive. Sometimes you had to live your own life instead of the life of all those who came before you. The life others expected and planned for you.

They ate, storing up energy for the morning chores, and listened to the radio. Marlon Jennings, on a local station, announced the ag report through forty-year-old speakers. Apparently, cows and hogs were up. While they let that soak in, Ariana accessed Weather Underground on her kitchen PC and clicked up an hour-by-hour report of the temperature and humidity for the day.

"I'll get the south end mended today," Ariana said.

Red sipped his coffee—a loud slurping sound followed by "Ah." No one paid attention.

"We had a storm a few days back," Red said. "Strangest thing I ever saw. Just big wind. Knocked the hell outta the barn, flicked hinges off the roof of the house like flies and kicked a tree down on the south end of the fence. I 'spect that's how Uncle Jesse got loose."

"I'm still replacing the Free Range signs on the highway. One of 'em blew clear to the Bar S."

So that's why he didn't see any signs on the way in. The storm had taken them all out.

"More coffee?" Tony asked, pot in hand and tilted toward Brax's cup.

"Drink while you can. That's what they tell me," Red said.

"I'm fine," Brax said. He wasn't as concerned about storing up caffeine as he was relieving himself of it later. He could just see it now, another thing he'd owe Ariana for—urine-destroyed grazing areas.

These next ninety days was going to be a big adjustment. Breakfast to Brax meant two Egg McMuffins and a large black coffee. If he was lucky enough to leave from home, Hazel would fix his favorite—pancake sandwich. Same insides as an Egg McMuffin, just different outsides. And she made the best coffee. He'd pack a supersize thermos and head out. But even with a handful of people, it was still jarring. The silence of the cab. The chatter in the kitchen. The aroma of home cooking. The smell of the road. And if he could eat fast enough, faster than Ariana, second and third helpings if he wanted them.

Brax kept quiet. He wasn't used to eating around people. Even at the truck stops, he'd sit away from folks. He'd keep his distance. Think about things. Life. The road. The next client for his business. Obviously, the rancher of the Sugar Trail and her hands were used to thinking out loud.

He hoped they didn't expect him to do the same.

"Where's everybody else?" Brax asked finally. He didn't know how many hands it took to run a ranch the size of the Sugar Trail, but when he agreed to pay his debt, he imagined a lot more than two, three if he counted Selena.

He looked up from his plate of nearly devoured home cooking. Tony glanced at Ariana. Red pushed his food around on his plate. Ariana stopped chewing. Red gave him a "you poor man, don't you know better than to ask such questions?" pat on the back. "She likes to torture us."

Ariana rolled her eyes. "Shut it up," she said and resumed eating.

"Ari runs a lean ship," Red said.

Tony chuckled. "Yeah, she does. We're also the only ones who can get along with her."

Ariana picked up a piece of hard, dry toast from her plate. Turned it, examining. Seemed to study the gradation from golden center to dark brown edges. "Just for that, I think you should muck out the stables with him," she said, motioning to Brax.

Tony smiled and his eyes twinkled. "I love it when you boss me around."

Brax noticed Tony's eyes just then. They'd grown intense and focused. His gaze hadn't faltered from Ariana's.

Brax couldn't tell if he was just flirting, or if there might be something between the two.

Funny, Tony didn't seem like her type.

And then he caught her smiling. It flashed across her face quicker than a strobe. But Brax caught it. He was surprised how good it looked on her. She should smile more often.

"We'll see," Ariana said finally.

Brax kept on eating, noticing how the three had an easy way with each other. Probably joked like this with each other every morning. Sat in the same places every morning. He ladled a thick helping of salsa over his remaining eggs, truly a fly on the wall.

She watched the man eat for a moment. He might have been a stranger in their kitchen, but he was no stranger to a good meal. His thickness alone told her that. But just the way he went after it on his plate gave her a twinge and a pause. She might actually have something in common with the guy.

"So, Ari. What's your idea? You gonna work him?"

She looked him up and down, slowly, thoroughly. Heat pooled at the small of his back, wrapped around his hips and settled between his thighs.

He took a deep breath, stared back at warm and golden eyes, luscious lips, thought *Down, boy* and waited for his sentence.

"First, he can check the fences. That way he'll get a feel for the place. Then I think barn duty oughta do it for a while."

"A while? You're talkin' at least a week."

Tony frowned. "Hell, it would take *me* a week, and I got the back for it. No offence, Brake."

"Brax," Brax said, indignance flattening his voice. He'd never understood why people had so much trouble with his name. "One syllable, four letters, one vowel. Sounds like jacks, slacks, tacks."

"Brax," Tony repeated, correctly this time.

"Then what?" Red asked. "And for the record, I like Big Rig better."

"Then we'll see," Ari said, finally turning away.

Good, Brax thought. Much more of her eyes on his flesh and he might have had to take her, right then and there, in front of her ranch hands. The woman sure did have a way with her eyes. And he'd never seen eyes the color of smooth caramels. But hers were. They softened her. Softened all the hard and heavy words she spoke. He wondered what they looked like when they were aroused and not merely interested and curious like they were now.

"You don't say much, do ya?" Tony asked.

"Nah, he don't say much," Red answered.

Ariana focused on her tea, tipped up the blue cup, draining the last drop.

"I can speak for myself," he said.

Then all eyes were on him. He took a breath. Another thing he always had to explain. The fact that he was a man of few words. He spoke when it was important. But that wasn't enough for some people.

"No," he said, finally. "I don't talk much."

"Good," Ariana said. "That means you won't have much to say when I tell you your chores each day."

Brax grunted. *I guess I walked into that one,* he thought.

Red mashed the last of his fried potatoes with his fork, gathering up the crumbs. He waited a beat before sliding the fork past his scruffy white beard and into his mouth. When he finished chewing, there was not a crumb left on his plate. Just the grease spots where the eggs and potatoes had been for a short while. "You want me ta take him over to the barn?"

Ariana pushed back her chair and stood. The legs scraped the creaky, worn linoleum and sounded like a cat meowing.

"Nah," she said and wiped her mouth with a bright white linen napkin. "He can ride with me."

She turned and cocked her head. "Come on, Big Rig. Let's break you in. Let's go south," she said, not letting him finish his last bite.

He got up without a word, placed his plate in the sink and nodded to Red and Tony.

"We'll be along directly," Red said.

Ariana gave Tony a reassuring pat on the arm. "Thanks," she said.

"You always thank me for breakfast when you know I'm glad to do it. I mean, I am the best cook here."

"That's why I'm thankful," Ariana admitted, thinking about heading out into the day that was still dark and sleeping.

"Ari?" Red said, wiping crumbs from his white beard.

"Yes," she said.

"Looks like Selena is trying to skip breakfast again."

"Let her sleep. We got an extra hand today," she said.

Chapter 8

Brax stepped outside the kitchen, and the darkness swallowed him like a thick black cape. Without the benefit of streetlights, building lights and car headlights, the cozy house on the hill stood alone in the final pitch-dark of morning. His eyes struggled to adjust.

He took a moment to tune his senses to the outdoors. The smell of fresh grass. The sound of the wind through the leaves. Crickets. Even the sound was open. Big and wide. Not like the tight overloud hum and rattle of his truck's engine.

He looked up and didn't recognize the sky. There were at least three times as many stars, and the brightest ones looked close enough to pluck and pocket.

Red walked up beside him, swirled a toothpick between two thin, pink lips and watching him stare at the sky. "Yeah. One poor fella just looked up and cried like he'd lost his mama."

"Or found her," Brax said.

Red tipped his hat to Brax. "Come on, Big Rig. You're with me." Red stepped out the front door. The heels of his boots clapping against the wood porch floor.

"Where are we going?" he asked, but Red was already off the porch and headed toward the stables.

The two had an easy ride against the perimeter of the property. They worked their way along the edge of each of the three thousand acres of the ranch. Red's eyes were pink rimmed, surrounded by wrinkled flesh and sharp as a hawk's. Just when Brax thought they wouldn't find anything to fix, Red would spot something.

The day had just started, but already, Brax was looking forward to the end of it.

Throughout the morning, they stacked fallen branches, trash and other debris left behind by the storm into piles. As they went, Red noted places in the fence to watch and identified weakened areas that needed immediate repair. To Brax's astonishment, the old guy would spot them before they rode up on them good.

"Looks like another one," he said, pointing to a place in the fence that looked perfectly normal to Brax. They rode up, stepped down from their horses and took a closer look.

"See that?" Red said.

Brax bent closer. Examined the wire thoroughly. Darned if there wasn't the equivalent of a hairline fracture where the line connected to the post.

"How'd you spot that from so far away?" Brax couldn't keep himself from asking.

Red pulled the twine from a gunny sack. Cut off a piece with wire stretchers, careful not to let the thorns pierce his thick leather gloves.

"The sun told me," he said.

Brax held on to the old wire while Red cut and spliced it with the new.

"The sun has a certain way of shining on things," he said. "Metal especially. It can shine on, shine off, or shine through. When it shines through, I know there's a problem."

He spun the wire where the two ends met. Twisted it quickly like he'd caught lightning in his fingers. When he finished, Brax took the old wire, wrapped it carefully into a ball and dropped it into his gunnysack.

"One down. We got about fifteen more of these."

They saddled up and rode on. An eternity of dirt ground, fence, grassy hillside and trees stretched out before them.

"How do you know there are fifteen more?"

"Well, well. You can talk when you wanna, huh?"

"Just curious is all," Brax admitted.

"I been on this ranch, or one just like it, since before Ariana was alive. Since before her mama was alive. My daddy used ta tell everybody that as soon as I could walk, I could run. And as soon as I started running, I ran from the house to the range and never left. I suspect that's mostly true. Sometimes it's like a torture when I have to go inside and leave all this—even for a night. Heck, when I get a mind, I just sleep outside."

Red's eyes looked dreamy, misty and content. Brax wondered what it was like to feel that way.

"Some people have to have those big surgeries when

they open your chest all the way up and fix your heart. I always thought that if they opened me up, I'd be what you call a…a…optical illusion. 'Cause all this," he said, gesturing widely and lovingly with his arms, "is what's in here. Wouldn't be one thing different.

"Ari's the same way. Which is why I can't get it to stay in my head why she wants to sell this place."

"She really wants to sell, huh?"

"Yep. That's why you bein' here is so important."

"I don't understand."

"When you took out Uncle Jesse, you took Ari's ace in the hole. She was the main draw. The land is good, but it's small. The herd is good, but it's small, too. But Uncle Jesse was big."

Brax remembered what the front end of his truck looked like the last time he saw it.

"You can say that again," he agreed.

"No Uncle Jesse, no sale."

"Because she won a prize?" Brax asked, the ordeal in the courthouse still fresh in his mind.

"Not a prize, *the* prize," Red said. "Jesse was a grand champion. That alone doubled not just her value, but the value of any calf she bore. And that is what Ari was hoping would sell this place. She'd tried for eight years to raise one heifer like her. And when she finally got one, *bam!*"

Brax's energy deflated like a punctured tire. He had no idea. Even when they'd discussed it in the court-house, he'd dismissed most of it as ranch talk. But it was more than that.

Much more.

"Now Ari's got to get this place in tip-top shape to make up for the lack of a prize-winning bull to sweeten the pot. So an extra pair of hands—especially ones the size of yours—are what's gonna get this place right."

Brax shook his head. That realization put him just a little off-kilter, but Run Amok with his powerful muscles and sure stride kept him steady.

Brax let the words and everything they meant settle over him like the sun that was coming up strong over the bluffs.

"There," Red said, and even though Brax couldn't see it, he knew as soon as they rode over and looked, they'd find something—something to make right.

Ariana kept the big man in the corner of her eyesight. He didn't walk like a cowboy, but if she had anything to do with it, he would soon enough.

He did have a swagger. A cocksure stride that told everyone within eyeshot that he was a bold, confident man. He wasn't likely to take anything off anyone. *Don't mess with me and I won't mess with you.*

But oh, did she want ta do some messin'!

He accompanied her outside and they got into her Ford F-350.

"So, no ring," she said, starting the engine and heading toward the ranch house barn. "You married?"

"No. Are you?"

"No," she answered quickly. "Girlfriend?"

"No. You?"

A cool hand of relief wrapped around her. She let out the breath she'd been holding. "I like to play it loose, you know? I'm not the hitched-up kind."

"That makes two of us."

She liked the sound of that even better. They could have all the fun they wanted for the next ninety days.

And when his time was up…well…his time was up. It was a good setup.

They kept quiet for the mile-and-a-half drive to the ranch house barn. The truck shook and shuddered over the uneven dirt road. Ariana rode easy with it. She'd been over the road so many times she knew when to dip, lean and brace for every rut, cut and hard track in the dirt. Brax didn't have her advantage, so the ride jostled him like a june bug in a jar. He tried to keep still, and put up a good fight, but it was no use. In the end, the land won just like it always did in that part of the world.

"Here we go," Ariana said, backing up to the barn.

The moment Ariana hopped out of the truck, Sirocco and Run Amok started to neigh, whinny and stamp their hooves in the hay. Brax joined her at the back of the truck where she unloaded a large bag of corn feed from the bed and carried it inside the barn.

She was greeted by a swarm of new flies. There must have been a million, literally.

"That damned Tony. Sometimes I think the only good he does around here is cook. He don't care much about nothin' else 'cept ropin'."

It was a four-stall barn. However, they only had two stallions in there now. She stopped at the halfway point between both horses, let the sack slide down into the hay and punched a hole in it with her thumb.

"Grab that bucket," she said.

Brax did as he was told and held the blue plastic bucket in place while she poured feed to the top. A handful of the dry corn rained down the side of the bucket as she pulled the sack up to stop the flow.

"Take the pin out, swing that gate open. His bucket's there behind him."

Brax nodded and did as he was told. Run Amok came forward, nearly knocking the bucket out of Brax's hand with his nose.

"Hurry up," Ariana said, feeling a little nervous for the man. He didn't have the first thought about how to handle a hungry horse.

"Tell him to let you pass," Ariana said.

Brax's eyes scowled with disbelief.

"Just talk to him."

"Whoa, there, boy. Now you move on back, Amok, and let me put this in your bucket." His voice was low and even. Calm. He actually sounded like he knew what he was doing for a moment there.

The animal snorted, tossed his head away from the blue bucket Brax carried and moved aside.

Brax's eyes widened, but only for a moment. Then they filled with concentration as he dumped the corn into the feeder and came out of the stall.

"Put the pin back," Ariana reminded him.

"Right," he said. "I don't want to be the cause of you losing yet another animal."

Ariana smiled. She couldn't help it. Since the man stepped into her truck in Cheyenne, he'd been the cause of her losing all her good sense, so losing an animal might just be another pickle in the jar.

Brax closed the gate and slid the pin back into the slot to hold it in place. Before she could do it, he bent down and filled the bucket again.

Ariana stood back, content to watch him work. She'd step in if Sirocco got jumpy.

"Okay, boy. Your turn," Brax said. He opened the gate the same way she had, stepped inside and kept talking. "I'll get you set up here and you can have all you want."

The horse nudged and brayed, trying to get to the feed. Eventually Sirocco gave Brax the room he needed to dump in the feed.

Brax came out the same way he'd come in and secured the gate.

"I'll bet you've never talked so much at one time in your whole life," Ariana said.

"And I'll bet that was your first smile in months."

The two stared at each other for a long time. The flies buzzing and lighting didn't break the spell between them, but laughter sure did. When neither of them could stand it any longer, they let go and laughed a good while.

Ariana felt happy and angry at the same time. Brax had hit her prized cow and now was intruding on her land. She wasn't real big on city folk and was only willing to endure them for her sister's sake.

But Brax was getting harder to dislike.

Ariana checked him out. His city boots already covered with hay, alfalfa and manure. His jeans already dusty and dirt-caked from the soil that was so dry this year and muck from the barn. And about a quarter of the million or so flies in the barn had already taken a liking to him.

And he didn't seem to mind any of it.

That was good. Much better than some of the 4-H kids that came and stayed periodically, or the occasional agribusiness student wanting to work for the summer. Unlike so many of them, he hadn't asked to wash his hands once.

After fixing fences all morning, he actually looked eager for more work. If only he knew.

"What's next?" he asked.

Ariana stepped back. Took in the sight of way too much to do. She'd knuckle Tony when she got the chance. It was really unfair to Brax to ask him to do this much so soon. But she'd get him started, round up Tony and have him help.

"You use that pitchfork there," she said, pointing to the thing hanging on the wall that was about as old as she was. "You load the wheelbarrow with the hay and alfalfa, then dump it in the manure spreader."

Brax stood tall. He was a barrel-chested man. Broad, sturdy shoulders. Straight back. He shouldn't have too much trouble.

"I'll switch out the horses," she said, then moved Run Amok and Sirocco to new stalls while Brax took the pitchfork down from the nail and moved the wheelbarrow closer.

"I'll pull up the spreader. Put it in place of my truck."

"And when it's full?" he asked, already heading to his chore.

"Tony will be here before then. He'll show you what to do."

Brax nodded and went to work.

Ariana should have driven away to the pasture or the corral. After all, there were bucket calves and orphaned colts on grain, horses to feed, a sick bull to doctor and fences to check.

She didn't go—at least not too far.

Instead she drove her pickup to the top of the far hill and parked. Close enough where she could watch and not be too noticeable.

The sun was coming up good now. It would be

another dry, hot day. At least Brax got to spend most of it in the shade of the barn. A fire hawk soared overhead, getting an early start on its hunting day. Again there wouldn't be enough clouds to temper the sun's angry heat that had punished Nebraska and most of the Midwest so early in the summer.

That was the thing she disliked most about ranching. Her powerlessness against Mother Nature. The fact that she and those who chose the western lifestyle were always at the mercy of weather. And this year, not even a rain dance had brought them relief.

Brax came out of the barn with his first load for the wheelbarrow. He was awkward and lost most of the hay before he could drop it in. If he kept on that way, his long week would easily stretch into two. And by the time he was finished, he'd need bed rest and liniment rubs for two more weeks after.

Hmm, she thought—imagining what it would be like to rub Cornhusker Lotion on Brax's aching muscles and hear him moan in pleasure. The image brought a sweet smile to Ariana's face and she lingered in that feeling.

He came out with another pitchforkful, more steady this time, and actually hit his mark.

He catches on quick, she thought.

He stood against the climbing sun, covered his eyes and stared in her direction. Taking the cue, Ariana tipped her hat and put her truck in gear. She had things to do and one of them, she decided, would be Brax.

"Ya think he knows he's overloading the barrel?"

Something about Brax made them all curious. Ariana, Tony and Red looked on from a hill while Brax tackled his big chore.

"No."

"He'll get it bogged and all of us will have to pull it out of the ditch."

"I don't know if you all have been payin' attention, but I get a new surprise out of him every day. He'll catch on."

Red pulled on the scraggly hairs of his beard. He'd pulled it like that for so many years his fingers had set tracks in it. "Twenty bucks says he figures it out."

"You must think somethin' about this city boy," Tony said.

"Not me," Red said, motioning toward Ariana.

Ariana adjusted herself atop Sirocco and smiled a little.

The attractive man had made her acutely aware of herself, her femininity and strangely enough her underwear. Her mother had always told her that to keep the ranch going she might have to act like a man on the outside, but that's where it stopped. She should always be a lady on the inside. To stay connected to the woman inside her, Ariana had ordered and worn Victoria Secret underwear since she was seventeen.

"There's a reason I didn't name you Sophie or Sally, Terry or Jo," her mother had said. "I wanted you to have a womanly name, 'cause out here with the men and the manure, it's easy to get separated from yourself. But soon as somebody says your name, you know, you are first and always a woman. A lady."

Yep, Brax made her want to mention her unmentionables, at least to him anyway.

Red and Tony rode on, but Ariana watched Brax work for a while longer. Pushing. Lifting. Pitching. Pulling. His arms hard as granite, muscles flexing, bulging. Veins constricting, pulsing. She watched and couldn't look away. She'd seen men working before, some harder than Brax. But his actions caught and held her attention. He moved right. She liked it. The way his brown skin looked oiled. Slick with sweat. The strain of his muscles. The power and strength behind the movements. Utterly hypnotic. She smiled. She couldn't help herself. She damned sure liked what she saw.

He looked up and paused for a moment. Watched her watching him. "What?" his expression asked. "Am I doing it wrong?"

"Yes. But I don't care. You look good doin' it like that."

His gaze became acute. Heated her with its intensity. He looked like he wanted to say something suggestive and sexy. Well, God bless it, she wanted to hear it. Needed to hear it. His mere presence on her land was becoming more unbearable by the second. Not because he was difficult. Not because he was incompetent or lazy. He was none of those things. He was, however, calling to Ariana's nature like nothing she'd ever felt. Just walking past him made the inside of her thighs quiver and she learned to walk gently or risk throwing herself into spontaneous orgasm. And if there was an orgasm coming to her, and she knew just by looking in his eyes not only that one was coming, but that it would be long and luxurious, she only wanted it from Brax. Not the fantasy of him. Not the suggestion of him or the idea. But the hands and hips and soul of the real thing.

No one won their stare down. Brax simply went back to working and Ariana continued watching, knowing that before the week was out, she would have him in her bed—one way or another.

* * *

"Ready for dinner?" Red asked.

"Dinner? It's lunchtime, isn't it?"

Red shook his scruffy head. "City folk," he said. "Out here we have breakfast, dinner and supper."

Brax straightened his back, felt the strain, shifted it until it cracked. Ah, that felt good. But progress in the barn didn't look good. No matter what he called it, he couldn't take a break now.

"I better keep working," he said, believing that if he stopped for too long, he'd end up spending his entire ninety days shoveling and that's it. There had to be something else in life besides doing chores and Brax was determined to get to it.

"You need to fuel up, otherwise you'll never get through it all."

"If I don't keep going, I'll never get through it all." Brax stared down at the corner of the first stall that looked as though he'd been using a teaspoon to clean it out. He was getting nowhere fast. And his arms felt like someone had taken the muscles and twisted them like rubber bands.

Red slapped him on the back. "The work here is hard. But we rest hard and we play hard. Right now it's time for rest."

Brax stuck the pitchfork down in nearly a foot of hay, alfalfa and muck. "Let's go," he said.

After a morning of horses, hay and flies in the barn, Brax found himself surprisingly ready for people and conversation. He had plenty of time to think between shovelfuls of muck. He wanted to know more about the ranch, more about Ariana. Mainly, he wanted to know more about how an African-American woman came to own a ranch in the middle of Nebraska.

They all arrived at once, Selena, Red, Ariana and him. The kitchen already smelled good from whatever Tony had cooking in pots and the oven.

They were all dirty and took turns in the mudroom washing the morning's dirt and grime from their hands.

Brax was covered, as were they all, from knee to ankle with dirt, grass and things best not thought of before a meal. Funny thing was none of them seemed to mind. They simply sat down at the table and waited.

"So, how was it?" Tony asked. He was stirring a pot of something brown and rich on the stove.

Brax's ego stood up tall. Chest puffed out and strutting. Macho Brax wanted to say, "Not bad. Cool. Piece of cake." Or better yet, "Man, I got this."

But Brax was a straight shooter. Life for him had just worked better that way. He wasn't about to start frontin' now just because he was surrounded by cowboys and a woman he found sexy as hell.

"I've had better mornings," he said, then reached for the glass of water sitting beside his plate.

"It's usually not like that," Tony admitted. "But lately, I've been busy with the rodeos and—"

"And shuckin' your chores," Ariana finished. She held a piece of hay between her teeth and chewed it like tobacco. "Well, don't worry much about tomorrow. You won't be too sore."

Ariana took a seat across from him. For the third time. She was direct, that was for sure. "No, it's the day after that you have to worry about. By then you're gonna be pretty stiff. Let me know if you need rubbing… liniment."

There was no mistaking the insinuation in Ariana's words and voice. The quiet and sudden stillness in the kitchen told Brax that everyone in the room had caught it. So, she was bold and direct. Well, he could take it and dish some, too.

"I don't know about liniment. I just may need to be rubbed."

"Like I said, you just let me know."

Damn, she didn't miss a beat. And Brax didn't want her to. Why had he been in relationships with mousy, demure women? Women who liked to giggle and be picked up? The woman sitting across from him—with her golden-brown hair, caramel eyes and cappuccino skin—didn't do anything she didn't want to do, laughed with her whole body and looked like she could pick *him* up if she wanted to. She was completely wrong for him and still he wanted to have her so badly that even knee-deep in horse manure he couldn't stop thinking about her.

Tony placed pot roast, tomato salad, glazed apples and biscuits on the table. Surrounded by real butter, homemade marmalade, fresh honey, Red wasted no time digging in.

Brax and the rest helped themselves and soon the kitchen was silent except for the sound of smacking, slurping and forks scraping plates. The fresh food was exquisite. Even Kuri couldn't cook this well and she was damned good.

"Tell me more about the history of the Sugar Trail," he said, trying to take his mind off the fact that in three months he'd have to give up all this good food.

"I wanna tell," Selena said.

"You go right ahead," Ariana said.

"I'm the fourth generation MacLeod on the Sugar Trail Ranch. Great-Great-Grandma Gunny came up from Tennessee to homestead when she was still a girl. She wasn't married then, but she was engaged to Jack Turner, who—"

"Left her like a sack of bad potatoes," Ariana interrupted.

"I'm telling the story!"

"Sorry," Ariana said, biting hard into a biscuit.

Brax helped himself to more pot roast and biscuits. Bump the salad. He'd worked too hard to waste time, energy and room on rabbit food. And there was a lot more work to do. He'd need the fullness of meat and carbs to get through it.

Spearing a large hunk of beef with his fork, he stuck it in his mouth and chewed slowly.

The meat all but melted in his mouth. It was heavenly. Flavorful. Tender. Juicy. Delicious. The best beef he'd ever tasted. He ate with deep appreciation. His chores were well worth this.

Ariana slid him a glance. "Good, huh?"

"What?" he said, catching a trickle of juice before it ran all the way down his chin.

"All that moaning you're doing. Sounds like you like it."

He stopped chewing. "Was I moaning?"

Selena giggled. "Yeah. And real loud, too."

"You know that's Uncle Jesse?" Ariana said nonchalantly—the same way one would say, "You know it's raining outside."

Brax stopped chewing immediately. A lump of remorse and disgust formed in his throat. He struggled for a few seconds but couldn't swallow it. It was as if everything in the room stopped moving like bullet time in *The Matrix.*

"Oh, now, Ari. Don't do that," Red admonished. "That's not Uncle Jesse."

A cool rain of relief washed over Brax. He took a bite of biscuit, stabbed an apple. "Cool," he said and kept right on eating and savoring. Selena continued her story.

"By the time she got her house built she was sixteen and pregnant with Great-Grandma JoJean."

"What year was that?" Brax asked and washed down a mouthful with water.

Ariana took a swig of water herself. "Turn of the century."

Selena shot her sister a scorching look. "Every chance she got, Great-Great-Grandma bought more land. She started out with seven hundred acres. Every generation of MacLeod women has added on at least five hundred acres—that is, until Ari. She started selling 'em."

"And I'm not going to stop until they're all sold."

"So, I don't get my turn!" Selena said, letting her fork go. It clinked against the blue-and-white china and fell to the table.

"Trust me," Ariana said. She scooped up the last few tomatoes onto her fork. "You really don't want a turn."

"You don't know what I want."

"Wait till you come back from Grand Island. You'll feel differently."

"Whatever," Selena said, her voice flattened with

sadness. She sounded the same way Ariana had sounded when Brax had hit the cow. Dejected and deflated.

They were a lot alike. He wondered if Ariana realized it.

Brax finished his meal, leaving barely a trail of grease or gravy on his plate. Surprisingly, he was eager to get back to work. He knew he'd be sore. Damned sore. But the exercise was exhilarating. He was waking up muscles that typically slept through the long drive from Savannah to Wyoming. Or anywhere else for that matter. And the physical labor kept his lust in check. At least for now. His attraction to Ariana was stronger than he realized. Even now, sitting across the table from her with dishes and food between them, surrounded by her people, all he wanted to do was pull her into his arms and kiss that juicy, weatherworn mouth of hers until her toes curled like those of the Wicked Witch of the East.

"Another helping?" Tony asked, already clearing the dishes.

"No," Brax said. He had to get back to the land. Back to settling his debt. Take his mind off Lady West. A temporary love thang was a bad idea right now—although a quickie right before he left might not be out of the question.

Chapter 9

Red was wrong, or at least Brax prayed that he was wrong. The next morning, after shoveling more muck-packed hay and alfalfa than he ever knew existed, Brax could barely move.

He'd overdone it. He knew that each time he loaded up the wheelbarrow. Each time he dumped that thing into the shredder. He was moving at a pace designed to impress. He'd started it when he saw Ariana drive that truck up the hill and stop. She wanted to watch. He wanted to give her something to see. So he'd forced his muscles to move in ways they weren't used to and at a pace they protested. Then when she finally drove off toward the pasture, he couldn't very well slow down or she'd know it was all for show. So he'd kept on and savored the break along with the food when they'd all taken lunch. Rejuvenated and refueled, he'd gone back to the barn with the same level of determination he'd had earlier that morning. And now every muscle, nerve and inch of skin on his body was paying a painful price. His muscles felt like burning concrete. Stiff and on fire.

If only Ariana hadn't shoveled that first load so swiftly. So perfectly. He wouldn't have felt so compelled to do it not only as good as she did, but better. And then when she watched him, that just added gas to the blaze. Now the fire was inside him and his tissues were going up in flames.

"Ah!" he said, forcing his arms into shirtsleeves. "Ssss," he hissed through his teeth. He worked to button the plaid shirt, but his hands were so sore and blistered from gripping that pitchfork—even with gloves on—he fought with each button before getting it cleanly through the holes.

They'd eaten breakfast at 6:00 a.m. yesterday. It was already 6:20 and he didn't even have his socks or boots on. With his aching body, he figured it would take another fifteen minutes just for that.

The knock on his door broke his concentration on buttoning the last button on his shirt, and the round piece of plastic slipped through his large throbbing fingers.

"Yes?" he said, standing still, struggling to put a "no worries" face on.

Ariana opened his door and gave him one of her now famous appraisals. This one swift and thorough. "You look like crap. Sore?"

"Nah," he lied. "Just got up too late. The solid quiet is good for sleeping." At least he told the truth about something.

She stepped into his room—looking every bit the

ranch queen. Sky-blue Wrangler shirt, Levi's blue jeans and Durango boots. She owned that world. Every move of her work-thickened body told him so.

"Really?" she said, strutting in. Her smile was big and bodacious. It looked good on her. "Let's see you wink."

"Why don't you just head on down to the kitchen? As soon as I throw on my socks and boots, I'll join you."

"Nah. We'll go together. I'll wait. But first I want to see you wink."

Damn, he thought. He hadn't moved a muscle since she stepped into the room. He was too concerned that any move he made would give away his agony and the fact that just breathing was dealing him a healthy fit. And he couldn't go out like some punk after the first day. Besides that, he had eighty-nine more days to go.

"Fake it till ya make it," his friend Race Jennings used to say. Brax decided that's exactly what he would do.

Brax braced himself, bucked up and winked. The moan that came from his lips immediately afterward gave everything away.

Ariana choked back a laugh.

"Here's something you oughta learn fast. Nothing gets past me. Not here. The fact that you hadn't even blinked since I came in tells me you're hurtin'."

She came up, close enough for Brax to smell her. She smelled like soap, shampoo and detergent. She took his hands in hers and drew them up to get a closer look.

Brax bit his lip, determined not to groan, moan, wince or sigh deeply.

"Well, would ya looka here?" Her rough thumbs circled his palms. "Big Rig, you're gonna have hands like mine soon."

She lowered his arms slowly, carefully. From his face, her gaze traveled down to the last button on his shirt. She reached out and buttoned it. Brax didn't know if the jolt he received was a reaction to his sore body or her delicate attention. He wished for a time when she was *un*-buttoning his shirt instead of the other way around.

"You wanna sit today out? So your body has a chance to recover?" she asked. Her eyes and voice grew soft with her questions. She was still only inches away.

Brax's heart beat strong and steady at her nearness. Her body heat. Her clean smell. Her concern.

He didn't want to take the day off. "Well..." he began.

Ariana's slap across his back came swift and sharp. It sent a pain like a hot poker sliding into his shoulder and out of his chest. This time he winced and moaned. It was a simple atta-boy gesture, but it nearly toppled him.

"Forget it, Big Rig. Get your boots on and get some breakfast. Hopefully there will be some left by the time you get downstairs. Selena likes you, so she'll probably save you something to eat."

Despite his pain, a crazy question entered Brax's head. "Do *you* like me?"

"Maybe."

She smiled then. It was fleeting and left as soon as it came.

Ariana sauntered back to the doorway. "Buck up, Rig. Chores don't go away just 'cause your strength does."

And with that comment she was out the door, her worn boots clapping against the hardwood stairs.

"I'll be right down!" Brax called after her.

His body had betrayed him, but his mind hadn't. This would be a day of mind over matter. He'd tough it out.

Get through another day of shoveling and take a long hot soak in the tub afterward. And he'd take it easier today. No showboating. Just good, steady work.

He walked over to where he'd left his boots beneath a wooden chair. His body yelled loudly in protest. He told it to shut up and get ready for the day.

Ariana didn't know everything. And he would prove that.

By the time he got downstairs and into the kitchen, he'd found a pocket of reserve energy and determination he didn't know he had. He hoped to get some of whatever he smelled cooking to give him the energy he'd need to at least make it through the morning and show Lady West she didn't know what the heck she was talking about.

When he walked into the kitchen, it was filled with bright and lively conversation, for so early in the morning. Everyone was up and, surprisingly, it was as if they'd been waiting for him.

They sat at the table, plates in front of them, but the plates were clean. They hadn't eaten yet.

They *had* been waiting.

A tradition, a ritual, Brax guessed. In the world he came from, you grabbed a bite whenever, wherever. But here, they ate together.

"Good morning," he said, trying to sound as normal as possible. He didn't want his voice to give away a strained night's sleep or the sense that he'd been run over by his own semi.

"You look wrung and twisted," Red said.

"Hope you're hungry," Tony said, getting up and

heading to the stove. He filled the kitchen table with the thickest bacon Brax had ever seen, Texas toast, scrambled eggs and onions with cheese sauce. They made room for this among the butter, salsa, honey, jam and tomato juice already on the table.

When Tony sat down, he blessed their food and one by one they passed the dishes around. No one said any more about Brax's haggard condition. Instead they discussed the weather, feedlots and the new calf. Brax made a note to check on it and the mother before the sun went down. He felt…a part of them somehow. Connected. He might be a stranger to everything else on that ranch, but he'd felt that calf when it was struggling inside its mother's womb. Even if it was a small one, there was a bond there.

The more he ate, the better he felt.

"So, ready for day two?" Red asked between big bites of bacon.

"Absolutely," Brax said, beating Ariana to the last piece of toast.

"Hey!" she said.

"Too slow," Brax said.

Selena, Tony and Red laughed at that. The tight-lipped expression on Ariana's face said that she didn't think it was funny. "We'll see who's slow. By dinner, you'll need a pitchfork to lift *you* up."

Brax took a big bite out of the heavily buttered toast. Real butter, he thought, as the smooth, sweet taste spread in his mouth. "We'll see," he responded.

When a twinge of pain shot through his sacroiliac, he kept chewing, kept the smug look on his face and thought, *Come on, eighty-nine days.*

When none of them could avoid work anymore, they all got up together. Tony had already started to clear and clean the dishes, to pack and store the leftover food.

With him and Red bringing up the rear, Brax walked as fast as he could in the direction of the door.

"Have a good morning, son," Red told him, slapping his hand.

When Brax opened his palm, there were four Advils there. A wave a relief and appreciation swept over him.

"I owe you," he mouthed.

"Don't think I won't collect," Red said.

"Why are you making him do the hardest job on the ranch, Ari?" Selena asked.

They'd ridden out to the north end where the newborn and mother were still separated from the rest of the herd. Cow and calf seemed to be doing well. The baby's legs were sure now. The mother rested and her calf nursed like it should. They would examine the calf today. Check it over. Make sure it was healthy and thriving.

Ariana pulled up her horse beside the pen. "He deserves it. He killed Uncle Jesse. Now he's here acting like he's large and in charge."

"Only because *you* are," Selena responded. She swung off her horse first, followed by Ariana. "All guys react to you the same why. They try to keep up."

Ariana swung off Sirocco. Patted the horse. Wrapped the reins around the fence. "But they can't. So they should stop trying."

The two approached the pen. The cattle there stirred and stared. They knew what was coming. Food. The herd came closer.

"You don't work the summer interns the way you're working him."

"It's only been one day," Ariana said.

"That's what I mean. You let him muck out that barn all afternoon. That's wrong, Ari. I can't believe he got out of bed this morning."

"Whatever," Ariana said.

"Whatever? You hate when *I* say whatever."

"I know," Ariana said. She couldn't think of anything else to say. No defense. No explanation.

Truth was, she was punishing him. For putting a pot-hole in her plan. Her prize Angus. Gone. Six thousand dollars. She didn't care about the insurance money. Insurance didn't do a thing to authenticate breeding stock. But blue ribbons did. And Jesse would have taken her all the way to the bank. All the way to Selena's secured future.

"If he's gonna last three months, you better go easy on him."

Ariana stared at her sister. All of eleven years old. She looked like she'd grown three inches in the last three months. And in the months since their mother had passed, she'd grown thirty years. Ariana had trouble the first few weeks after their mother died. Bouts of uncontrollable crying. Days where she worked herself to exhaustion. And a week where she just didn't want to get out of bed. During that awful time, Selena had taken over as head of the ranch. She'd stepped in and at times treated Ariana as if she were the younger one instead of the other way around. What finally snapped Ariana out of her grief was the way Selena had melded with the land. With the ranch. She saw the young girl becoming hard-bitten and callused. It was a pain just as great as, if not greater than, losing their mother. That's when Ariana knew. She couldn't save herself. But she had to save her sister.

She'd been on a mission to sell the ranch ever since.

A ranch that came with prize-winning cattle brought a fine price. The kind that would set them up nicely in the city.

"When do you leave?" she asked her sister.

"Three days," Selena answered.

Selena'd been indifferent about the City Swap Program from the start. It was the opposite of the 4-H program, taking ranch and farm kids off the land and into the city. The kids stayed in campus dorm rooms over the summer while the college students were gone and spent the summer creating and running a mock corporation.

They came back with a slice of city life that helped them know and understand there are alternatives to hay and horses. That life doesn't stop at the end of the pasture.

"You'll have a great time," Ariana said, almost wishing that she could go. She'd never spent any significant amount of time off the ranch. She couldn't wait until they were away and gone.

They finished feeding the herd. They'd already watered and grained the horses, colts and orphaned calves that morning. They'd checked the windmill and filled all their vehicles with gas. The only things left before dinner were checking on the calf—which they were doing—and tending to a sick bull in the south end of the pasture.

Compared to what Brax was doing, their job was sweet and easy.

"Maybe I owe him an apology," Ariana said. "I should give him light duty this afternoon. Count head or clean up the tool barn."

"You like him, don't you?" Selena asked.

Ariana stared at her sister, not sure how to answer. They never had secrets between them. They weren't raised that way. But there was no way to admit to her young sister that a stranger was driving her crazy with sensual thoughts. Thoughts and visions of naked bodies—his and hers—tumbling over each other in the heat of the night.

Well, she guessed she didn't have to say all that.

Selena continued her probe. "He's handsome. Don't you think he's handsome?"

Ariana was lost in her thoughts and heard her sister's question like a distant whisper.

"Yes," Ariana said.

"So you like him?" Selena asked.

"Yes," Ariana answered.

"I like you, too," came a deep voice from behind her.

Ariana turned. Brax stood behind her. Covered with dirt, straw. Horse waste. He was filthy but looked tired and eager at the same time.

"You set me up," Ariana said to her sister, realizing that Brax had ridden up on Run Amok and she'd been so deep in a fantasy, she hadn't even heard him.

"Yep," Selena admitted. "I sure did."

"What are you doing here?" Ariana asked Brax. "You can't be finished with the barn."

"I came to see them," he said, pointing to the cow and her calf. They'd moved nearer to the herd, but not much. Baby was sticking close to her mother.

The concern in Brax's face was too acute for Ariana

to tell him the realities of ranch life. He was so far gone already. It was too late to tell him not to get attached. He had to know that the calf he pulled could just as easily end up on his plate or in a burger at a regional restaurant, or as a breed cow on another ranch or as a pair of steel-toed work boots.

But she could see by the way he looked at the calf, underneath all that muscle, manliness and muck, he had a kind and caring heart.

Yeppers. It was too late. He was already gone. She took a long look at him, just the way she liked to, and hoped that she wasn't already gone, too.

"I'm going to find Red," Selena said, stepping back from the fence. She headed toward her horse in short, quick steps.

Ariana actually felt good about being alone with Brax. But she didn't want her sister to feel like she had to leave the *adults* alone. "Why?"

"You two look like you've been dying to kiss each other since yesterday. I'm eleven. I still think that's gross. But I know you guys don't. So see you later."

Selena swung up on her horse, made a *zchic-zchic* sound with her tongue and teeth and galloped off toward the ranch house.

Ariana shook her head. Selena was as open and honest as she was. A blessing and a curse.

Brax moved beside her. Bent over the wooden fence and braced himself on the top plank. He moved slowly. Methodically. She could tell he was sore. He bore it well. Propped his foot against the lowest wooden board. Stared straight into the pen. Kept his eye on the newest family member.

Aside from looking a bit uncomfortable, he looked like he belonged. He blended into the scenery nicely. Hard-bitten for a city guy. He'd take a nice cowboy photo. A souvenir for when he left. If people didn't know better, they'd swear he belonged right where he was. On a ranch, under the sun, overseeing the livestock.

"They look good. The calf looks strong."

"Not that you know what a strong calf looks like."

"Not that I know," he repeated.

For a moment, she thought he was mocking her. But she heard the sunrise in his voice. The sunset in his tone. Sincerity. Concern.

She wasn't the only one who could tell the honest truth.

The two animals stayed together, a slight distance from the herd but never more than a few feet away from each other. The mother chewed her cud while the calf nuzzled for a teat.

"They're so close. The mother never lets more than ten or fifteen feet get between her and the calf. And if the calf gets ornery and goes outside that range, she calls for it."

Brax slapped away a big fly and frowned with awe. "Damn thing comes every time."

"Yeah," Ariana said. "They're close. At least at first. Sometimes their whole lives or at least until we sell the calves."

"When do you do that?"

"When they're about a year. That's about ten years in people terms."

"Umm."

"You feed them water and grain?"

"Yep," he said.

Ariana was about to ask why he was still there, but the expression on his face told her there was something deeply personal going on here. More than just the fact that he helped pull that calf out. As closed as Brax seemed, she figured that he'd tell her why he spent spare moments here if and when he wanted her to know.

Ariana leaned into the fence, adjusted her hat, took a peek at the sky. The clouds seemed as unsettled as her soul. Dark tumbling, rumbling masses. Thick thunderclouds, threatening a hard rain. They brought strong winds. Kept everything dust-covered and dry. Until they cracked open and God cried.

Ariana wanted the rain. A cooling, slow, steady downpour for two, maybe three hours per day for a week would catch them up. It would be muddy beyond all belief, but when the sun came out, so would the green. And they needed the green.

Buyers wouldn't see the dry weather, the dry state. They would only see her land and how the steady sun had turned her grass pastures to dust.

Her mother and her grandmother had called the Sugar Trail the desert of the plains. Most of the time they were wrong. The Trail was as lush and green and thick with vegetation as any place else in the country. And from what she could tell in traveling to fairs and competitions, maybe even more so. But when it was bone-dry, only a constant drenching could saturate it.

"How's the barn?" she asked, turning like he turned, trying to take her mind off the sudden throbbing between her legs. She leaned against the fence just like he did, in a way she'd done a million times before.

"It's still there," he said.

She left it at that. There was a lot of work to do. She was grateful for his hand. And with Selena leaving the next day, Brax would really be useful.

Both she and Brax looked on while the cow hovered over her calf, while the calf nursed, and while they never moved too far from each other.

Unlike his family. He and his brother and sister had spent most of their lives apart. And from his conversation with his sister earlier, even technology was conspiring to keep them apart.

"So, how's it going?"

"How's it going?" Brax asked, keeping his head tilted skyward. "How do you think it's going? I'm stuck. Slingin' crap by the pound. There are more flies here than I knew existed on the entire earth. These people live in the middle of the country, but they sound like they're from the dirty-dirty. And at the end of the day, I go to the ranch house covered in dust, horse hooey, flies and hay."

"Ugh!"

"The barn I'm working in looks like it would take six men seven weeks to clean."

Brax could hear his sister's stomach churning.

"Well, don't let me keep you, then," she said.

"Don't you dare hang up. I need to talk to someone who doesn't sound like the next word coming from her mouth is 'Boy howdy!'"

"Okay, but what's that noise?"

Brax stretched his body even higher. "It's the freaking signal. Out here, getting a signal is like getting free money. It almost never happens."

The line cracked like crunched cellophane. Brax

pulled the phone away from his hear hoping it would subside. "Picture me, on top of a hill stretching my neck like a giraffe."

"That's a picture I'd love to see. Is it a camera pho—"

"Honey! Honey!"

The signal fizzled one last time and went out. Not only was it nearly impossible to get a signal out there, but when he did, the poor signal wreaked havoc on the battery.

"Aggh!" Brax grumbled. He'd do what he had to do, but the sooner he got the heck outta Dodge, the better.

Outta Dodge, he thought. *How appropriate.*

"Thanks for waiting for me this morning," he said, returning his thoughts to the present.

Ariana was shocked. Big Rig was talking. Like he wanted to carry on a conversation. Maybe he'd walked all this way to tell her something. She decided to listen and engage. Who knew if she'd get another chance within the next three months?

"You're welcome. We eat together around here. It's just how we do it."

"I usually eat by myself, so it's different."

"I'll bet a lot of things are different," she said.

"Yeah. I've been trying to call my brother all morning. It's like my cell phone is dead."

"Out here, it might as well be. You might be able to get reception on a high hill. Other than that, forget it. You'll have to use the house phone."

"I don't want to run up your bill."

"Don't worry about it. You won't be here long enough to run up a bill."

He turned toward her then. Gave her a good look. He

could dish out as good as he could take. It was the same kind of look she was so fond of giving him. "The work never stops does it?"

"No. Long days. Short nights. It's all we know."

Brax fell quiet. *Well, that went fast,* Ariana thought. She liked him so much better when he was vocal. She wondered what she could do to keep him talking.

"Wanna see the sire?" she asked.

He turned to her, didn't say a word, but intrigue raised his brows.

"Come on," she said.

The wind picked up. It was almost dinnertime and she was right on schedule with her chores. As a matter of fact, visiting the bull would put them ahead of schedule.

They left the corral and walked to Sirocco, where Ariana swung up first, then Brax climbed up behind her with a stern grunt.

"Okay?" she asked.

"Okay," he answered.

"Come on," she said.

Mindful of his overtaxed body, she led them on a slow trot along a cow path.

"You barely move," he said, after a few moments.

"What?" she asked, not understanding what he meant.

"Your hips, your body. The horse is going. I'm all over the place trying like the devil not to fall off this sucker, but you're barely moving."

"I've been riding since I could walk," she said. "Actually, my mother used to tell this story about how fascinated I was with horses. To hear her tell it, I came out of the womb that way. She said I rode my first pony when I was six months old. As soon as I could sit up, she put me on a horse and claimed I rode it.

"Of course I don't remember that. Red says it's true, though.

"What about you? Your parents have stories about you driving trucks while you were still in diapers?" she asked, imagining the man probably had some funny stories about himself and an 18-wheeler.

"No. No stories. I was a foster child. I didn't stay anywhere long enough to have memories like that."

Ariana took a breath. He sounded in more pain now than he had been that morning. Even when she'd said the word *parents,* his arms had stiffened around her. His body had grown tense.

"I'm sorry," she said. She couldn't imagine life without strong ties and ideals of family.

"No need. I wasn't beaten. I wasn't neglected. I wasn't mistreated. Just shifted around. I never got too comfortable, but I never wanted for anything."

"Sounds like mistreatment to me. Every time you turn around, you're being shipped off to a different family. How did you survive?"

"How did you survive *your* childhood?" he asked, obviously insulted and angered by her question.

"You just survive," he said finally.

She let the topic drop, not wanting to open that box again. There were clearly some raw issues living there. Issues Ariana didn't want to get caught up in.

In the early morning hours, however, Ariana found herself very caught up—in keeping an eye on her new hand. She and Brax were both night people. Wanting to be awake and active when the evening was darkest. Ariana had heard her mother say as much about Selena when she was a baby.

"She's fighting sleep," she'd said. "Afraid she's gonna miss something."

Maybe that was the case with her and Brax. Both able to function on very little sleep. Both getting their blood up when everyone else had bedded down.

She watched that night, the way she had all day.

He was riding. With some kind of quiet fury or vengeance. She could tell that until his *sentence,* Brax hadn't spent much time on a horse. The fact that he was on one now, walking, trotting, turning and pulling the horse up, showed her that he had every intention of rectifying that truth in his life.

"You're going to be sore," she wanted to call out from the widow's walk on the roof of her ranch. In the stark night, she was sure her voice would carry. But she was more sure of something else: Brax was a man who didn't enter into anything lightly. She knew he was aware of the risk to his groin muscles and wanted to do it anyway.

Riding was a crucial part of running the ranch. If Brax was going to be more than merely effective, mastering the back of a horse was not optional but required.

Ariana had never known anyone, besides her own mother, with such strong determination. She would be content to relax on the roof and watch him work with Run Amok until the sun came up.

Strong powerful muscle on top of strong powerful muscle. In the moonlight, Ariana didn't know which animal was more beautiful.

Looked like he'd finally figured it out. You don't really train or tame the horse. The horse tamed you. Trained you how to treat it. As soon as you obeyed, you and the horse could function as one almost as closely as a man and woman making love.

Ariana flushed hotly at that thought. She'd like nothing better than to make love with Brax. The man came to her place with a full-grown swagger. Not something he had to develop by life on the range. She couldn't stop her mind from conjuring up thoughts of gazing into his intense eyes from underneath his weight, being covered by the heat of his skin, teasing him into a slow ellipsis over her thighs.

The space between her legs responded instantly to her musings, throbbing strong and wet urges. Ariana pressed her hands against the hot space, closed her thighs and kept watching, imagining that she was the animal he was riding, attempting to tame and break him in.

She sighed, rubbed slow, closed her eyes. August couldn't come soon enough.

Chapter 10

Ariana did more watching Brax eat than she did eat herself, which was unusual. Eating was one of the high activities of her day. She did so enjoy a good meal. And Tony could cook his round Colombian behind off. But this morning, she was more interested in Brax than she was her food.

For the past few days, he'd darn near worn himself out. He baled hay faster than Ariana knew was possible. By evening time, he could barely drag himself back to the house.

But he did.

She wanted the work done, true, but she didn't see any sense in him working himself the way he did. But he sure was fun to watch. Every muscle in his torso straining with each lift, turn and dump, his biceps straining against his shirts in a fierce way. Ariana kept watching just to see if today was the day when the seams would finally give out and hard corded muscles would burst the double stitching.

They never did. And neither did he. But she was afraid that any day, Brax would come back exhausted, or worse, injured. If that happened he'd be no use to her and she'd feel guilty as blue sin.

She could tell the workload and fast pace were getting to him. He was moving slow this morning. Talking less than his usual nontalking self. And he was eating, but not with the same ravenousness he originally had about Tony's cooking.

Just a few weeks, and he was worn down already.

When he got up to leave, she felt compelled to say something to him. All she could come up with was "Don't work too hard."

The rest of the day, she stayed away from the barn. She didn't want to see Brax work himself into the ground no matter how good his muscles looked bulging under his shirt. So when he came limping in with Red that evening, she had no idea how whopped out he was.

Red helped Brax into the chair. Brax groaned in obvious pain, his mouth tightening into a grimace.

"He worked too hard," Red said.

Brax sat back and the imitation La-Z-Boy darn near disappeared behind him. He sure was a big man, Ariana thought. He dropped his head back. His arms went slack at his sides, and he let his legs go straight out in front of him. He closed his eyes and groaned again as if even that small movement hurt.

Red stood back. Crossed one long, thin arm over the other. "Ain't no supermen out this way, son. Just cowboys. And a cowboy knows when to push it and when to take it easy. By the way you're carryin' on, I'd say you best take it easy for the next two days."

Ariana shook her head. She had animals that were good for nothin'. But a hand…that was just plain bad business. "Where does it hurt?" she asked.

Red huffed and leaned against the wall. "Better to ask him where he ain't hurtin'."

"Where don't it hurt?" Ariana asked.

"My big toe," Brax said, not moving, barely breathing, lying as still as a fence post and looking just as long.

"I'll be fine. I just need to sit here a moment."

"Sit!" Ariana and Red said together.

Men! Ariana thought. All week long, he'd been on a mission to prove how tough he was. Tougher than the ranch. And when the ranch beat him out, he still wouldn't admit it. Men could be so darn hardheaded. And this one, with his square jaw and determined eyes, looked like he had the hardest head of them all!

"You may not realize it, Big Rig, but you're lying down in that chair. You ain't sittin'," Red chuckled.

"Umm," he said, sounding too tired to argue.

Ariana conceded defeat the way Brax should have days ago. "What you need is a long, hot bath in fresh sage. And some Cornhusker Lotion. And a good night's sleep."

Red nodded. "Uh-huh. Starting right now. So come on there…Big Rig. Let me help you up."

"Oh, please," Ariana responded. "The only reason you leanin' against that wall is because you can barely move yourself. I know you were out there tryin' to keep up with him. But you're no spring foal, Red."

"I know what I am!" he snapped. "And I know what I can do. Now, I'm about to help this man upstairs."

Ariana laughed inside. "Move out of the way, wrinkly."

She jabbed him playfully with her elbow. He bent over quickly and kissed her on the cheek. A wise, fatherly kiss. She loved the old coot. He was the closest thing she had to a dad. Sometimes she'd wished he was her father. Scraggly hair, gruff beard, tobacco chewing, whiskey drinking. She'd take it all. Willie Nelson fans, eat your heart out. She had Red Findley.

"I'll go run the bathwater," Ariana said and headed upstairs. It was the first time she'd let herself think about a naked man in her house. And the fact that it was a big, handsome, muscle-bound, sexy, African-American man made her smile and get warm in special places—places that were supposed to stay asleep for another four months.

Fat chance with Brax around.

Brax was a liar. He'd told them that he hurt every place except his big toe. Truth was, his big toe hurt, too. Everywhere hurt and hurt bad. What was he thinking? But he didn't have to ask that question. If he was honest, he knew exactly what he was thinking. He was trying to be big and bad and impress that beautiful, finer than the finest fine woman by working his butt off. But God had a sense of humor and the only thing Brax managed to do was work himself into the ground. And now he'd fallen and he couldn't get up. Not even with help.

"You're tryin' too hard, son," Red said.

Brax couldn't move, but he made himself talk. "It's my first time mucking a barn."

"I ain't talkin' 'bout that barn and you know it."

Brax groaned. Could the ache in his body get any worse?

"I'm blind, but I ain't old."

Brax cracked one eye open. "What?" he asked.

"You understand me."

Brax was in way too much pain to set him straight.

"Now you got her attention, that's for sure. But you can't put a rush on it. She and her womenfolk don't play it that way."

"How does she play it?" Brax asked, feigning curiosity. Or was he?

"Like an old banjo, son. Careful. *Real* careful. And slow."

Slow. Brax had no intention of doing anything around here slow. He wanted to get back to his life as soon as possible. He didn't care how fine Ariana was.

"Ready," she said, coming back down the stairs.

"He's all yours," Red said.

Brax opened his eyes all the way and saw Willie Nelson head out toward the kitchen.

"You need any help?" Red asked.

"No," Ariana said, and came over to where Brax was sprawled out in the chair. "Ready, Big Rig?"

Brax gritted his teeth and braced himself for inevitable pain. "Ready," he said.

Ariana slid an arm behind his back beneath his shoulder blades, surprising Brax with how strong it felt. He reached up with his arm and wrapped it around her in the same way.

"On two."

"Two?" he said.

"One…"

"Wait!"

"Two!" she said, and lifted with unexpected strength.

Brax shifted his weight from his behind to his feet and pushed up with all his remaining energy.

The groan that escaped his lips sounded wild and foreign even to himself. Nonetheless, he was on his feet.

Standing next to Ariana felt good. She kept him upright. Sturdy. She was strong beside him and her strength and agility held him with assurance. He felt confident and assured in her ability to hold him up.

"Take it easy," she said.

He held on tighter. His muscles had stiffened since he'd sat down. She bore his weight and held him tighter.

"I don't think I have a choice," he answered.

They climbed the stairs awkwardly, but they climbed them. As hard as he'd worked that day, a hot bath sounded like salvation. He just hoped that his sweat wasn't offensive, as close as he and Ariana were now.

They reached the top of the stairs and maneuvered down the hall to the bathroom.

"I can take it from here," he said. His back was spasming in all directions and he hoped his last statement wasn't another lie.

She gave him another one of those thorough appraisals. Quicker this time. Not nearly as hot and searing, but just as moving. Brax made a note to give her something to look at...when his body didn't feel mangled.

"You sure?"

"One hundred percent."

She let go and he walked stoop-backed toward the bathroom sink.

"Don't you mean eighty-eight percent?"

He took easy steps toward the stool across from the linen shelves. "Was that a joke?"

Ariana frowned. "I can be funny."

"Well, now, *that's* hysterical," Brax said, thinking that if he could chuckle just then, he would have. But that high-sided bathtub with the steam and thin layer of bubbles floating on top of the water called out to him and his aching spine.

Ariana stepped into the hallway. "I'll be back to check on you," she said, closing the door behind her.

Brax moved as fast as he could while still keeping the piercing pain away. It took him fifteen minutes to get undressed and another three to get into the tub. He could have used her help to lower himself into the deep bath. Luckily, he made it himself and the still-hot water surrounded him in a wonderfully wet, steaming, hot cocoon.

"Ah," came his grateful response. He leaned back and settled into the water that came up to his shoulder blades. A light woodsy scent floated up and made him inhale deeply.

The tight muscles in his back relaxed. The spasms slowed. He leaned back and closed his eyes. The image of the bathroom with its sun-yellow walls, distressed wood paneling and brass fixtures gave way to warm oblivion. The bathwater made soft swishing sounds as he settled in. The aroma of natural herbs soothed his aching soul.

He had really overdone it. He didn't think he'd actually thrown out his back, but back strain was a definite possibility. He sank deeper into the water.

He'd only been soaking a few minutes and found

himself so relaxed, he started to drift. *Show-off,* he admonished himself. Was she really so good-looking and attractive that all of his machismo made him want to strut around like Bob Villa on overdrive? Oh, who was he kidding? The answer was *hell, yeah.*

Terrible. He was acting like a pimple-faced adolescent. Funny. He was enjoying himself playing this little wink-and-grin game with Lady West. Like high-school students who look and look away.

Against his better judgment, he laughed at that.

"What's so funny?" came a familiar voice.

If he hadn't been so concerned that he'd wrench his neck, he would have turned around. "Nothing," he said. Then the fact that she'd just walked in on him sank in. "Don't you country folk knock?"

"Not when there're city folk around. We don't trust you."

She came around beside him as if she'd done it one hundred times. "So, feeling better?"

"Feeling violated. I *am* naked."

"Trust me, I've seen a naked man before."

"Not this man."

"What's the difference?"

"Trust me. There's a difference."

Brax didn't cover himself. There were enough bubbles in the water to do that. Besides, he was still reluctant to move for fear that his muscles might yell and shatter glass.

"Water still hot?"

Brax shifted ever so slightly. "Yes."

"If you need help getting out..."

"I won't, but thanks anyway."

Bold woman, he thought as she left. Forward. Fearless. He smiled. He liked that. A lot.

Against the protests of his neck, shoulders, back and arms, Brax found the soap and a washcloth and washed off the day's dust and dirt and grime.

And what did I get for my foolhardiness? he wondered, not able to let his foolish behavior go. A bath and laughter. Well, better he make a fool of himself early on and have the rest of the time to redeem himself than have his stupid stunt go on for weeks, erasing all doubt that he was a nincompoop.

He liked the shape and depth of the tub. It was oversize and accommodated his bulk well. He had plenty of room to wash and soak and relax without feeling crowded. It looked custom-made. It was well designed. If Brax had his way, he'd spend much more time in it.

Forty-five minutes later he'd washed both himself and the tub thoroughly and was headed to his room to chill out for the rest of the evening.

Unfortunately, Ariana had other plans.

The only thing Brax had been able to do since he got into his room was close the door and collapse facedown on the bed. He'd barely covered his backside with his towel before Ariana walked into the room.

"How ya doin'?" she asked.

His body was too tired to react. "I don't get it. Does it work differently out here on the ranch? It must work differently, 'cause where I'm from we knock, announce our presence or just plain leave folks alone until we're invited in."

Ariana sat on the bed next to him. The bed sank with her weight, and his body leaned toward her. "We don't have time for all that formality out here. We have work to do. Now, do you feel better or not?"

"Yeah," he said, wanting to turn over and stretch. "I feel better…better as in I never want to walk again."

"Well, we can take the truck or an ATV from now on."

"I didn't say I didn't want to ride. I enjoy our rides. It's walking that's dealing me a fit now."

"That's the spirit. We'll get you bowlegged and boot-licked in no time."

Brax wouldn't mind being licked, but he sure didn't want that kind of attention wasted on his boots. "So, what's on your agenda?"

"I been puttin' off that ol' toolshed for weeks. I don't mind gettin' the tools out, it's just puttin' 'em back where they belong is where I pull up a little short."

"Not a finisher, huh?"

"What do you mean?"

"For some people, the excitement for something comes at the beginning and tapers off at the end."

"I don't know about that. It sure ain't true when it comes to good cookin'. I enjoy every bite. The first one and the last."

Brax laughed and went warm. He'd never in his life used the word *delightful* to describe anything or anyone. Ariana was truly delightful and everything that encompassed that meaning. Just seeing the sweet twinkle in her eyes lit him up all over. And to know that there was a wise, bold soul behind that delight, it made him want to be just as wise and bold as she.

Maybe he was feeling better. He chanced an attempt to pull himself up on the bed. The pain that sliced through him was blinding.

"It's mostly your back?" she asked.

"Yes."

"Okay," she said.

Brax heard some noises like a jar being opened. He lifted his head but couldn't turn it far enough in her direction to see what she was doing.

"Put your head down," she said in a voice softer than usual. "Relax."

"Don't put anything on me that stinks. No eucalyptus. No menthol. Nothing icy hot or anything with the word *gay* in it."

"Shut up. It'll work better that way."

Brax was about to protest again, when warm hands came down on his lower back and pressed firmly. The sensation was luscious and Brax softened like putty. A few expletives of appreciation popped into his head, but instead of saying them, he just moaned—loudly.

"You're not the first one to mistreat his back around here. I've laid hands on Tony, Red and over half the hands and interns that have worked the Sugar Trail. So enjoy. I'm pretty good at this."

"And not at all modest," Brax responded.

"Why beat around the bush? The truth is the truth. Everything else gets in the way, takes too much time or costs money. I like to keep things simple."

Ariana's hands coaxed out all the tension left in his body, and Brax thought that what she was doing wasn't simple at all. The way she worked each section of his back loosened the knots, broke the strain and smoothed out the spasms bordered on perfection. It was like she had four hands instead of two and each one of them knew exactly how to touch him to make him feel good—real good.

Despite the manly image he held for himself, he melted like whipped butter. "Since we're being truthful, let me ask you something. Are you like this with all men or just me?"

"What do you mean?"

"Well, you're giving a massage to a darn-near naked man that you've only known a week. I could be a pervert or something."

"Please, I can break a wild horse and gut a pig. I can take you."

She blew a thin breath through her lips and then said, "City folk. You think you know everything."

In a move that Brax prayed he wouldn't pay for later, he turned, grabbed Ariana by the forearms and flipped her down on the bed. Now their positions were reversed and he stared down into her beautiful face.

"You country folk," he said. "Too naive."

Ariana's eyes grew wide and soft at the same time. The attraction and admiration in them was so strong he felt it on his body, like her hands had been only a second ago.

They gazed at each other for the longest second in the history of Brax's life. He wanted to kiss her so badly. But he wasn't nearly as forward as she had been with him, and even though he'd had several mothers, they'd all taught him the same things about how to respect a woman.

He loosened his grip, but didn't let go.

"It's just you," she said, sitting up.

Brax let her go. She stood and collected herself. Placed the lid back on a can of Bag Balm salve.

"Put some pillows around your back when you lie down. Another hot bath might not be a bad idea, either. If you need to rest tomorrow, that's not a problem." She walked toward the door but stopped before heading out. “Just get better and get back to work,” she said and disappeared out into the hallway.

Good thing, too. Brax didn’t know what he was going to do about the erection between his legs. He hadn’t bothered to hide it and she didn’t seem like the type to miss something like that.

Brax lay down carefully on the bed. He wouldn’t be any good tomorrow. He knew that already. His back needed rest. And his mind needed to wrap itself around the idea that he and Ariana would most certainly be lovers. From the look in her eyes and his reaction to it, they would be back on his bed soon. Very soon.

Chapter 11

The next morning, Brax stayed in bed. His back was noticeably better and he wanted to keep it that way. He hadn't been there long, but he'd noted a few outlets that needed rewiring, as well as a loose wall panel in the living room, and some fallen cabinet shelves that needed to be reset. It was light duty, but he'd be damned if he'd sit around and do nothing or take over for Tony and cook. That was out.

"Mornin', Big Rig," Red said, poking his head in the bedroom. He carried a plate heaping with sausage, fried eggs and toast. The wonderful smell woke up Brax's stomach and he sat up with care.

Red and Brax cleared off the end table and Red set the plate there and handed him a fork.

"Good lookin' out," Brax said.

Red looked back with a blurry-eyed, red-rimmed blink. "Huh?"

"Thank you," Brax said and dug in.

Just as he'd imagined. Best sausage he'd ever tasted.

"Dadgum if that ain't fresh," Brax said, speaking the way he knew the old man would.

"Yep. Just quit oinkin' this mornin'."

Brax eyed the wrinkled man with suspicion.

"Don't make it so easy, son. You take all the fun out of pullin' your leg if you're just gonna hand it to me like that."

Brax laughed so hard he thought he might choke on that good-tasting food. He didn't and kept right on eating.

"She likes you," Red said. He was leaning against the wall, his eyes fixed on some chew that he'd just removed from his pocket.

"So she says," Brax answered. He remembered Ariana's advice. Tell the truth. Keep it simple.

"She told you."

"Yeah." Brax bit into the toast. Almost took out the whole slice.

Real butter, he thought. Delectable. He slid his thumb in his mouth to make sure he got all of the juice.

Smacking. Now, that was a no-no. But he couldn't help himself. The food was too fresh and too good to use proper etiquette. Proper etiquette would be an insult to how good it tasted.

"I'm getting the same kinda smoke signals from you." The chew garbled Red's voice. Made it sound covered up and held back.

Brax kept eating and sidestepped the question and Ariana's advice about the truth.

"Maybe." He wondered why Red was heading into his territory. Did he and Ariana have a May/December thing happening? Was the old codger checkin' for the competition?

"Throw that nasty question out of your head. I love Ari, but not like that. I swear, you're about as see-through as a windshield."

"According to you all, that's a good thing, right?"

Red let his chew go early. He walked over to the other side of the room, picked up the trash can and spat.

The room suddenly smelled as though Red had lit up a Jamaican cigar.

"Looka here. I've loved that little girl before she loved herself. And if she's taken a likin' to you… well…that means somethin' 'cause that type a'thing don't happen too often 'round here. She's too smart to take to a slick dude. So that's a good one on you. But I want you to know something…you make her cry or hurt her in any type a'way, and you'll wish it was you that got hit 'stead a'Uncle Jesse."

Brax smiled. He couldn't help it. To have someone in your life who cared about you that much. Brax had a brother and a sister, but they had only recently reunited after years of separation and foster homes. There was no one in his life who had his back like that.

Ariana was truly fortunate.

"Do I need to repeat myself?"

"No, sir," Brax answered with as much respect as he could lavish on those two words.

And he took them to heart. Even without Red's threat. Brax had been raised all over, but he'd been raised. He'd pay his debt and do it with dignity and respect.

And he'd make sure that Red saw it.

"You take it easy today. Get yourself well."

"I will," Brax said, but Red was already out the door. And Brax was already planning ways in which he would make good on his promise.

Taking it easy for about three hours, Brax fixed everything on his mental list and even managed to throw in a knob tightening for all the doors and most of the cabinets in the kitchen. He unplugged a slow drain, fixed a leaky faucet, reglued three bathroom tiles and two floor tiles. Even taking his time, he breezed through the jobs thinking for the first time of home maintenance as light work.

Compared to mucking out a barn, pulling a pickup with a chain by his teeth was light work. He'd never tell, or listen to, any jokes about ranchers or farmers ever again.

He'd made himself a pot of coffee and took a break. Brax stepped outside where the sun was as strong as the coffee in his cup. He sat on the porch, noting that his back was sore, definitely, but he liked using his muscles. Pushing them. He enjoyed the physicality. And now he knew where the boundaries were, so he could work up to his threshold.

Just the way his body felt mostly, before the injury. His biceps, triceps, glutes and quads all warm, hot and humming. He was starting to loosen and tighten at the same time. He felt more flexible, yet his arms and upper thighs felt like granite.

If he just used his head from now on, stopped showing off, he might just recondition his body before this was all over.

Brax tested his muscles by walking to the end of the long driveway and retrieving the mail. The box had been stuffed with magazines. *AG Week. American Cattleman. Nebraska Stockman.* What looked like bills from feedlots. Even one from the vet. But what caught his eye was the package. Addressed specifically to Ariana MacLeod rather than the Sugar Trail Ranch. The return address was Columbus, Ohio, and the company was Victoria's Secret.

Brax bit his lip as his imagination ran wild. He wished he was Superman and had X-ray vision.

He shook the box as if that would give him a clue as to what was inside. It didn't. And he knew thinking about it would drive him crazy.

First of all, was it for her? Of course it was for her. It wouldn't be for Selena. Maybe it was a present for someone. God, no. It had to be Ari's.

Brax placed all the other mail by the computer on the kitchen counter, but he didn't know if Ariana wanted her secret out in the open, so he went upstairs to find a more appropriate place.

He didn't think that glancing around her room would break his word to Red, so he took a quick look around her bedroom. Then he placed the package on her bed and the gods smiled. There on a small dressing table sat a Victoria's Secret catalog. And as luck, and lust, would have it, four pages had turned-down corners. On each page, a bra and thong set was circled. Mostly lacy and white. Brax swallowed—hard—and thought he might be breaking out in a sweat. Images of Ariana wearing the lingerie sets moved slowly in his mind. Like a runway model, Ariana strutted her stuff. In his mind, she paused, thrust out a round hip, turned and headed backstage for a quick change.

He saw everything in perfect detail and vivid color. He closed the catalog and replaced it. It seemed Lady West was more lady and less west than he imagined.

He headed back downstairs with a long whistle. He pulled on his collar and headed for the fan. Damn, it was hot in that house.

Chapter 12

A day of rest and he was back at it. That, coupled with the sensations of touching Brax's skin, and Ariana couldn't take her mind off him and his beautiful, naked body.

She wanted to see it again.

"You can handle a pitchfork pretty well. How well do you think you can handle me?" Her mind had forced out the words before her mouth had a chance to clamp shut and prevent them from coming out.

"You don't pull any punches."

"Why should I? The wind, the land, the livestock...they don't pull any punches. They tell it just like it is. If the sky is unsettled, the wind will let you know it. If the soil needs moisture, the crops will let you know it. If a horse doesn't want to be ridden, it will stop or throw you off. Simple. Direct. Straightforward. You don't get mixed up out here. You always know where you stand. I like it that way."

"What about when you leave?"

"It's an adjustment I'll have to make. Selena's future is too important not to."

Brax sized her up the way she'd been doing him ever since he arrived. He took his time with his appraisal, careful to appreciate all Ariana had to offer. "So, are you saying that you won't stop or throw me off?"

"I'm just asking if you're up for the challenge."

"Challenge? What challenge? I'm not sixteen and inexperienced."

"And I'm not some city girl, grinning in the mirror, ready to burst into giggles just because you hold my hand. You gotta work me, just like everything else out here."

He rode closer then, close enough so that she could see the determination in his eyes. "Have I disappointed you so far?"

"No."

They rode farther.

"So, do you say that to every man you lock your eye on, or just me?"

"Just you."

"Well, you got me all wrong, Lady West. I may not know much about what goes on on a ranch, but when it comes to a woman's body, sex, lovemaking, I ride high in that pasture. You have any *special requests*… you let me know."

Ariana stopped her horse and stared back at Brax. "What kind of special requests?"

A light shone from his eyes. Sexy and confident as hell. He was serious, yet a soft smile claimed his mouth. "How do you like to come? Hard and fast? Slow and long? Do you like to cry or laugh? Something in between?"

They kept riding. He could tell she was intrigued.

"You like a waiter? 'May I take your order?'"

"Umm-hmm. That's how I do. When you're with me, you'll get exactly what you want. Have it your way. Every day."

Ariana liked that idea. She'd never had a man "take her order" before. And then something Brax said struck her as strange. "Laugh? Do you tell jokes during sex?"

This time Brax stopped. Turned his horse to where Ariana had dropped back behind him. "Lust laughs. Haven't you ever had them…where it's so good, it brings a smile to your face?"

Ariana frowned. She didn't think she'd had anything like that. Not with Stew anyway. The others were such nondescript occurrences, she didn't remember much about them.

"An orgasm is an orgasm," she said, deciding that Brax was just making stuff up now to make himself sound better. He didn't need to do that. She'd already made up her mind.

Brax's jaw went slack. He gave her another appraising glance. This time, he saw it. The toughness, the hardness, the no-nonsense rigidness. Why she walked so hard and smiled so little. "You've never had one, have you?"

Ariana put a hand to her hip and engaged her neck. He smiled at that. Black women, he thought. In the city, on the road, on a ranch. They were all alike and he loved that.

"I've had plenty of orgasms!" she asserted.

"You sure?"

"Of course I'm sure. I know my own body."

* * *

Before Ariana could get down from Sirocco, Brax was off Run Amok and offering his hand. She smiled and allowed him to help her down.

"Thank you," she said.

"Anytime."

The morning forecast had said partly cloudy skies and a high of ninety. The first part of the morning looked like the forecaster would be dead-on. But sliding into the afternoon, the clouds were beginning to turn steel-gray and the wind picked up by gusts.

Ariana wondered if they needed to brace for another storm. If they had another windstorm like the previous one, they'd have a lot more to fix and repair. She prayed that another animal didn't get loose and wander away like Uncle Jesse.

Brax's hand, despite how it must ache, held her firmly. His touch was warm and even though she'd dismounted her horse more times than she would ever be able to count, his grip was welcome and protective. She felt perfectly safe.

The sensation was strange. With her never having depended on a man for that kind of reassurance, it felt foreign. She was suddenly self-conscious, not wanting to get used to a sensation that was temporary and would be gone at the end of three months. But still…

"Can you fill that water barrel for me?" Ariana asked, trying to think of anything to get him to move away. Take his sensuality and bury it beneath hay and grain or cover it over with straw. Anything to make him unappealing until the work was done.

Somehow, Brax's brown eyes found the tiny amount

of sunshine peeking through the cloud cover and sparkled with it. Before her heart could melt under his gaze, she turned away and headed toward her grain silo.

"I'll get the feed," she said, ordering her foolish heart to ignore itself. *No emotions,* she repeated in her head. *Disconnect,* she ordered herself. Just like with the animals, Brax's time with her was transitory. And it worked. The farther she walked, the more she ticked off the distance between them. Words floated in her mind. *Pull away. Push back. Step off.* She grabbed a feed bucket, opened the silo door and stuck the bucket into the grain. She got it as full as she could carry and headed toward her truck parked in the driveway.

At the same time, Brax made his way back from the water hose, carrying the aluminum pan full. They reached the truck at the same time and placed the water and grain in the bed.

"What now?" he asked.

"Now we visit the sick," she said. "Come on."

They got in the truck and headed off toward the east end. She stopped once to let down the barbed-wire fence so they could drive over.

"How do you do that without cutting your hands?" Brax asked.

"Practice," she said. Funny, she was so used to handling the fence, she never gave it a second thought. She could see how someone who wasn't familiar with the wire could get barbs caught in their skin.

"And you don't worry about puncturing the truck tires?" he asked after they drove into the east pasture.

"No. The barbs are short, so they don't do any damage."

Brax nodded and then moaned. As the truck rode

over the rough terrain of the land, it must have been taking a toll on the man's body. She slowed down.

"Don't slow down because of me," he insisted.

"Don't act like you're not in pain because of me," she countered.

Brax managed a weak smile. She caught it out of the corner of her eye.

"Truth is, Ariana, I don't know if I'll be able to get out of this truck."

They both laughed at that. It felt good to laugh with Brax. Ariana felt like a barrier between them had fallen. Just the fact that he'd said her name made her relax. Feel soft. Womanly. Suddenly, it was like she didn't know what to do with herself. All this in such a short time. What would she be like after a month? Two months?

She had to admit. Aside from Tony, she didn't come into prolonged contact with men her age on a regular basis. Not to mention handsome, well-built, truck-driving, determined, African-American men. Just having him in the seat next to her made her anxious and curious as to what those gentle lips tasted like.

"Whoa!" he said, as a serious dip in the pasture violently jostled them both.

"Don't worry, she won't roll," Ariana assured him. She adjusted her direction and steered the truck toward more level terrain.

Even though the truck still jostled them a bit, Ariana felt Brax go still. "What?" she asked.

"Is all this yours?"

"Yes," she said.

"As far as I can see?"

"As far as you can see," she answered.

"Damn."

It was true. On this part of her land they could see for miles, and for all three thousand acres of those miles, they all belonged to Ariana and her sister. Most days, she didn't think about that. She only focused on being a caretaker of her sister, Red and the animals that shared the land with them. Now and then, she was overwhelmed by the fact that for as far as she could walk, the ground beneath her feet was tilled and wrested with by her family. Their blood, sweat and soul had become part of the soil. When Brax made his observation, it drove that truth home. The awe in his voice made her realize more acutely than ever what was so easy for her to forget and ignore.

They drove on for ten more minutes. Ariana didn't say a word. She didn't need to. Her land was saying it all. And it was talking loudly to Brax. She could tell by the attention he was paying to the hills and valleys. The trees. The colts and mares running in the next pasture. And all the land. His eyes were piercing as he studied it all. Like he was faced with a gigantic meal and was trying to figure out an attack plan to eat and digest it all.

When they came over the hill and drove toward the bull lying on its side, the expression on Brax's face changed and he looked as though he might have trouble even taking a bite out of his meal.

As they neared the animal, Brax sat at attention, ignoring the agony slicing through his back. "What's wrong with him?"

The poor thing was obviously in more pain than he was. He was massive. Easily two thousand pounds and the darn thing was sick. Shoulder bones poked up through his thick skin.

He was covered in flies and barely moving.

"Come on," Ariana said.

She was good at that. Ordering people around. Brax had made a note to mention that to her, but the sight of the ill animal made him think twice and three times.

She didn't have to say another word. Brax ignored his aching limbs and headed toward the water bin in the back of the truck.

"We don't know what's wrong with him," she said, grabbing the grain bucket. "We found him on his side one day. His legs were swollen and he'd already started to lose a lot of weight. We've been shooting him with antibiotics ever since, but he's not responding. For three days, he didn't eat anything, but yesterday, he started eating."

The animal struggled as they approached. Even looked as though he was trying to get up. Brax couldn't tell if he was trying to charge them or run. Either way, Brax was cautious in case the animal regained his strength and didn't like being approached by humans.

But as soon as Brax came up with his exit strategy, he let it go. The Angus, as big as a couch, collapsed with a deep-throated sigh.

"Put the water as close to his mouth as you can," Ariana said.

Brax did as she asked. No sooner had he gotten close than the animal stirred again, struggling to move and raise itself. Ariana set her bucket down quickly and stepped behind the bull. She placed her hands on his shoulders and talked to it like it could understand every word.

"Easy, boy. We just want to get you stronger. We've

got water and corn. And you're gonna get your strength back. Now take it easy. Drink some water."

The animal sat up and lowered its head toward where Brax had placed the pail and stepped back.

A large, dry pink tongue slid out of the bull's mouth and lapped slowly at the water. Ariana continued talking, soothing. Calming. "That's it. Drink all you want."

While Ariana kept the animal calm, Brax went over to where she'd left the grain, picked it up and placed it beside the water pail.

Immediately, the bull switched and nearly slammed its face into the corn. It moaned deeply and ate quickly.

Ariana stepped away. "He couldn't do that two days ago. He's getting some strength, but not healing. If he's not up tomorrow, I'll give him another shot of antibiotics."

"What if it doesn't work?" Brax asked, surprised at his own concern.

"Then it doesn't work," she said.

Suddenly Brax didn't want to hear the details. He didn't need to. He could imagine them. They would continue to bring food and water until the bull stopped eating. After that, it was dust to dust for the enormous animal. Another bullet between the eyes, he imagined.

Life on the ranch. No attachments. He got it.

Ariana walked around to where the bull struggled to eat and drink and pushed the bucket and barrel closer. "That's it, big guy. You keep at it. We'll be back to check on you this evening."

The bull stopped eating for a moment and bent his neck toward Ariana as if he understood every word. She gave him a strong pound on thc flank, then turned toward the truck.

The wind had picked up even more. It blew dust and dirt into their faces. Ariana kept her pace. Brax spat out the grit from between his teeth.

"What about the flies?" Brax asked, bringing up the rear and taking a healthy eyeful of Ariana's round derrière.

"The flies keep the parasites off his hide."

"I always thought flies were parasites."

"Shows what you know."

"Well, I do know one thing," Brax said, heading toward the truck. Every muscle in his body cursed and hollered and knotted up into tiny stabbing points. "I'm not going to be any good tomorrow."

They both got in the truck and Ariana drove toward the house. Images of himself prone, Ariana bringing him water and biscuits in a bucket, played slowly through Brax's mind.

"I'm sorry about that, about workin' you so hard so soon," she said finally.

"No, I'm sorry," he said. "I want to make sure you know how bad I feel for hitting Uncle Jesse."

She nodded. "Thank you," she said and visibly relaxed. Her shoulders went slack and she sat all the way back in the seat. Had she been holding that tension since he got there?

The wind continued to strengthen. Ariana gripped the steering wheel tighter. Angled the truck to the smoother path. It wasn't long before they arrived at the fence. Ariana didn't bother to put the truck in Park, just took her foot off the clutch and jumped out. Leaving the door open, she reached down, picked up the barbed wire and reset it. Then she was back into the truck just as swiftly as she'd slid out.

So easy with her surroundings, Brax noted. He wasn't that easy with anything. Ariana had a way with barbed wire he never had with Hazel. No matter what he did, he couldn't avoid her sharp edges. By the time they split up, they were both cut and bleeding.

He could learn a lot just from watching the way Ariana treated things: her sister, a bull, even a fence. She had a way with it all. And if Brax wasn't careful, she'd have a way with him, too.

Chapter 13

Ariana woke up the next morning, determined to cut Brax some slack. She'd told him after dinner yesterday that he didn't have to go back to the barn. He didn't listen and had gone anyway. Then she'd told him after supper that he didn't have to go back to the barn the next day. He could water and grain instead. He could count the cattle. He could ride with Red and fix the fences.

He refused.

He moved slowly that morning, but he moved. Steadily and deliberately toward the barn. Determined to finish what he'd started.

"Stubborn fool," Ariana said.

"Ain't that the cougar callin' the mountain lion a polecat!"

Red was always sayin' somethin' crazy like that, and Ariana loved him for it. The wise man in the shadows.

He kept her sane. He was the voice of reason when she needed it. The cause of laughter when she needed that. And always the glue holding everything she did together. He'd been around since she was a kid. When her mother died, he'd stepped in like a slow roll of clean air and had been her rock.

And she would never say she didn't know what she would do without him. Ariana knew exactly what she would do without him. She would shrivel up and become useless.

"I'm nothing like that," she said, speaking of Red's comment. He was trying to insinuate that she and Brax were alike. But that couldn't be further from the truth, could it?

"Are you kidding? If he was redboned like you, you two would look alike."

Ariana and Red led their horses along the perimeter of the ranch. Checking for strains and damage to the fence and trying to fight the high winds that hadn't died down from the previous day. "You don't even know him," Ariana asserted.

"I know he got up extra early this morning and was in that barn hours while you were still turning over snoring."

"I don't snore."

"Oh, please. I can hear you from my place."

Red's place was on the edge of her family's property. He lived in the original homestead built by her great-great-grandmother. It was a tiny three-room house that was a half step above a log cabin. But Red seemed perfectly happy there. And having him living on the property made her feel like every part of her land was in good hands.

"What?"

"Didn't know that, did ya?"

"How do you know?"

"Mr. Insomnia told me."

"But it's too dark to work so early. How did he see what he was doing?"

"I don't know. Maybe he took a lamp with him. But he was up and so was I."

"Like I said…stubborn."

"Hmph," Red said.

He knew when to give up an argument. And she wasn't about to admit that she and Brax were the least bit alike.

"So, you gonna go easy on him or what?" Red asked.

"Why is everyone so concerned about how I treat this man? This is the fella that ran over Uncle Jesse."

"He didn't *run over* her."

"Might as well have."

"He just seems like a nice fella is all. You don't want to go burnin' him out before he gets lit good."

That was true. After dinner, she would insist that he do something different. And she wouldn't take no for any kind of answer.

Ariana reflected that in spite of the fact that Brax was serving a *sentence* on her ranch, he seemed to be a decent guy. "He *is* a nice man, isn't he, Red?"

"Sure seems to be, Ari. He sure seems to be."

"I'll see you at the house for dinner?" Ariana said.

"Never miss it," Red said. "If you see Tony, send him out this way!"

"Okay!" Ariana said, already riding toward the barn. Apparently, Tony was nothing like Brax. Tony was content not to do any hard work. He came out of the house and into the pasture occasionally to water and grain the animals. But mostly, he was content to cook, clean, and rope calves on the weekends.

She rode up to the barn and found Brax deep into his chore. Just as she imagined, the spreader was nearly full. Now would be a good time for a break and a drive. Watching how hard Brax was working, maybe just a break.

"Need a break?" she asked, stepping out of the pickup.

He kept hauling, as if he hadn't heard. Hauling, sweating and breathing hard. The sun outside mixed with the shadows inside and made Brax looked larger than life. With his hat, boots and jeans, he was starting to look like a real live cowboy. Damned authentic.

"Give me twenty minutes. I should be at a good stopping point by then."

"What? You think the hay is going somewhere? It'll be here when we get back."

"True," Brax said, bringing out a forkload. He carried it with a practiced arm now. An arm that had a rhythm and routine. He dumped it quickly and returned to the clean spot in the stall.

The horses brayed at her approach. Greedy. She was sure Brax fed them already.

"If I stop now," he called, voice straining with his labor. "Something awful might happen."

"Like what?"

"Like my back locking up, or my legs refusing to move ever again in life." He gave her a quick appraisal. "You know, something like that."

Ariana walked through a wall of flies into the dark of the barn. "I say we take our chances."

Brax straightened and stuck the pitchfork into the thick refuse. "It's your dime," he said.

The wind hadn't died down any. If anything, it had picked up and the temperature had cooled. A long penetrating rainstorm would be a good thing for her ranch right now. Grazing pasture was getting scarce. The drought and hot temperatures had seen to that. She suspected that might be why she had a sick bull, but she didn't know in what way. But she did know that unless it was a torrential downpour that caused flooding, any amount of rain would be a God gift.

As she drove, Brax sank all the way into the seat. He let his head fall back and closed his eyes.

"I know it's a lot of work," she said.

"I know you know," he answered.

"You don't have to work like a crazy man."

"I don't know any other way to be," he said. "If I do something, I do it. Not a little. Not lighthearted. Not half-assed. It's done. And it's done well."

Ariana liked the sound of that. "Where were you last summer? I had two interns who weren't worth a nest of gnats."

"To be honest, I'm not trying to be here for three months. I really want to get this over with. Pay off my debt and get back to my life."

Ariana had a strange reaction to that. She was looking forward to three months with a man like him on her ranch. Just the way he looked at her and the way he allowed her to look at him. It reminded her that she was a woman, even in muck-covered boots. And that feminine touch, which her mother insisted she never lose, made all the difference with Brax on the ranch.

"Is that a problem?" he asked.

"No," she said. "No sense you stickin' 'round when your debt is paid."

Brax grunted his agreement. "So, where we goin'?"

"Choke Hill," she said.

Brax's head lolled over toward her. He opened one eye. "If you mean ta choke me, you go right on ahead, 'cause I'm too dog tired ta stop ya."

"Spoken like a true cowboy!" she said.

Ariana drove on and up toward the hill. The pickup rocked and dipped with the ruts and uneven terrain. She stopped between pastures to open the fences and drive through. Brax kept quiet the whole time. She was saddened by the thought that he might be asleep by the time they arrived. As hard as he'd been working, she wouldn't want to wake him just to see the view.

When they reached the top, Ariana put the truck in Park and cut the engine. Brax lifted his head slowly from the seat and opened his eyes.

"That was bumpy, but restful," he said.

She smiled and he smiled back.

A line of trees and bushes spread off to their left and right. Ahead of them lay five hundred or so acres of her land. They got out of the truck and Ariana walked to where the front bumper brushed against a vine of choke cherries. She picked a few and popped one in her mouth.

"Choke cherries," she said. "You ever have any?"

Brax reached down and grabbed a few of the round red berries. "Yeah," he said. "I used to eat these when I was a kid. These and blackberries."

He leaned against the truck. Crossed one thick leg

lips. That round and voluptuous mouth that had taken over his imagination since he first saw her.

With restraint tossed aside like a branch in that storm, he bent down to taste what his soul had been hungry for for days.

Brax tried to breathe normally. To relax. But Ariana's lips were the sweetest taste he'd ever had in his mouth. Greed consumed him. Instantly. He wanted more. Pressed to take more.

He licked her mouth with his tongue. Tasting every inch. Every wrinkle and soft place. He added his teeth, running them across the flesh of her lips, and began to suck. Softly at first. Then as his need rose, he took from her more urgently, sucked, pulled and licked more sweetly and moaned as she fed him eagerly.

She reached up, pulled him closer, pressed her body tighter.

The inside of her mouth was soft, moist, wet with desire. His body wasted no time in reacting. His blood rushed like hot lava in his veins and straight to his groin where his erection had already started tightening and growing. He pulled her closer, wanting her to know how his body responded to her. How strong his need was.

She moaned deliciously in his mouth.

He realized that if he didn't pull back now, he might not be able to later. And if Ariana wasn't willing, if her reaction to their kiss had come from her fear of the storm, well, he couldn't pressure her. Whatever happened next between them, if anything did, would be on her.

He pulled back. Her lips followed. Apparently he wasn't the only one who couldn't get enough.

"Whoa," he said. "Slow down."

"Why?" she asked breathlessly.

"Because we just survived a storm. And we need to go see if there's damage." Brax heard himself say the words, believing that the only real damage would occur if he could never taste Ariana's honey-sweet lips again.

He reached up, touched her drenched hair. It was soft and wet against his fingers. Her head moved in the direction of his palm.

She was ready. Willing. Her eyes drowsy with desire. When he'd stepped back, she stepped forward. Pressed her hands against his chest.

He groaned and placed his hands on top of hers.

Why did he feel a need to be respectable and forthright when her eyes, her body said *you can have this. Take it—take me?*

This flew in the face of his newly confirmed bachelorhood. After Hazel, he'd made a decision to live carefree, no strings attached. Here was a beautiful woman offering his first taste of that lifestyle since his decision to live it, and he was turning it down. Well, he'd slap himself upside the head later. Right now he needed to put some rational distance between his mouth and hers and see if anyone was hurt.

He planted a soft, reassuring kiss on her forehead. "Let's go," he said.

Ariana was sick. Not physically. Just emotionally. She was thankful that Selena, Red and Tony survived the storm just like she and Brax had. But her ranch hadn't been as lucky. Although there was no major damage, there was enough debris to keep them on cleanup detail for over a week. Trees uprooted. Branches strewn.

Bushes tossed to heck. Not to mention shingles off roofs. Barn doors blown crooked and a mile or two of downed fence.

"We're just startin' to recover from the last storm," she said at breakfast.

"At least this one came with rain," Red said.

That was small consolation, she thought as she sat at the kitchen table scooting her breakfast around on her plate. The men, on the other hand, had no problems cleaning their plates and carrying on as if it were business as usual.

But if Ariana knew one thing for sure, this new day was anything but business as usual. Along with her ranch, her life had been turned upside down—or at least her emotions had been.

The kiss she'd shared with Brax had kept her in a constant state of sensual awareness. Ariana liked to go out in the early morning sometimes, catch the first fresh air of the day before anyone was up. But last night, Ariana stayed in her room. She didn't want to chance running into a restless Brax in the wee hours when her good sense was probably still asleep and couldn't override anything that resembled bad judgment.

So tender. So damned tender. She'd never been kissed like that. With so much force and care at the same time. She wanted more and was so glad that all the cleanup work ahead of her would keep her from following Brax around like a foal nagging him for one more chance. One more kiss.

"Look, Ari. We'll clean it up. Don't worry," Tony said, rubbing her arm.

Ariana smiled inside when she saw Brax's gaze lock

on where Tony's hand settled on her forearm. He took a swallow of coffee and looked away.

Jealous already, she thought and wondered how protective he would be of her after they slept together. Funny, now that he was wearing jeans instead of his city clothes, all she wanted was for them to come off.

"I'll check the windmill," Selena said, then gulped a glass of milk.

"You finish packing," Ariana said.

Selena placed an empty glass on the table and rolled her eyes.

Ariana ignored her sister. "Red, why don't you and Tony take the perimeter and the fence? Brax and I will take the interior and the animals. We'll water and grain and count."

"Sure, give us the tough duty," Red said.

"Ari's been through it recently. She deserves to take it easy," Tony said and punctuated his statement with a kiss on her cheek.

"Okay," Brax said, standing abruptly and looking slightly agitated. "We should probably get going, then."

Red and Tony stared at Brax with questioning looks. Ariana knew exactly what was going on.

"Might as well," she said, standing, as well, and following outside. When they were out of earshot, she said, "Awful possessive, aren't you?"

"Yes, I am."

"Kinda soon, ain't it?"

"Maybe," he said.

They both got into the truck. Gave each other a good appraisal before Ariana started it up.

Brax let out a breath and stared out the passenger-side window. "Okay, yeah. I had a reaction. I don't know why."

"I do." She smiled, feeling bold in a way she hadn't before. A way different from roping cattle and breaking colts. "It was the kiss. The kiss came over you. And now you feel like I'm your territory. Or at least my body is. Males mark their territory all the time."

"That's what you think, huh? That I was marking my territory?"

"Something like that."

He turned and gave her a look she didn't like. One that gazed at her with disdain and distaste. She'd made him mad, hurt him or both. Ariana didn't feel good about either. "I'm sorry. My mouth is always getting me into trouble."

"In more ways than one," he responded.

"Are you angry?" she asked, noting the tightness in his voice and the clipped expression on his face.

"Yes," he said, turning away once more.

Ariana stopped the truck and put it in Park. They had too much work to do to become enemies now. And with over two months left in his "sentence," it would be torture to go through that whole time like opponents with attitudes.

"Are you angry with *me?*" she asked, afraid of the answer, but needing to know nonetheless.

"No," he said.

Ariana waited. Kept her hands to herself instead of touching him the way she wanted to.

"I'm mad at me. I wanted you yesterday—"

"Hell, I *still* want you," Ariana declared.

Brax chuckled. That seemed to break the tension

between them. He reached toward her. Ran the backs of his fingers across her hair. The gesture felt heavenly and brought strong memory of his kiss back to her lips. Her body. The man was so sexy. The heat in his eyes alone was enough to start a serious brush fire. She took a deep breath and prayed that he never stopped touching her. "I was trying to do the honorable thing and not take advantage. Then when Tony touched you and kissed you, well, my ego went into overdrive."

"I'll say. You looked like you wanted to smash his face."

"How about drive a cattle brand down his throat?"

"Daggone. You got it bad," Ariana said, grateful that he hadn't stopped touching her hair and enjoying every stroke.

"Well, just for the record, I still want you, too."

Ariana released a long sigh. After she'd practically put herself on a platter and been refused, she was glad that he was at least interested. Maybe even as interested as she was.

"Red and Tony should be gone from the house by now. We could—"

"Hold up, Lady West. Not so fast. Why don't we—?"

When Ariana took his hand and put his finger in her mouth, he shut up quick and let her slow, swirling tongue inside the tight wet of her mouth send shock waves through him. After only a few seconds, he wanted to unzip his pants, set his erection free and beg her to divert her talented tongue to where he ached most.

Suddenly she stopped and Brax's whole world stopped with her.

"I'm sorry," she said.

"Don't be."

"I don't want you to think I'm some kind of homestead 'ho. I mean, we haven't known each other long."

"How long does it take to know what we want?" he said, feeling like he'd make a huge mistake in not taking Ariana up on her offer.

"Let's just get through the day," she said.

Brax looked down at the large bulge in his pants. "How?"

"The best way we can," she said. Her voice was thick, sex-deepened like she was just about to have an orgasm or had just had one. He loved the sound and thought fondly of bringing that sound out of her again... and again.

"So, what happens now?" Brax asked, cursing himself. Twice. Now that he was so hard he could nail her to a wall, she was putting on the brakes.

Story of his life, he thought as yet again he was denied the very thing he'd dared to feel something about.

"We have an affair. A two-month affair. As hot, quick, torrid or languid as we want. And when it's over, it's over."

"Sounds like a plan. When do we start?" he asked, noting that there'd been no change in his groin area. He wanted her and the promise of her mouth in the worst way.

"Let's just clean up the ranch first. Heck, we both may be jumping the gunnysack. If we are, we'll find that out, right? Maybe we'll be too tired or find out that we're really not that attracted to each other when we're done."

Brax rubbed himself in the most sensual way she'd ever seen. Obviously, he was trying to adjust himself in his pants, but to Ariana, it was an act of sensual aggression. It made her throb and moisten up. "Oh-kay. So maybe we're puttin' off the inevitable. But suddenly I'd feel better about myself if I didn't give up the goods so fast."

"Gotcha," Brax said.

Yes, you do, Ariana thought, starting up the truck engine. *Ya got me gate, hook, fence line and sinkhole.*

Brax groaned painfully. How long would he have to wait? he wondered. "The bull is in your corral," he said.

Ariana smiled and steered the truck out toward the pasture. "You catch on fast."

Brax strummed his fingers against the passenger-side door, thinking that catching on was the only thing with her he planned on doing fast. When it came to her body, he was going to make sure he took his time. The longer she made him wait, the longer he would take with her. Get his fill. Punish and please her at the same time. And one thing was for certain, he would not make the time between then and now easy for her.

Chapter 14

The storm didn't make it easy going in the pasture. Brax and Ariana filled up the truck bed to brimming with branches, weeds and other debris. At first, she found it difficult to concentrate. Every time he moved, reached out, bent to pick something up, walked, breathed, she found herself wanting to be on the receiving end of all his movements. She wanted his hands on her body, his arms around her, his breath in her ear. They had opened Pandora's box and it was big, sprawling like her ranch and all out in the open so there was nowhere to hide. She kept catching herself watching him, moving toward him. Using every excuse to touch him, brush up against him, be in his line of sight. It was as if she'd suddenly lost her mind. She couldn't help herself. It wouldn't have been so bad if Brax hadn't behaved as his usual self-contained, inverted self. The man of few words. While she threw herself at him, he threw himself at the task. They'd skipped dinner and cleared the interiors of her land well before four. The only chore left was to count head. They made another sweep and that's when they saw it, or rather her.

The new mother. The Angus that had just given birth. She was laid flat, the top half of her body burned black as tar.

"What the hell?" Brax said.

Ariana's stomach clenched into an all too familiar ball. "Lightning. We lose two to five head a year to severe storms."

The two approached the animal tentatively, the smell of charred flesh still singeing the air.

"We've been pretty lucky this year. This is the first one we've lost. Hopefully the only one. With Uncle Jesse gone, we really can't afford more accidents."

Brax nodded, his expression pensive. Pained. He walked around the animal, speechless and concerned.

"What about the calf?" he asked.

"It grows up without a mother," Ariana answered. "We'll take care of it until it can take care of itself. It's not unusual."

"It's not ideal, either."

"Well, no," she said, reacting to the seriousness in his voice. "But it happens. *We* can handle it."

Brax nodded. "So, what about the carcass?"

"Usually, I'd call a rendering truck. But it's been so dry this year and food has been so scarce for everyone, I think I'll just let the turkey vultures do what they do."

The pained expression returned with full force. Brax

looked as though she were speaking about a human being instead of an animal.

"Don't get attached, remember?"

He moved his gaze from the charred carcass to her, "I remember," he said with a voice as dead as the cow.

Ariana had counted up to eighty-three head when she noticed something out of the ordinary. It was a steer—brown with small white spots on its left flank. She didn't have to read the tag to know it belonged to the Bar S. Hank Snooden's steers were always getting out. It was as if the castration hadn't worked and all his steers lived to come over and root around Ariana's heifers. They were proof that castration didn't always eliminate the urge to mate. No matter what, as she'd seen in all of her thirty-four years on the Sugar Trail, the urge to mate, procreate, reproduce, release sexual energy was one of the strongest God ever created. Hank's steers didn't know what had happened to them or at least they acted like they didn't know.

Three of them were always testing the wire, finding the weak point, breaking through whenever they could.

Most of the time, she'd catch them before they got in, but a couple of times, she'd caught this one—red ear tag 1226—posting up on one of her heifers. The poor thing probably couldn't figure out what was wrong once he got up there.

That's why most ranchers kept the steers and bulls separate. Or at least kept them in check behind a secure and sturdy fence.

Hank wasn't that way. He was just too easy with everything and everybody. Ariana stepped down off her horse, let the fence down and tried to shoo the steer in on foot.

He was too stubborn, so she got back on her horse and guided the steer across the fence that way. When the steer was a good distance back on his side of the pasture, Ariana put the fence back up and continued counting.

She looked off in the distance and saw number eighty-four.

Her chore list was long that morning—replace a patch of barn siding, replenish the water tank, check the tires on her pickup, call Willows for an update on potential buyers—but her mind was shortsighted. The only thing it could remember with any certainty and detail was how strong and powerful Brax's back felt beneath her hands. How her fingers felt like they were rubbing satin-covered steel. And the delicious shivers moved up from her wrists and spread like a brush fire throughout the rest of her body every time she pulled a moan from him. She smiled every time she thought of how easy it had been to do that.

The men she knew, the cowboys, had muscles that were tightly coiled like ropes. They had hard muscles, yes. But the muscles were long and tight. They were built like greyhounds. Brax was more of a boxer. His muscles came in thick solid blocks.

Brax had responded to her touch in a way that relaxed her, too. Made her comfortable being so near his naked body she could taste the soap he used by breathing his aroma..

Delicious!

His skin was such a rich brown. Unlike her soft brown that reddened when touched deep into the tissues, his color never faltered. It remained a deep sable. She could have touched him like that for hours and still wanted more. When she stopped, her hands drooped at the wrists like they were sad.

She slashed a bag of grain open with her pocketknife and dumped the cracked corn into the feed trough.

Yes, sir. Her memory was short and stuck on the way Brax had had his way. Flipped her like a flapjack. Gave her the best view of her life, next to the hilltop view of her land. That Brax was something else. So different than what she'd expected.

Now she couldn't help but wonder how he would surprise her next.

With the rest of her list forgotten, Ariana headed back to the house. She told herself it was time to get an early dinner and then start on the rest of her chores. The real reason was to check on Brax, see what he was doing. Watch him move if he was moving. Rub his back if he wasn't. Anything to touch him again. Be underneath him again. Feel like a woman again.

"Get up, Sirocco," Ariana said, thrusting her boot heels into the horse's flank. She snapped the reins and the horse changed from a quick trot to a gallop.

Ariana smiled. She hadn't run her horse in a long time. Both she and Sirocco cut through the wind like they had become a single force running on the open plains. It was times like these that Ariana loved—moving with the horse, the give and surefootedness of Sirocco as she drove them both on. They couldn't have been freer if they'd left the ground and grown wings. Not even gravity could hold them.

It was the perfect marriage of strength and power beneath her. Muscle and purpose. Sirocco ran on as if he knew Ariana's thoughts, her desire to break free. It was a wish they both shared. And these were the times when both their wishes came true.

Moving too fast for the sun to settle on them, Ariana hunched forward. Got close. Let her nose lead like Sirocco's. A cloud of dust rose behind them. Her breath came in large snatches like the horse's heartbeat.

When she got close to the house and brought the horse up slowly, Ariana knew that she'd had a much-needed release of pent-up emotion. She knew also that no matter how hard, fast, and far she rode, it would never be enough. The only one who could get her over Brax was Brax. And the only way he could do it was to make love to her. Until that happened, Ariana and Sirocco made good friends with the wind.

When she finally got to the house and the stable, she was panting as much as the horse. Ariana stepped off Sirocco and walked him the rest of the way to fresh water and hay in a big trough in the corral.

Sirocco swung his head and neighed at bit, happy he was let loose, if only for a few marvelous moments. Ariana patted the horse and made quick work of removing his harness and saddle.

I'm going to miss that when I sell, her mind told her. *How's it going to be, holed up in a house like a hen in a chicken coop? How are you going to keep the crazy away?*

The best way I can, she told herself and headed inside the house.

Ariana's pulse quickened and she had to fight her

exuberance to skip through the house calling Brax's name. She wanted to see him. Bad. She wanted to smell him. Watch the way his eyes grew intense when he looked at her.

Less than a week later, Ariana found that the hardest job she had was not tending to her ranch, it was trying to stay on Brax's radar. But like when he first arrived and threw himself into barn work, he'd now thrown himself into the watering and graining of the motherless calf. And not just the calf, all of her animals had a caretaker. Brax made sure they were fed and counted. He kept the windmill turning. Kept the pens and stalls clean. He took to the livestock and they'd taken to him. Talk about a cowboy. He strutted around her land as if the animals belonged to him and she was a visitor.

Red and Tony went along with it probably because they were so grateful to have another hand around, they let him do whatever. They even took orders from him and had bonded to the point where she was starting to feel left out.

After a week passed, Ariana was more restless than she'd ever been in her life. Brax had pushed away from her and her ranch. Surprisingly, letting her see him be the hardest worker on the Sugar Trail was the sexiest thing he could have done. He left every morning clean and eager. He came back every evening covered in his work and worn out. And her land was much the better for it. He was paying off his debt and then some.

Ariana wanted him more than she'd wanted any man in the entire thirty-four years of her life.

"Save some of that energy," she said, climbing up into the barn loft.

Brax had nearly emptied the entire loft of hay and alfalfa, sending it down into the stalls for the horses. She would have to stock up again soon.

"Horses get hungry," he said.

"So do people," Ariana said in her deepest, most sensual, *I want you* voice.

Over the past few days, she'd let up on her flirtation and pursuit. But her libido hadn't let up. So she'd decided that morning to *step up her game.* At least she thought that's what it was called.

There were just two months left, but she felt like she was running out of time and that the connection she'd shared with Brax was being lost.

He broke off a layer from the brick of alfalfa, then took a small pitchfork and hurled it down into Run Amok's stall. The horse whinnied his pleasure.

Then Brax turned to look at her. Ariana had taken special care with her hair and clothing that morning. Not the typical pulled-back ponytail. Not her regular Wrangler shirt and jeans. Her hair was loose and her black shirt and black jeans by Miss Sixty, her favorite designer. She hoped Brax approved.

He took his time checking her out. "You look good," he said, leaning an elbow against the pitchfork.

"So do you," she said. She got close. Real close. Took a few steps around him, then came back to face him. His eyes never left hers.

"You interested in takin' a break?"

He smiled. "What kind of break?"

She took the pitchfork away. Threw it to the other side of the loft.

"This kind," she said, stepping forward. Before he

could react one way or another, she kissed him, full-on. She'd wanted a slow build and some kind of restraint on her part.

She didn't get that. And neither did Brax. What they both got was the full onslaught of all the pent-up energy she'd kept in check for the past two weeks. She nearly knocked him down with it.

When he stumbled back and their kiss was broken, they were both a bit breathless and surprised by the intensity of her passion.

"Ariana—" Brax said, stopping her hands that were already reaching out for him again. Seeking his warmth and comfort.

"What?"

"Slow down," he said, fighting off her advance, using arm movements like wax on/wax off.

Ariana's acute need turned into maddening frustration. "Slow down! I've been slow for two weeks. And you've been cool as January frost."

He frowned with a half smile. "Cool as what?"

She backed away. "I thought we had an agreement."

Brax removed his work gloves. "I thought we did, too."

"Well, don't do me any favors and sleep with the horny cowgirl the day before you leave. I'm not a charity case."

"Look, I'm here to repay a debt. I'm going to repay it with chores out here, not chores in your bedroom."

Ariana placed her hands on her hips. She hoped the gesture would mask the pain she felt from Brax's words. "I never said—"

"I know you never said. But your actions just spoke a different message. And I wanted my intentions here to be perfectly clear."

"Oh, you don't have to worry about that. They *are* perfectly clear."

Ariana shook herself to pull herself together.

"Ari," Brax began.

"Ari?" she repeated, stepping backward. "That's awful familiar, don't you think? I mean, callin' me that might give me the wrong impression."

Brax's body went slack and he reached out for her, but Ariana didn't want his consolation. What she wanted was to get away. Her feelings were hurt. And for someone used to getting her way, the thought that she couldn't get what she wanted was strange and confusing. She wasn't used to it and didn't know how to act. But she did know that she needed to get away from him and figure it out.

She took one last look at him before she headed down the ladder. She wanted to remember what had attracted her to him in the first place. Everything was still there—his determination, chestnut-brown skin, his piercing brown eyes, the five o'clock shadow that always showed up at three, his all-brawn body. Even his penchant for silence and the fact that he would not take "I can't do it" for an answer. And now that she committed it to memory, she knew exactly what to shield herself against. What to build a barrier for. And what to fight a weakness to.

Ariana left embarrassed, disappointed and extremely hurt. Her reaction surprised her and she made a promise to herself that Brax Ambrose was off-limits. He wasn't the only one who could keep busy and stay distant on the ranch. But damn, it would be hard.

Brax had trouble working the rest of that day. He kept seeing Ariana's face, the way her body went limp as if all the strength had been stolen from it, and the disappointment in her caramel-brown eyes. It haunted him for hours. Supper, a spirited talk with Red and Tony afterward and a hot shower didn't erase the lingering image. Even in his sleep, he kept seeing Ariana, sensing her hurt and feeling guilty. Finally, when he'd grown tired of tossing from one cold side of his bed to the other, he got up and decided a walk might do him some good.

He headed out into the pitch-dark of the early morning and didn't come back until the day had just begun to break.

As he approached the house, he noticed a figure sitting on the roof. He didn't have to get close to know it was Ariana. He could make out her silhouette anywhere. He'd memorized every curve, every shape of her body. She probably thought he didn't pay attention to her, didn't watch her. Didn't see her watch him. But he did.

And now, after weeks working the property, he knew every bat of her lashes. Every way she snapped the reins on her horse. How she liked to stand with one ear to the farthest end of the pasture and listen for the whip-poor-wills. The way she kept an eye on her sister before she left for the city. How she would sometimes stare at the top of Choke Hill for minutes on end and look so very sad. And how sometimes at night, when she couldn't sleep, she'd climb up on the roof and watch the sunset.

"Were you here when I left?"

"Yes," she said. She sat on the flattest part of the roof where the left and right side came together surrounded by a wooden railing, with her legs crossed and her eyes toward the sky.

"You watched me go and didn't say anything?"

"I didn't want to give you the wrong impression," she said. Her voice was so full of sarcasm it hurt him to hear it. Suddenly he realized why it was so difficult for him to sleep.

With a heavy heart, he stepped to the end of the porch and began to climb up. When he reached the top, he swung over the railing, took a seat next to her and looked to the east where the sun was waking up the sky.

"I come up here when I need some perspective on things. When I need to pull back and think clearly."

"It must be nice to just unwind when you want to, then jump back up when you're ready. I've never had that option."

A timid sun hid behind a rolling body of clouds. A few rebellious rays illuminated grassy dunes and expansive lowlands of the prairie wilderness.

Brax continued. "I've been disconnected from everything. I don't remember a time in my life when I felt any real connection to anything. Not when I was a kid. Not when I was growing up. Not until…now."

Brax's heart pounded like the thunder in the storm they had ridden. He knew she could hear it. She had to be able to hear it. She didn't act like it, though. She didn't move. She just stared at the sunrise and wrapped her arms around her knees.

"I'm a truck driver for a reason, Ari. It suits me. It means I don't have to be any one place for any long period of time. It means I can keep moving." He paused for a moment. Not wanting to continue, but knowing he had to.

"You said, don't get attached. I'm the king of unattachment. And then I came here. And for a while, the first few days, this place felt like prison. All I wanted was to serve my time and be released. Then came the storm and that kiss. It made me want to stand still for a moment. But what did me in was when we found that cow, and I realized that that calf that I helped bring into the world was as alone as I was. No strings. No attachments. No connections. I realized that I didn't want to go through life like that anymore."

Ariana turned slowly from the sunrise to look at him. The red and yellow rays peeling back the black sky illuminated her face. Made it shine with curiosity.

"I had plans to become a swinging bachelor and to live the carefree life I've never lived before. No commitments. Just fun. But a man like me wasn't built for fun. Not that kind anyway. I know that there's no way I could ever kiss you again. Not with the *agreement* that we made.

"I'm growing up, Ari. And a decision to use you for two months, or for us to use each other, doesn't seem like a very grown-up thing to do. If I've hurt you or led you on, I'm sorry."

She turned toward the sunrise again. Her expression never changed. "Maybe I overreacted. I'm not used to being denied, Brax."

"I can tell," he said honestly.

She touched him. First on the forearm and then on the thigh. Her eyes darkened, even in the growing sunlight, and every sense in Brax's body came awake.

"Don't deny me, Brax. Please. I want you so bad, I can't think anymore. I can't breathe."

Her hand trembled against his. He held it. Caressed it. Indulged himself in the feel of it.

Dear God, he wanted her just as badly. Maybe even more so. "Ari—"

"Screw the two months. Don't you know why I can't sleep? Why I haven't been able to sleep in weeks? Screw the two months, Brax, I want—"

He didn't let her finish her sentence. His heart couldn't hear it. Just in case things didn't work out between them, better he didn't have a promise from her lips haunting him.

Better to live now, he thought, and covered her lips with his.

Chapter 15

Ariana surrendered, determined to keep her fierce need tamed. She'd wanted to be touched by a man like Brax for a long, long time. She opened her mouth, let him in. He smelled like the bath he had taken before he went to bed, he tasted like the hay he probably picked on his walk. He felt like a blessing. Warm. New. Marvelous. And capable of bringing her deep joy.

His tongue searched for hers. Swiftly. Determinedly. Powerfully. His breath hot on her lips. She shivered with anticipation and drew herself nearer to her pleasure that started in her mouth and moved in long swift lines and pulses down her body. Reaching out like hot greedy fingers, teasing, touching, nibbling. Sampling.

And she was just as greedy. Leaning against his body. Wrapping her arms tightly around his neck. Taking.

He tasted her and fed her at the same time.

His kiss was a deep, dizzying promise of pleasure to come. And she wanted everything.

The skies that had never truly settled from the storm sent strong winds across her back and face. Warmth from the rising sun caressed her skin. And then there was Brax, smoothing, soothing.

She sent her deep moan into the wind and Brax set her free.

His hands, his fingers, touched her tenderly. Methodically. Creating a trail from the nape of her neck to her shoulders to the top of her breasts. The path ignited and caught fire on her skin. She lost her breath and came up for air.

"You taste good," he said.

She placed her hands on the side of his handsome face. His eyes were dark, even in the rising day. Dangerously seductive. She caught sight of her own reflection in them, her expression much the same. Gone into the sexual abyss. There was nothing she wouldn't do or deny to please or be pleased by him.

He took her hand as if to lead her back inside.

"Can we do it here?" she asked, the throbbing between her legs deep and insistent.

"Wherever you want," Brax said.

Ariana barely recognized his voice or her own. They sounded sex-drugged, like other people had started to speak through their mouths—other people who didn't care where they were or who saw. Only that their needs were satisfied.

The pleasure throbbing inside her turned into a need so sharp, it hurt. She gasped with the sensation. She'd never felt something so painful. So delicious.

"Ah, Brax! Please…touch me," she pleaded, hoping that would stop the terrible ache.

"Like this?" he asked, and slid his fingers between her wet opening where she opened and flowed like a brook. He fingered her with long, strong strokes.

"Ah!" she said, savoring the sensation. But only briefly. The pain built again.

She didn't know what to do, how to save herself. No one had ever brought her this far before. She prayed Brax knew how to bring her back from the brink or take her all the way over.

"Brax…ssss…it feels so good…I, I can't take it."

He plunged his hand deeper. Ariana cried out and felt her juices sliding down between Brax's fingers.

"Damn, you're wet," he said and kissed her.

By that time, her mind was gone. She'd lost it the second he started sliding his fingers in and out of her like a piston. She held on while her hips danced wildly with the rhythm all on their own.

She could control nothing.

"So, tell me, Lady West," he whispered in her ear.

"W-what?" she asked. Her voice trembled out the word as she stuttered.

He kissed her forehead. Her temple. Her cheek. "Is it good?" He kissed her jawline. "Do you like it?"

"Uu-uh, Brax…yes!"

"Am I good?" he asked.

"Yes!"

He was more deft than anything she could have imagined. Downright skillful. He touched her, turned his fingers, circled them inside her, plunged them deep, vibrated them against her walls like he'd been born with his hand inside her. He changed her mood like her clit was a remote control. She squeezed her eyes shut and panted from the pleasure. When she opened them, Brax gazed at her with interest and the bold expression of a man in complete control. He was watching her. Programming her with his hand and watching the changes his skill produced.

And she loved it!

And she liked the new sound her body made from it. Slick and wet and needy. Like rain falling between her legs.

A sense of strength and weakness radiated in large, powerful waves. She wanted to watch, too, as Brax worked his arm back and forth—in and out. Worked his arm. Worked his hand. Worked her. Ariana sucked air between her teeth and bucked wildly as if she were an unbroken bronc in her own bull pen.

The more his hand rocked inside her, the more she lifted her hips to meet it. If he moved left, so did she. Right and she was there. She didn't want him to ever stop touching her this way. She felt like she would die if their connection ended.

When he pulled his hand back, she groaned in protest and clawed at his body selfishly. "No! Please! Don't stop!"

"I want to taste you," he said.

Ariana sighed and leaned forward to kiss his tender mouth. But instead of meeting her, Brax bent and stuck his tongue inside the soft sensitive place where her feelings for him flowed so freely it felt as though she'd sprung a leak.

The soft forceful warmth of his tongue jolted her so

completely as he licked, she screamed into the early morning and birds asleep in a nearby tree startled and took flight.

"You're so free. So open. So giving," he said.

She heard him say the words and realized he must not know. She couldn't refuse him if the world depended on it. She couldn't say no. Couldn't stop him. Couldn't hold anything back. She wondered if he knew a woman was being born on that roof. He was bringing her to life. And she was determined to experience and feel all that life could offer her.

She flung her arms out to her sides. Opened her legs as wide as she could. She let go of everything and like the newborn she was began to cry.

All this time she'd believed that being in control was important. She was so, so wrong. Ariana gazed at Brax through her tears. Tender concern filled his face. Not just raw lust. He cared about her. She saw it in his eyes and that above all else plunged her over.

She let out the scream that had been tightly wound inside her waiting to be set free since the moment they first touched. It wasn't loud. It wouldn't break glass or any records for decibels. But it was long, full of bliss and the joy of being made complete. The sound made her feel lovely. But most of all, well loved.

She lay there for a second, all of her senses open and in overdrive. She breathed hard and tingled from head to toe.

"I've wanted you since you hit Uncle Jesse," she admitted.

"With the way your eyes hurled buckshot at me, I sure couldn't tell."

"In my mind I was thinking, 'You careless, fine, handsome, reckless man.' I didn't know whether to slap you or slide my tongue in your mouth."

"I'm glad you went the tongue route."

"You haven't seen or felt a tongue route…yet."

"Well, don't make me wait too long."

"How 'bout now?" she asked, stroking his thigh.

Brax lay beside her smiling, as big as a wheelbarrow. "Let's just say you owe me."

She frowned, wanting the rest of him. "Don't worry," he said and stroked her inner thigh. "I always collect on a debt."

Brax's blood cooled as he sensed her turning away from him. "Like someone once asked me, what's spookin' ya?"

"Me, I guess. It's like you turned me inside out or something. Just way too exposed if you ask me."

He leaned against the white wooden fence. Planted the heel of his boot against the two-by-four. "Sometimes being exposed is a good thing. Besides…you didn't seem to mind when you were waking up in the morning screamin' my name. I like you when you're exposed. You're beautiful when you're exposed."

"I could end up wanting you to stay longer than three months."

"Don't worry. I won't."

"I feel like somebody…well, you…turned a light-bulb on inside me. I must be sparklin' like the Baker's Field fireworks show."

"Woman, will you shut up?" he said, pulling her to his chest quick and kissing her hard.

"I don't know what to do with these feelin's. They

keep wantin' to bust out of me. All the time. I keep wranglin' 'em in like they can be roped, but it don't seem to help too much."

"So, what are you saying?"

"I'm saying I'm way too confused to make you a habit or anything like it. At least not until this... whatever this is wears off."

"And if it doesn't?"

"Oh, Lordy. Then I'll be in way more trouble than I know what to do with."

Brax grinned and echoed her words. "Oh, Lordy. You sound like you're from the Deep South."

"People tell me I sound just like my mama. Red says it's my mouth that's moving, but it's her voice that's comin' out.

"And people say she sounds like *her* mama. And that she sounded like hers and on back. The tale is that Great-Great-Grandma Gunny lived in Nebraska, but she never really left Tennessee. I was twenty-eight years old before I really got that meanin'. Do you get it?"

"Yeah. I get it."

"I'm sure that over the generations, something about the way the MacLeod women speak changed, but I guess it's not enough to make a big difference.

"With city folks, it ain't the sound of the words, it's the words themselves. You-all don't fence in nothin' ya say."

"I thought you liked to lay it on the line."

"I do. And I lay it. I don't throw it or smash it down or drill it in. But city folks, oh, no offence!"

"No harm, no foul."

"Well, you let your words do any ol' thing. Run any kinda way. I mean, they seem to come out so fast and hard, I wonder sometimes if you really know what you're sayin'. I mean, pssh, don't get me started."

"Why not?"

"Well, 'cause I would say that half the time you don't seem to know what you're doin', either. I think if you-all could fit twenty-four hours into six, you would."

A blast of laughter shot from Brax louder than he'd ever heard it. Damn, the way her mind worked. Easy and complex at the same time. Ariana, just like this place, was a breath of fresh air. Brax felt like he was breathing for the first time in his life.

"You better not be laughing at me. I'm pretty handy with a hot brand." Her smile was big, honest, full of sweet play and beauty.

"Don't you know you've already branded me?"

Her playful expression dissolved into wonderment. She blinked several times and sucked in a breath.

Brax pointed to his heart. "Property of the Sugar Trail Ranch—Ariana MacLeod, proprietor."

"You like my place?"

"I've been alive for forty years, but none of it mattered until four weeks ago."

"But what about the ranch?"

Brax had to reassure her that he wasn't still the slow-talking Big Rig he'd been when he first arrived. He'd found his heart on this ranch and his soul in her. He wanted them both. Loved them both.

"I love your ranch, Ariana. So much I wish it was my own."

They nuzzled against each other, spooned in an embrace of pure bliss. In Ariana's dreams, the Sugar

Trail did belong to Brax and in that beautiful fantasy, moving away to the big city was the last thing she wanted to do.

Chapter 16

The hours in the day had moved faster than Brax could sense them. He'd discovered that nobody around here wore watches. After a while, he didn't need one, either. The sky, the temperature, the energy of the animals, and his body told him what time of day it was. Even the scent on the air—full or light, pungent or earthy—told him better than a second hand ever could which chore he needed to move to next. By the time he took a breath, his chores had come to an end and he grabbed some reading material and headed up the stairs to bed.

He stopped as soon as he got to the landing and saw Ari. She stood just at the door of Selena's room. Staring in, half-smiling, half-sad. It was obvious that she missed her sister. The push-pull of emotions played like delicate shadows across her face. Ari fingered her collar with one hand parked on her round hip.

"You miss her," Brax said, more statement than question.

"Yeah. She's my only family. When she's gone, well, it's like I just don't know what to do with myself.

"I know she's my sister, but she's also like a daughter. Everything I do is for her. I want her to be happy."

Brax strode next to Ari. Close enough to sense the warmth of her body. "Are *you* happy?"

"Me?" she said and recoiled as if he'd asked her the most ridiculous question on earth.

He kissed into her hair and down to the top of her head, inhaling all the *j*'s—jasmine, juniper, jimsonweed. They were all her and he loved them. "Yeah, you."

Ariana put her arm around his waist. He took a deep breath, letting the care and possessiveness of her move sink into him. She turned toward him a little. Snuggled close like a child herself. "I don't think about me, much. It's just safer that way."

He didn't like the sound of that. "Safer how?"

"If I think about me, it squeezes out thinkin' about the Sugar Trail, about Selena, about Tony and even Red. There's only so much room up there. After a while, things start ta fall out."

He pulled her tighter. "Well, we'll just have to change that."

"Not tonight," she said. She must have sensed that it wouldn't take much for her to make him forget about the magazine in his hand.

He kissed her full on the mouth. It was a gentle rolling kiss to draw out her tension, pull away her anxiety. He'd take it all one lick, one tongue flick, one lip suck at a time. He worked her mouth skillfully, sweetly. Tenderly.

He kneaded the soft flesh inside her mouth, pulsing his tongue along her cheeks, reassuring, touching, licking. He tasted each lip—sucked each one by softly pushing and pulling until the lavish sensation opened moans in them both.

Ariana pulled back gently. “Good night, Brax.”

Inside Brax yelled, *Why? No! Let’s make love now!* He smiled, took half a step back and said, “See you in the morning.”

She moved to go, but the magazine caught her eye. “What’s that?”

This time he chuckled. “*American Cattlemen.* I started reading it earlier and thought I’d finish the article in my room before turning in.”

Ariana slow-footed it down the hallway. She looked tired. “Anything interesting?”

“Surprisingly, yes. A Wyoming guy wrote an article about winterizing your ranch.”

“Why is that surprising?” she asked, stopping at her door. Brax certainly enjoyed watching her walk. Now that he’d gotten an eyeful, he headed toward his room. “The surprising part is that I understand it.”

They both laughed at that and shared a long, connected gaze that made the blood flowing in Brax’s heart feel like a stampede and sent his libido into overdrive.

“Good night, Lady West.”

Ariana’s gaze never faltered, only deepened before she stepped inside. “Good night, Brax.”

Brax stepped into his room and threw the magazine on the bed. Forget that article, he thought. His next stop was either a cold shower or another night of walking in the pitch-dark.

* * *

Four hours later, at 2:00 a.m., he slammed the magazine closed and headed out toward the evening and the darkness that never turned him away.

Brax hadn't been a guest at the Sugar Trail for two weeks before he discovered a mouse nest inside one of the barrels of grain in the hay loft. In the city, anywhere in the city, if he'd found such an unpleasant surprise, he would have been appalled, and thrown the damned thing out, dismantling it in the process. But out here, he'd actually paused to look at the nest and realized with the bits of gray and tufts of yellow, seeds, twigs, and the like, it looked like a soft place for a rodent to bed down. Instead of throwing it away, he left it, thinking that that's all most folks want, just a soft place to lay their heads when the day's living winds down.

He stepped outside and as always, the night swallowed him whole. Typically, there was that second, where he unconsciously checked his hearing. A minute thing. Checking the equipment to make sure it was working properly. A pause and a deep, concentrated listen. This time he didn't do that. He didn't need to. He knew he was the only loud sound maker. Following the path his boots had made for weeks now. Down past the barn, past the pen, down toward the road where his feet really did sink in like sand. Smoosh, smoosh, crunch, smoosh. His boots fell heavily against the earth. Deeper it seemed. He'd probably gained seven or eight pounds since he'd been there. He ate good, so some of it might have been fat. But he suspected the bulk of it was muscle. And he liked that. Liked the tightness in his arms. The definition. The cut. The flexibility. The new and improved version of himself.

Just him and God now. In the ink-black of night that covered him like an enormous friendly hand, his eyes barely made out the terrain ahead. A stab of green chickweed leaf. The silhouette of a line of pine trees. One with branches sticking out like thin arms with leaves that touched him like fingers. Like family. The crunch of his steps punctuated the occasional hoot of the barn owl that lived just behind the house. He'd noted the recent bulk of the owl, the absence of the mouse, and had a good idea as to what had happened.

Brax was a night owl himself. So was Ariana. Oh, they could both handle their business during the day, but when darkness winked out the sun, they both still had energy. In the past Brax had been driven to build or fix things at night. But lately that night energy had become more contemplative, reflective. Sometimes he walked or just sat and thought. He thought about each day more, what he accomplished. He found himself thinking about the next day in a more complete and attentive way. Planning more specific goals. He was grateful for his solitude. Most evenings, Ariana would be up, sitting on the widow's walk like a queen surveying her queen-dom, deep in thought as if she were trying to solve every problem on earth, or just plain happy—a woman loving life and everything about herself.

How do you get there? Brax wondered. He reviewed his life and realized that for the most part, he'd been peaceful but never at peace. The closest he'd ever come was…truth be told…this ranch.

"What you and Ari have against beds and sleepin' in 'em, I'll never understand."

That was one thing Brax could make out in the darkness without any problem. Red's silver-gray beard picked up the moonlight and reflected it like a fuzzy thicket of silver hanging on the chin of his bright and buoyant face.

"Where you comin' from this time a'night?" Brax asked.

"Water tank. It's been so hot. And with the nights not coolin' off like normal, I just had to take me a dip."

"In the tank!" Brax asked incredulously.

"Yeah. You cleaned it today, right? Ari said that the darned thing ain't been that clean since we bought it. So I figure, take me a dip tonight before the critters get to it tomorrow."

Brax noted the man's shirt half buttoned and the towel draped off his arm.

"I got an extra towel if you wanna partake."

The man's old eyes danced like a six-year-old's even in all the coal-black and shadow of the late, late evening.

It was hot, Brax reasoned. And it wasn't like he hadn't heard them mention trough-bathing in earlier conversations. And if he did say so himself, he'd done a damn good job cleaning that sucker out.

"Thanks," he said, talking the towel.

"Don't mention it," Red said. "On second thought, mention it to me later."

Brax headed off toward the more open and spacious part of the ranch deeper into the range.

"I'm serious. I want to hear all about it!" Red said behind him.

Crazy coot, Brax thought, already stripping down in his mind and easing himself into the water for a cool dip that was just what his overtaxed muscles needed to loosen up.

Brax approached the place where he'd spent the

entire day, emptying, cleaning, even scraping the inside of the big bin where the cattle came to get their fill of water. The windmill kept the water level high and stable. Brax counted the hours in his mind and tried to estimate how many dead flies might be in the water by now. The strangest part of that equation was not the number of flies—which he pegged at about eight—but the fact that he didn't care.

He looked around, not sure why. He knew Ariana was the only other person fool enough to be up at this hour. And he hadn't seen any trace of her. Damn it. He stripped down to bare skin and had to admit, he was surprised by the way his own body looked in the deep moonlight. For a moment, he ran a hand over his biceps, triceps and delts. He flexed a bit, admiring the definition and tight way his muscles had grown solid and bulked up. When a sharp twinge on his right buttocks made him slap his own behind, he stepped quickly over the side and into the tub.

"Damn mosquitoes!" he said and eased down into the round corrugated metal container.

The water was warm, almost tropical from the evening sun and warm earth. He leaned against the rim that was slightly cooler than the water and closed his eyes. He didn't have to try hard for his imagination to take over. He was in Tahiti. No, Puerto Vallarta. No, he needed some African boom-bam in this fantasy. He was in Tunisia. And there was a woman there. A beautiful woman who looked just like—

The head popping up out of the water didn't surprise him, but his reaction did. His whole body had stiffened, he'd fisted his right hand to swing, before he realized who was in the tank with him.

"Ariana!" he said. "What the hell are you doing out here? *In* here?"

She gasped for air and brought her hands to her face several times to clear away the water before she finally spoke. "Hidin'. Takin' a bath. What does it look like?"

Brax squinted, wishing that his eyes could adjust a bit more to the darkness. She was definitely naked. The water barely covered the tops of her breasts. The curls of her hair defied even the water. They were slicked back, but just barely. A few simply did their own unruly thing, sticking out from the sides of her hair and jutting up at the top. Like the bugs he didn't give a damn about that. If she only knew how she looked to him, she'd… probably kick him off the ranch.

"I'm sorry, what was the question?"

"I said, 'What does it—' oh, never mind. Just go on back to the house now, so I can finish."

"Finish what?" he asked.

"Relaxing!" she answered, emphasizing the "ing."

"Like you worked hard today," Brax said.

"I work hard every day."

"When? All I ever see you do is order men around."

"I work as hard as any man in this county. I don't just order men around…although that *is* fun."

Brax heard the smile in her voice even if he couldn't see it clearly in the darkness. "Why were you hiding?"

"'Cause I'm in here with my nakedness. Which is why you have to leave."

"I don't think so. I earned this soak. And tomorrow, the cattle will fill this thing up with cow spit." Brax grunted. Truth was he wasn't about to get out, not with

Ariana naked in here with him. Not without some strong persuasion.

Naked. The word ricocheted in his mind like a hard rubber ball bouncing in a tiny room. From his mind to his veins. From his veins to his—

Brax clenched his teeth. He was hard enough to break bricks. It didn't help that Ariana must have been moving on her side of the tank. The water washed over his manhood in soft warm waves. He tried to turn his involuntary moan into a groan, but Ariana wasn't stupid.

"You're not doing anything funny over there, are you?"

"The only funny thing is the fact I'm actually going to be a gentleman in this situation and keep my hands to myself."

"What's funny about that?"

Brax considered her question. Roaming his hands all over a wet and willing beautiful woman or…behaving. "You're right. There's nothing funny about that."

They sat for a while, night voices adding occasionally to their own. Crickets. Cicadas. A strong breeze rustling the tree leaves. The swish of the water as they both adjusted inside the tank.

It was hell.

The best Brax could hope for was that his manhood would settle all the way down so that he could get out with dignity, dress and half walk—mostly sprint—back to the house and an ice-cold shower and maybe some of that Cornhusker Lotion he'd noticed in the bathroom.

He wasn't even inside her and all he could think was, *Baby, stop movin'.*

"How you coming with that manure spreader?" she asked.

"Works like a charm. I'll be done by tomorrow."

"Tomorrow? But it takes a week."

"Maybe for Tony," Brax heard himself say, too obviously bragging.

"You think so?"

Brax grunted his agreement.

"I guess he'd do better if he *admired* himself."

"What?" Brax asked; then her meaning came clear.

Ariana lifted her left arm out of the water, flexed it, stared at it and flexed it again, repeating his exact motions of a few moments ago.

The water fell from her skin and sounded like a small rain shower and stirred up more feelings and an aroma he couldn't quite place.

"What's that smell?" he asked.

"Your first chore tomorrow. I poured rose oil in the water before I got in. I just wanted a little..."

"Ambience?"

"That's it!"

Suddenly Brax remembered his earlier encounter with Red. "Was that before or after Red?"

"Red? What about Red?"

"I ran into him. Before I got in this thing. He said he'd just come from here."

"Red?"

"Yes, Red."

"That old grunt. He was pullin' your leg."

"But he had a towel."

Brax searched his memory but couldn't recall Red looking the least bit wet.

"Are you sure it was Red?"

He decided that ridiculous question deserved a ridiculous answer. He felt like a ten-year-old boy, silly and playful. "You're right. I think it was Hank from next door. Or it might have been his wife. She looks like Red."

"Butt-head," she said and flicked a big wave of water at him.

Brax reciprocated with his own wave of water. "Bevis!"

Ariana laughed and shielded herself unsuccessfully from the water, then stopped abruptly. "I don't get it," she said with all seriousness.

Damn, Brax thought. She was so innocently sweet and honest, he just wanted to grab her up into his arms and kiss her until they both came from the force of it. As a matter of fact, Brax sat up, braced his hands against the bottom of the tank and slid toward her.

"Don't think you're gonna come over here with your big hands and splash me."

He moved closer. "Why not?"

She covered up a little. Sat back against the rim. "I'm warning you. I'm good at splashing. I won the Kimball County splash championship when I was three."

Brax laughed, deep in his throat. The sound came out thicker, stronger. More amorous than he'd realized. He slid closer.

"Good at splashing. Good at kissing, too." He slid against her. Their skin was touching beneath the water.

She didn't pull away.

"I mean, you get a championship medal for that in my book." His heart beat extrastrong in his chest. He placed a finger beneath her chin and lifted it toward him.

Her eyes grew wide and her bottom lip quivered. "Round here they don't give out medals. Just ribbons."

"Um-hum," Brax said.

Suddenly the dark didn't matter. He saw her lips clearly. They had his name written all over them. He'd left it there the first time they'd kissed, and he was determined not to let it fade.

He took his time running his tongue over the lips he hadn't been able to get off his mind all day. He memorized the smoothness, the creases, the pointed and corner places. His lips yielded easily, completely and she brought her arms around his neck. Pulled him closer.

The water dripped down his back. Igniting his senses. He drew in to her, wrapped his arms around her. Her hair tickled the side of his face. Brushed across the top of his arm in gentle waves like the ones they made in the water.

Closer.

He slid his hand from the wet softness of her back to her neck and up into the tangled dampness of her hair. He grabbed and pulled the thick, silky strands that held his captivation and caught his soul.

Her arms circled around him, pulling as urgently as he felt.

In that moment he had to back away or the sensation would take him too quickly. Rush at him so fast it would all be over too soon.

He slid back.

"Well," she said, blinking. "You sure know how to take a girl's breath away."

"Not a girl's. Yours," he said.

"Definitely mine. What else can you do?"

Wouldn't he love to show her? Brax didn't have a condom. He hadn't thought he would need one and under normal circumstances, he wouldn't have been out in the middle of the prairie where the nearest Walgreens was half a state away.

And she looked so hot and willing. Ariana proved out his thoughts as she opened her legs to accept him. He floated closer, pressed his arousal against the inside of her thigh. Teasing her. Torturing himself.

Ariana stroked his arm, kneaded the flesh to his shoulders where they traced wet circles and lines against his skin. Her touch was firm, commanding. Not timid or tentative like some others he'd been with.

Some women didn't know how to touch a man. They didn't realize how forceful they could be, how rough, and still get a man off.

Ariana knew.

"No condoms," Brax whispered in her ear. He was in pain. Acute suffering that radiated like a fire from his loins. So intense he was sure he was sweating, water or no.

He nibbled her neck, flicked the tip of his tongue against her throat. Pulled her earlobe gently with his teeth into his mouth.

Ariana groaned and wrapped her legs around him like she was jumping on her favorite horse.

"Ari," he said, dragging out the syllables in his sex-drugged state. "We don't have—"

"Touch me," she said. "Like on the roof."

He didn't recognize her voice. Deeper. More forceful. Full of lust.

She was driving him crazy. He kissed her with all the passion he felt and slid his fingers inside her. The sensation of her opening to him, molding to his fingers, inviting him was so intense that the only thing he could do was breathe.

She opened to him like a hand in offering. And Brax wanted it all.

"You give so much," he said, placing his mouth on her left nipple and drinking in big gulps. Ariana's head fell back, giving him full access.

She was a volcano raging against him. He knew he'd been born to cool her fire or, better yet, keep it stoked.

He used his hand like a rudder to send hard waves of water slamming against her most sensitive area, one after the other.

Ariana closed her eyes and opened her mouth. "Uh-oo-ahhh!"

Instead of holding tighter, she let go. But it was that act of her release—of opening completely—that drew him closer to her than any embrace ever could.

When he inserted two fingers and then three, he rubbed the shape of infinity into her soft, gentle walls, her hands enclosed around his arousal in a hot and strong embrace. Her caress was a command as her fingers worked his hard length and sweet agony flooded his entire body. The only answer: surrender and explode.

Their hands moved together. Up and down. In and out. The sound of water surging, splashing only heightened his need to please and be pleased. And he wouldn't—couldn't—stop until they filled the dark and quiet night with the sound of Ariana screaming his name.

Forget Stew, and all the other slow-walking men she'd been with in her life. Ariana had no idea anything this good could happen inside anyone's body without it just bustin' open from the feelin'.

Her mind wouldn't tell her what to do, but her body

seemed to know all about it. It twisted and turned every way from Saturday, humped and gyrated like she was on one of them buckin' machines. She had simply lost her ever-sweet mind.

And she didn't care, not one bit.

Her body felt as if it were half-ice and half-fire. Love flowed inside her like warm honey. She panted—out of breath and out of resistance. He'd captured every part of her. With each plunge of his hand, he claimed her.

Ariana couldn't remember being this pleased or this surprised by herself. Or thinking that it was okay to let a man take over.

She wanted him to take over and to do whatever to make those feelings come again—the ones where she tightened around his hands and the vibrations there sent her hips flapping like Old Glory on a windy day and her heart pounded like thunder marching through her land.

She grabbed him tighter, loving the way his skin was soft and hard together, and opened her mouth to name the feeling that spread out from his hand to the edge of her body and made her explode.

"Braaxxxxxx!"

He was right. She'd never had one before him. And if she got her way, she wouldn't share this feeling with anyone but him ever again.

Chapter 17

After three and three-fourths hours of sleep, Ariana got up, showered and headed out to the pasture. She wanted to get a quick start on the day, so that she could slow it down with Brax. After his hard work, he deserved a rest. And so did she. Ariana wanted a break from all of the long-distance lusting she was doing. It was time for some up-close and personal drooling.

Ariana rode out to where Brax was up to his shoulders in fence posts. He'd been digging holes for them all morning. A wave of guilt expanded inside her. Another reason she wanted to give him a break was so he didn't strain his back, just in case…

Ariana brought Sirocco up close, just as Brax packed the dirt around the post, upper arms flexing as he drove the dirt in with the shovel and the flat of his boot.

He was still a bit awkward, but so determined it didn't matter, which amounted to sexy in her book.

He looked up, sweaty and intense.

"How's it going?" she asked.

"You tell me," he said.

He'd done a more than fair job. Better than some who'd been doing it for a lot longer. Almost as good as Tony or Red.

She had no doubt the post would hold.

"Looks good," she said, taking her gaze off the pole and draping it all over Brax.

A shiver down her back let her know he could give as good as he got. His eyes reached back, caressed her. "Real good," he said, chuckling. "You look like a glass of champagne sittin' on that horse."

Ariana felt like champagne just then. Light. Golden. Bubbly. "Thirsty?"

Brax's resolve crumbled to dust. He made a soft pallet out of fresh hay and alfalfa, then laid her down gently, reverently on the bed. Ariana took a deep breath and gazed up expectantly from where the vision of her looking ripe for lovemaking made his rising need hard to control.

He decided it was time for a confession.

He reached down to the top button on her blouse. "You know, you're all wrong for me. Not my type at all."

His words were sincere and came out husky, soaked in lust and need.

"Really?" she asked, laying her arms back against the hay. "How so?"

One button open. Two. "Well, for starters, your accent is as thick as molasses. Now, I'm a brother from the south, but you can hardly hear my accent."

"I hear it," she said and licked her lips.

Three buttons. Four. Five.

"Umm," he said, eyes locked on the soft brown flesh of her stomach, her chest. All the places he would taste and tease.

"And a Nebraska girl? I mean, come on." Last button. His heartbeat quickened. "I need someone a bit more cosmopolitan."

"Is that so?" she asked, beginning to rock her hips as he ran a finger down the silky center of her body.

"I'm city folk, remember? Big Rig." His finger stopped at the top of her jeans. Circled her belly button. Coaxed a moan.

"Big…yes. Big Rig." She closed her eyes, already letting go, turning herself over to him. His manhood tightened painfully. Urgently.

Not yet, he told himself.

"Please, Brax," she said, reaching down to unbutton her jeans.

"And that," he responded, grabbing her hands and holding them over her head. He bent. Kissed her stomach, licked and caressed the sweet flesh with his tongue, drawing a long throaty moan from Ariana's lips. "I need a woman who needs me. Sometimes I'm away for days. And, well, you—"

He raised himself up then. Stared into her eyes trying to stop his soul from tumbling out of his mouth. "You just seem like the type of woman who wouldn't wait."

She squirmed then, her eyes staring back, drunk with passion. "I *can't* wait, Brax. Please…"

Her pleading fueled his lust like gasoline on fire.

"And I can't do anything except love you, and love is just, well, out of the question, so you see..."

His lips ravaged hers, sating the need he had to taste her delicious mouth. "You are all wrong for me, Ariana."

He let go of her hands, unzipped her jeans and slid his fingers deep inside her. "All wrong."

"Aaah, ss-ah," she moaned and ground her hips against his hand.

She was soft, hot and slick with arousal. He had to be careful, control the tempo, or his hand sliding against her juices would be so loud, someone might hear.

"S-so, does that mean it's o-over?" she asked, then moaned with acute pleasure as her juices ran like a great river.

"It's not over until—"

"The fat lady sings?" she managed.

Brax brought her deftly to her peak and Ariana surrendered all. "No. We ride off into the sunset."

"I'm coming, Brax. I'm coming."

"Oh, yeah?"

"Yes!"

"Um," he said, and kissed her opening.

He watched. Amazed at the emotions changing her face. This was a real woman he was touching. Full-bodied. "Don't rush, baby."

"Oh-h..."

"Take your time."

But Ariana didn't have any time left and as Brax positioned himself to enter her, she exploded into blissful oblivion. He was prepared this time, so when he protected her and slid inside, the day fell away to a bright hot sun and the sounds of their delicious joining.

* * *

"Where're we going?" Brax asked. After spending exquisite time in his arms making love, Ariana was bursting with energy and determination.

They'd ridden in silence for fifteen minutes or so. Ariana took good mental notes. It wouldn't be long before he and Run Amok bonded. It was already happening. They both reacted to each other, each glad to see the other, Brax frequently bringing the horse extra oats and apples, brushing him for longer periods. She realized something special was going on when she caught the city slicker actually talking to the horse. As though he was carrying on a conversation. Something he still hadn't done much of with her. At least, not verbally anyway.

"Green Hill," she said, flicking Sirocco's reins. "Come on!"

She didn't think Brax had run his horse yet. Fast trot, she'd seen. But it was her turn to push him the way he'd been pushing her.

She checked him, out of the corner of her eye. He kept up and stayed on. Rode right.

When they made it to the top of the hill, it was nearly dinnertime, only Ariana was hungry for something other than Tony's good cooking.

"This is it," she said, as out of breath and exhilarated as her horse. "The center of everything."

Ariana's heart was both happy and sad. Her happiest memories and most tragic combined at the top of that hill. Bright blue sky and rolling green grass for as long as she cared to look. And she looked often. When she was happy. When she missed her mother. When she had a decision to make.

Ariana believed she had a decision to make. What her body craved was so much more than intimacy. What it already felt made her afraid and sweet-grinned at the same time.

"If I owned this land, no one could ever get me to leave this point," Brax said. He gave Run Amok a solid and appreciative pat on the neck and then swung down. The stallion snorted and rocked his head, expecting a treat. Brax didn't disappoint. He pulled an apple from his saddlebag and held it to Run Amok's mouth. The horse ate contentedly.

"This hill and I are good friends, that's for sure," Ariana admitted.

"Sometimes, when I'm supposed to be doing chores, or I need some by-myself time, I come up here at sunrise to watch the day begin or at sunset to watch it end."

They both glanced up just as a large bird soared overhead. Eagle. Ariana pegged the wingspan at about six feet. They both tracked his air play. Dipping. Gliding. Banking. Mastering the wind.

"They say eagles are the only birds that fly just for the hell of it."

Ariana waited, hoping Brax would continue.

"They often fly because they can. Not for prey, or a mate, or a place to build a nest. Just because. Just because they *like* it," he said.

"Some Native American tribes believe that man is the beginnin' of the evolutionary chain and the high points are the animals. Eagles for sure," she added.

Brax looked up, shaded his eyes with his hand. "So we evolve into them instead of the other way around?"

"Yeah."

Brax fed Run Amok the last of his apple and brought him close to where Ariana stood with Sirocco. "What do *you* believe?"

"I believe that we are born to take care of the earth in order to take care of ourselves. And when we've done all we were put here to do, we go to a place where we can rest."

Brax nodded. "Sounds reasonable to me."

"Come on," she said. "There are some folks I want you to meet."

They tied their horses to a sage brush and climbed the rest of the way to the summit.

There were days when Ariana didn't have the strength to make the short climb. Memories of her mother and grandmother that could have made her strong stole her energy and left unbearable grief in their place.

But not today. Ariana, surefooted up the sand and rock path, climbed slowly so that Brax could keep up.

"Just over here," she said, reaching the top and motioning to a lush tree-covered area overlooking the ranch.

"It's unbelievable," Brax said. "If I hadn't seen this with my own eyes… Who would have believed… in Nebraska?"

The Sugar Trail was the tail end of a big valley. At the farthest edge of the sand hills, the land was lush. It rose and fell like a wild paradise for miles. A paradise untouched by time.

"There are other really high places on the ranch, but this is my favorite. I love the view. It makes me grateful. You know? Keeps me humble and beholden to God for all this. It keeps things in perspective, that's for sure. Every time I fool myself into believin' I have a problem,

I come up here. It sets my mind right. Helps me see how little and insignificant some things are."

"And how beautiful and majestic others are," Brax added, eyes burning into hers.

"Yes, well…that is why I brought you up here."

"I just wouldn't feel right carryin' on with you without you meetin' my folks. Just wouldn't be proper."

Ariana's breaths came raggedly. Apprehension tightened like a thick cord around her stomach. Her hands shook. And she couldn't figure out if she was tired from bringing Brax up the hill or nervous about visiting her mother's grave.

She missed her mother sorely. At times she felt so disconnected from the world, so severed, because her tie and lifeline was her mother and her mother was gone. After her mother had passed, Ariana's world had unraveled like a stray thread. God sure had a way with people's lives, she reasoned, leaving her and her sister alone to handle a ranch by themselves.

Selling it would be Ariana's first moment of peace in six years.

They walked along the overlook and what Ariana called "God's Garden." One thing the Lord did get right was the flowers growing on the summit and the arrangement of trees. A man or a woman could not have created a better display with yard tools and a certificate in landscaping. The view always made her breathe deeply and smile. Especially this time of year when the sun was strongest and the wildflowers grew so tall and full.

"Yeah, Big Rig. Ever since you got here, I've had this overwhelming urge to slap your behind."

Brax crossed his arms over his barrel chest. Looked smug. "Don't fight the feelin', Lady West."

Obviously, he didn't know who he was dealing with. Maybe city women didn't know how to go for what they knew, but ranch women sure did. She sized up his firm, round behind, took aim and swung.

Before she could bring her arm forward all the way, Brax caught it and used it to pull her against him.

Her blood caught fire. They stood there. Shirt to shirt. Inhaling each other. Her nipples already alive and aching for his mouth, she pressed closer. Teasing herself and him. His eyes said, *Make a move.* She wanted to, more than anything. And if he was still interested after he met her family, she would. Without delay.

"This is Gunny MacLeod, my great-great-grandmother," she said to Brax as they moved toward the row of headstones. "She came on the heels of the Exodusters 'round the turn of the century. She'd heard that the government was giving land away in Nebraska. All you had to do was live on it for five years and it was yours. So that's just what she did. She headed out this way with her sister MaeSally and her husband, Boaz. The three of them built the house where Red lives. I 'spect they would have stayed on for the five years, but Boaz got consumption. MaeSally took care of him the whole time while Grandma Gunny took on the chores of raisin' the cows and chickens they'd bartered for. Well, Boaz fought real hard, but the sickness took too much out of him and he died. MaeSally followed soon behind him. My mother never said if it was because she got sick or was just so heartbroken behind him dying and leaving her just when they was 'bout to start fresh in a new place.

"That's when the curse started."

"Curse? Are you telling me there's a curse on your land?"

"Not the land. Just the women who work it. No matter what, we have the worst luck with men. Mama called it a curse. My grandmother called it the curse. Because that's what Gunny called it. And it seems to be pretty much true."

Brax frowned in disbelief.

"Yeah, they all look like you. Thinkin' they know what's what, till the curse comes on 'em. Then they believe."

"Them who?" he asked.

"Men. The ones who come makin' time. Soon as their time runs out, that's when they believe."

"So men who've dated women in your family end up dying?" he asked, disbelief thinning his words.

"No! That really would be a curse, wouldn't it?" Ariana pushed back a stray curl.

"The men just never stick. Some*thing*, some*body* always comes along to push them away. And we end up alone." She lowered her head and her voice. God, how she was tired of being alone. Even with Selena, Red and Tony, she had no companion. No one to turn to. Maybe in the city…

"So, tell me about JoJean," he said, pointing to the next headstone.

"She's Gunny's daughter. She's the one that turned the homestead from a step above sharecroppin' to a right farm. The Sugar Trail had everything then. Chickens, goats, hogs. Alfalfa. Corn. By then, the state had passed the Kincaid Act. After your five years of homesteading, you could bid on land right next to yours."

"Bid? Like an auction?"

"Well…not really. Basically, it came down to, you planted where you wanted to expand until somebody objected. So Grandma Jo kept plantin' and expandin' till she ran into Cofield's land. They liked each other right away and was married so fast, nobody could believe it. And then, one day Cofield was fetchin' water from the well, and a bolt of lightning struck him down."

"Damn," Brax said, recoiling. "Thought you said the curse didn't kill people."

"Oh, he didn't die."

"He didn't?"

"No. But it was the third time he'd been struck since he married Grandma. So he disappeared after that. He told Grandma Jo the Sugar Trail was a bad fix. Said he was leaving and asked her to come with him. But she didn't want to leave the land."

Brax shook his head. "And her?"

"That's my grandma Gunny. I barely remember her, but what I do remember is that she was a large woman. Tall like a man, and thick—like me."

Brax smiled. "Umm."

"She was the hunter. She had more shotguns than anyone I've ever known and went huntin' nearly every day. When I was little, we ate a lot of deer, possum, raccoon, squirrel, pheasant, turkey. All fresh from her gun.

"And she knew how to clean, skin and cook up all that stuff. I feel bad. I couldn't skin a raccoon if you paid me."

"That makes two of us," Brax said.

"Well, out of all the MacLeod women, she actually got married and stayed married."

"Really?"

"Jack Turner. They were married right here, under the big tree. And they stayed married for twenty years."

"Sounds like the curse skipped them."

"It does kinda sound like that. And it would have, if it weren't for the fact that the man posing as Jack wasn't him. He'd come across Jack on a train, hit the poor man in the head, stolen his money and started calling himself by the man's name."

"Old-time identity theft. I don't believe it."

"I'm telling you. That's the power of the curse. Gunny found out when the real Jack showed up to settle a dept the imposter had run up. Well, she went and got one of her shotguns and chased him off the land."

"After twenty years of marriage?"

"Yeah. Sounds crazy."

"What happened then?"

"She took up with the real Jack for a while, but that only lasted about a year. Then he went back to his wife and children."

"Oh, man," Brax said. "I hate to hear how your mother was cursed. It seems to get stronger year after year."

Ariana sucked in a deep breath. She and her mother didn't talk much about her father. She only knew that her mother had loved her father in a crazy, "can't see two feet in front of me" kind of way. The same way he had loved her. But her father's family was against the union, so eventually, the pressure to please his family won and Ariana's father left. Out of all the curse stories, she couldn't bring herself to talk about this one. And she'd so believed that she would be able to at least tell Brax. The only man she'd ever considered telling the story to.

"My mother never married my father. She got pregnant and he left. The only other time he came back, my mother got pregnant with Selena. No one has seen him since."

She lowered her head almost all the way then. No longer able to hold it up. She couldn't believe how much talking about her past, her family, had taken out of her.

Before she knew anything else, Brax's finger slipped under her chin. He lifted her head and stared into her eyes, a smile of reassurance riding the hard, handsome features of his face.

"There's only a curse if you believe there's a curse," he said. "If you choose not to believe, then the women in your family went through some unfortunate times with men…that doesn't mean you will, too."

"Really?" she asked. "You can't prove that by my relationships so far."

"Well, maybe that's about to change."

Suddenly the entire outdoors got hot. Rain-forest hot. Sultry. Ariana could barely breathe.

His mouth was so close. Was he going to kiss her? Was he throwing his hat into the ring as her salvation?

When Brax's cell phone rang, it startled both of them.

His eyes cooled, but stayed friendly, and just a bit amorous. He pulled the phone from his back pocket and flipped it open. "If Shyla is still on the payroll, I'm going to—"

And just like that, the moment was stolen. Brax covered the mouthpiece, mouthed the words "I'm sorry," paced away from her family and Ariana was left in the middle of her world, alone.

Chapter 18

They had been talking about the Kimball County Fair and the Fourth of July celebration for weeks. Every year, Ariana, Red and Tony upheld their tradition of attending the fair and watching the fireworks. This year they'd agreed to let an outsider in—Brax. And Brax was determined not to give them any reason to regret their decision. The least he could do was look like he fit in. He told himself that was the biggest reason he was going shopping. Brax had learned to lie to himself well over the years. He packed away the real reason he was ready to whip out his credit card like Deadwood Dick—he wanted to impress Ari and at least get her to stop teasing him about his clothes.

Under the pretenses of needing some personal items, Brax persuaded Red to "run him to town."

Red kept one wrinkled hand on the steering wheel of

his '73 Ford pickup and the other on his spit can. "So, whadaya think?"

"I think you all have a good thing going here. I wouldn't have believed that taking care of land and animals could be as fulfilling as it is. As noble."

Red grunted and spat into a Coke can that had to go back three branding campaigns. "I mean the girl. You like her?"

Even the thought of Ariana at the fringes of his mind brought warmth of contentment, pride and the rise of an emotion Brax cared not to name at the moment.

"Yes," he said.

"Good, 'cause she sure thinks on you with pink sunshine."

Brax let go a laugh. Pink sunshine. That's exactly how he would refer to Ariana and the effect she had on his heart. He was done for. All in. She had it. Had him. And that's all there was to it. If this was country lovin', he wanted nothing more of the city. She smelled like every dream he'd ever had about a woman. Her moans sounded like the very epitome of female surrender.

Red's old pickup jostled and bounced over the uneven country road. Dirt and gravel pinged on the underside of the truck, and the back wheels stirred up a cloud of dust that threatened to beat them into town.

"She tell you that?" Brax asked, trying to keep his need to know as subtle as possible.

"Sure did!" Spit.

"What'd she say?" Brax asked, before his mouth could catch the words and stuff them back into a young and smitten side of his heart.

Red spat first, then chuckled into his cup. "Don't you know nothin', workin' here, yet? It ain't what she said. It's the way she been hummin' and singin' round here like a new radio. You think you gonna see some fireworks tomorrow, but she'd got 'em goin' off in her eyes for some days now. And she don't seem ta wanna be more than two feet away from you. The fact that you headin' in town with me must be puttin' her into an awful scurry." Spit. Spit.

Brax's ego inflated like a big tire on a monster truck. "Yeah," he said with relief in his voice and a smile on his lips.

When they got to town, Red went over for a cup of coffee and Brax headed into Buckey's General. He knew exactly what he wanted and wasted no time picking out three shirts, two pairs of jeans, a hat and an expensive pair of boots. He'd overheard Tony once saying that the trick to getting that crisp, cowboy, *stranger in town, just got off a horse* look was to buy the clothes a size smaller than you actually wore.

And there was something else he couldn't wait for, either. Brax pulled a box of condoms from a shelf and almost laughed at the looks he got then. It was a small town. Everyone in the store knew where he was staying, and now they knew what he was doing while he stayed there. But his memory was too hot, too fresh to care. He licked the tips of his fingers compulsively, as if he would find Ari's sweet essence still there from the previous night.

He exited Buckey's considering the upcoming fair. It was going to be a long day, but not nearly as long as the night he had planned.

* * *

Ariana was so jittery, she couldn't stop her hands from shaking. She stood in front of her floor-length mirror buttoning the last button on her tan lace blouse, and tucked it into her jeans skirt. The same tan lace adorned the seams of the skirt. She matched the blouse and skirt with tan boots—her best pair—and a tan Stetson.

She didn't know if she looked good, but she sure felt good. Underneath, she wore her latest Victoria's Secret set, the one she ordered after seeing Brax tired and sweaty from digging postholes for the new fence.

She never wore perfume. She did today. Some Between the Sheets just behind the ears. And inside her wrists. And her cleavage. And the backs of her knees. She sprayed the crooks of her arms with the perfume and checked herself once more.

Her heart jumped at the thought racing in her head. She had to say it out loud to get it off her soul. "You were wrong, Mama. The curse doesn't last always. Not for all of us. I love him, Mama. *So* much. It's gotta end with me."

Ariana took a deep breath and turned toward the door.

They were down there. Red, Tony and Brax. Waiting. They were all going to the fair, but she and Brax were going on a date. Everyone knew it. They probably expected her to dress for the occasion. Well, when it came to Brax these days, she aimed to please. 'Cause he sure as shootin' did.

That wave of heat, which visited her every time she thought about Brax, covered her again. It made her take that big pretty bow from around her ponytail and shake her hair loose. Her curls bounced around her face and hit softly against her shoulders.

She was ready.

"Don't get her on any of those rides."

"The only thing she can ride is a horse."

"Those big contraptions make her throw up."

"And funnel cakes make her fart, so don't get her any of those, either."

"But she loves chicken on a stick."

"Anything on a stick!"

Even from the top of the stairs, she heard them clearly. Red and Tony laughed like they'd just told the funniest joke in the world. Red laughed so hard he started coughing. Ariana hoped that he didn't have any of his chew in. Her kitchen would be sprayed brown for sure.

"What I really like is you two on a stick. Now, that's a treat!" she said, then shut her mouth. She wasn't sure if she'd ever be able to speak again.

Ariana was only slightly aware of the whistles, knee slaps and the expletive that left Brax's mouth. Something about how good she looked. She thought she heard Red saying something about mighty fine. But the mighty fine one in the room was Brax Ambrose. She just stopped at the foot of the stairs and stared. The shirt, the jeans, the boots and the hat. He didn't look like the real thing.

He was the real thing.

He looked more like a rancher than half the ranchers she knew. She could tell by the way his thigh muscles pushed against the denim so hard; her body temperature rose like steam. And the fact that she had to force herself to stop glancing down at the bulging fly.

She wanted to touch him and never stop. He looked so good, like he'd been born outside, on the ranch, under the stars, kissed by the wilderness and nursed by the plains.

When she finally got up her nerve to look Brax in the eye, she couldn't see his face. All she saw was her reflection, bright and twinkling in his eyes. The image sent her insides fluttering like ten big-winged butterflies.

Masses of people crowded the streets in loose family groups wearing their country casual. Most folks had smiles on their faces and food in their hands. Those who didn't were waiting in long vendor lines for nachos, hot dogs or slices of pizza as big as your face.

Brax had no idea there were so many people in the entire state of Nebraska—forget the surrounding towns. So far that morning, he'd seen at least a thousand and from the steady stream of folks coming through the entrance, there were several thousand more on the way.

He and Ariana had wasted no time leaving Red and Tony behind and going off on their own to walk the blocked-off streets of Kimball among the vendor booths, rides and animal-petting stations. The town had been transformed into an impressive fair.

Brax licked his lips. The movement brought a vibration of heat between Ariana's legs like the swift flick of a tongue—Brax's tongue—and made her hands tremble all over again.

"Lookin' good, Lady West."

"You look good, too, Brax. You look like…like you were born to wear those clothes."

Chocolate-brown, button-down shirt with long sleeves and two front pockets. Classic fit, indigo jeans held up by a thick belt with a silver buckle. Black roper boots. And he topped the whole thing off with a chocolate Stetson. Ariana sighed her approval. No more city dude. Even Big Rig was gone.

For a moment, she was so taken by the new cowboy in her presence, she couldn't remember her last name, her first kiss or how to get back to her ranch.

"I'll take that as a compliment," Brax said, smiling.

She loved the way his mouth drew back, the way his luscious lips showed off teeth as white as new flour.

It was like seeing a cowboy for the first time and recognizing the power and honor of that role. He'd changed, she'd like to think, for her.

That day, Ariana got everything she wanted. Even chicken on a stick. As they walked among the farmers, locals, out-of-towners and children, Brax denied her nothing.

In the past, no matter how good a man looked to her, there always seemed to be something not quite right. Some men were built funny, like Hank Snooden, who was big on top and had a low waist, so even though he was about six feet tall, he looked kinda short. Stew had a nice body—a great body—but he also had a right eye that sometimes wandered sideways all on its own. And then there was Tony. Her Tony, who had flirted with her like crazy one summer until she hired him. He'd really loved her then. Maybe he still did and hid it well. She knew that's what kept him coming back as a hand summer after summer, until his taste for wrangling caught on. After that, Ariana was no longer his main concern. And that made her happy. She loved Tony. He was the brother she wished her mother could have given birth to.

As for Brax, he must have known how she stared at him. Sometimes it was because she liked the way he looked and sometimes it was because she was trying to find something wrong.

He can't be perfect, her mind kept telling her, and she kept looking. Even now, as they strolled down Chestnut Street carrying the longest chicken on a sticks that Ariana had ever seen, the only blemish that came to her mind was how little he talked. If she could change anything, it would be that. The real Brax didn't come out to play often and when he did, he went right back inside. For quite a while.

Ariana finished a large bite of chicken and said, "Tell me a story."

The frown on Brax's face came quickly and intensely. Like he was from another country and thought he'd been insulted in another language. "What? Like Goldilocks?"

"No, ya polecat. I guess what I want to hear is *your* story. Tell me your story."

Brax pulled off the last bite of chicken from his stick and tossed the stick in a trash barrel. If he thought a big hunk of meat was going to keep him from having to talk, he didn't know much.

"That may keep your mouth busy now, but the fair goes on till midnight."

The soft concession in his eyes told her she'd won. Brax swallowed a big gulp of soda and took her arm.

Shock and surprise vaulted through her and felt as sweet as strawberry milk. She moved closer so he could get a better grip.

"I grew up in Georgia. Mostly Savannah. But I've lived some in Atlanta and Red Oaks. My mom left my father when I was three and he left me when I was three and a half.

"Spent my entire childhood in the system."

Ariana wasn't sure what that meant, but it sounded bad.

"By the time I was sixteen, I'd been in ten different homes. Most of them nice decent people, but for whatever reason—death, lost job, pregnancy, house fire, you name it—it happened to me—I always ended up moving to another home."

"Sounds like a june bug lightin' on a different flower. Never settlin' on just one."

"Yeah. That might have something to do with why I drive a truck. I just can't stand being in one place for too long. I feel uncomfortable. I get restless. Driving keeps me sane."

They strolled past the bingo tent, a beer garden and three 4-H exhibits, neither of them paying much attention to anything besides each other.

"So, you like being a driver? I know plenty of 'em, but we just never sat down and talked, you know? I don't think too much on what happens to my heifers after they get on the truck. All the places they go. All the things they see. What's that like?"

Brax took another sip of his cola. He pulled long and hard like the thoughts in his head were that soda and he had to work to get them to come free.

"I don't know what it's like," he said finally. His voice sounded gray and overcast like a low-hanging raincloud.

"You said you been driving for fifteen years."

"I did, but the only thing I really saw in those years

was the road. Everything else was a blur through the side window. Out of focus."

"Sounds fascinatin'," she said.

"It is, if you like seeing the world from a distance. My only company was road signs and calendar girls." Brax remembered one calendar girl in particular, Morgan Allgood. Her picture had kept him on time for an entire month.

"Distance'd be a nice change." Ariana drew herself up, her eyes sparkling with her thoughts. "Just for a week, I'd like to know what it's like to go to work someplace that's not swarmin' with flies."

"I've been on a time schedule for the past fifteen years. The schedule never included much rest, stopping or looking around."

Ariana's heart felt like a sack of grain had just been dumped on it. "You must be hard to love."

He stopped then. And because he was holding her arm, she stopped, too. He turned to her, his eyes a blend of shock and concern. "I used to be. I realize that now. But when it comes to you, I don't ever want to be that again."

"What do you mean, Big Rig?" she asked teasingly, in case she was reading him wrong. In case he was playing with her heart.

"I mean, I love you, Ariana MacLeod. And if there's a good God in heaven, you love me, too."

Ariana reeled in astonishment. She felt a rush of heat to her face and she stood gaping in stunned silence.

In her mind, she jumped into Brax's arms, tossed her head back, screamed with delight and covered his face with kisses. In her mind, she was the happiest woman in the whole dang county.

In her mind.

But in real life, she held tighter to the man she loved. Looked him in the eye dead-on. His face was hard and worried. She'd never seen him so vulnerable. Not even when he realized that Uncle Jesse was a she and that he was liable for all the damage he'd caused.

She'd watched him so often. Working so hard like his life depended on him getting the posts in just right. Windrow hay or water and grain the animals without a mistake. He'd done everything there was to do around her ranch. She'd seen it with her own eyes. He took to it good.

But could she take to him?

"Ari?" he said, his voice impatient and constricted.

"I love you, Brax. For a while now, actually."

His face softened and his eyes brightened. His shoulders went slack and he bent to kiss her, but she pulled back.

"What's wrong?" he asked.

"Nothin's wrong. It just is what it is, I guess."

Brax stepped back. "Do we need to sit down?" he asked, but he meant, "Do I need to sit down?" Her "I love you" sounded like she'd pushed it through a door that was still partially closed. The sound of it tightened his stomach and he was desperate to know why she was holding back when in their most intimate moments, she'd been completely and unabashedly open.

"No. Let's keep walkin'."

They passed three more chicken-on-a-stick vendors, plus a Dippin' Dots booth, a cotton candy stand and a magician doing sleight-of-hand tricks for children. The smell of funnel cakes and cinnamon-coated almonds, along with onions and peppers fought for attention of their senses, stomachs and pockets as they walked. Brax's stomach hardened with each step until it turned into a tight fist and he couldn't stand it anymore.

"Okay, Ariana. Spill it."

She guided him over to a white wooden bench where they sat down. One of the few places on the crowded street that wasn't taken. Probably because there was no shade and the sun had made a bold entrance about an hour ago, brightening the clear ice-blue sky with barely a trace of clouds.

Ariana's bare shoulders glistened with a thin layer of perspiration from the heat. For a moment, the only thing on Brax's mind was licking the sweat off Ariana's beautiful skin.

"I love you."

"So you said," he said, suddenly craving the honeyed taste of her flesh, but feeling cautious.

"In thirty days, or less at the rate you're goin', you'll be all done and on your way back to…where are you from?"

"Savannah."

"I've never said 'I love you' to a man before. Ever. Have you said it before? No, don't answer that. Of course you've said it before. I mean, look at you. You've probably been in love three, four, maybe six times."

"I wouldn't say that," Brax said.

"Well, what would you say? Isn't loving someone different from being in love? And since this has never happened to me, how do I know?"

"Why are you pulling up?"

"The women in my family fare better when we keep our wits about us. My mind tells me to be cautious."

"Your mind?" Brax asked, thinking about how he had all but lost his. Here he was —no cell phone, no cable, no civilization—on his own private version of the TV show *Lost,* and his wits had vanished a long time ago. Falling for Ariana was the most outlandish thing he'd done in his entire life. But he'd had no choice. He couldn't *not* love her. Not want to be with her. Now. Forever.

"I can love you, Brax, but I could never marry you. And you need to know that."

"Your mind?" he repeated, ignoring everything she'd just said and realizing he couldn't hear any more.

"Yes," she said in that two-syllable way she had of speaking. The way he loved.

He got up, blood raging in his veins and the heat of anger rising to his head. "What does your heart say?"

"Brax..."

"It's hot out here. You said you wanted to see the butter sculpture, so you'd better get going, before it melts."

She stood then, shaky, like his heart. "I'm sorry," she said.

Just then a couple with two romping boys came over. They were loaded with hot dogs and drinks in big white paper cups. "You guys leaving?"

"*I* am," Brax said.

With the sting of rejection propelling him away, he headed for the fair entrance. He couldn't take one more moment of being turned away. He'd had too much of that in his life. And this from Ariana was unbearable. He needed to move.

"Where are you going?" she called after him. Her words were barely audible in his agitated state.

Home, he wanted to say. Then he realized, all his life

he'd had a residence, but he'd never had a home, and now maybe he never would.

"Away from here." He couldn't look back, but felt her standing there, bare-shouldered, golden hair flowing, caramel eyes pleading. He took an emotional picture—he could use his mind for that at least—and walked away.

Chapter 19

The afternoon drifted by in a fog. The statues made of butter, the baby tigers, the jugglers, twelve-inch corn dogs and the Angus show that Uncle Jesse would have been a part of and most likely won. One big ol' nasty blur. Her stomach was tied so tight, Ariana had to stop at only one chicken on a stick instead of her usual three.

No matter what she did, where she went or how she tried, the only thing she could see clearly was Brax and how she'd hurt him.

When she found Tony at the horse arena, she was so relieved she could barely speak. All she wanted right then was to go home.

"Are you sure you want to leave now? We haven't even seen the hog show or the fireworks."

"I'm not in the mood for fireworks, Tony. At least, not anymore."

Tony frowned and pulled his head back. "What did you do, tell him about the curse?"

"Not exactly, but kinda."

"Holy crap, Ari. You've been wrappin' yourself up in that excuse like an old quilt."

"Are you gonna take me home or not?"

Tony nodded and she walked with him in her sexiest clothes feeling anything but.

As close as Sugar Trail was—a whole ten miles away—it was the longest ride of her life. She questioned her reaction to Brax's declaration every mile of the way.

She had to be honest. She could not keep the truth from him. MacLeod women were at their best when men were their companions—for a moment or for years and years. But as soon as they moved beyond that, their lives would break apart in some horrific way. A miscarriage. Abandonment. Illness.

The legacy was too strong to ignore. And it wasn't just her own life she had to think about. Selena's life was just as important if not more so than her own.

She remembered their last phone call. Selena didn't have the exuberance in her voice that Ariana expected.

"So, what have they got you doing?"

"We've been doing lots of volunteer work all over the city. Nursing homes mostly. We visited museums. Went to a play and an opera. Last night we had dinner at a sushi restaurant."

"Tell me what it's like again."

"Crowded," Selena said. "I feel like I should keep my arms against my sides. And it's noisy. Everyone talking. Cars and trucks zooming. And they have what they call

a skyline. Lots of big buildings. It's pretty at night, but it blocks out too much of the sky."

"What about the people? Are they nice to you?"

"Yeah. They're too busy to be mean. At least so far anyway."

"I ask you this every time, but do you like it?"

"I don't dislike it."

"Do you think it could grow on you?"

"Maybe."

Ariana swatted at a yellow mud dauber, disappointment sinking into a ball at the pit of her stomach. Selena wasn't having the grand amazing time Ariana thought she would. From her own mouth, it wasn't a bad time, just not so fabulous she couldn't wait to live there.

Ariana pressed her back against the seat in Tony's truck. It squeaked with the movement as she wondered what she could do to get Selena's heart spinnin' like a windmill in a cyclone. The same way Ariana's did every time Brax came down for breakfast.

The ball in her stomach tightened into a rock with sharp edges. She'd grown accustomed to seeing him in the morning. And at night, well, she crossed her right leg over her left and squeezed her thighs together to still the throbbing. Just the thought—

"You all right over there?" Tony asked.

"No, Tony. I'm so far from all right I don't even remember what all right feels like anymore."

"So you love him, too."

"When I'm with him, I feel like milk chocolate—rich, creamy. Like I could just melt in his mouth."

"Too…much…info. Just yes or no. And I promise. I'll only be jealous for a minute."

Ariana's heart felt like sunup and sundown at the same time. Bright and peaceful. She smiled. "I love him, Tony."

Saying it made Ariana feel sweet and strong like molasses and hard leather.

A sharp silence fell between her and her longtime friend. The man who was just as much her brother as Selena was her sister.

"You said—"

"I know what I said," he responded, lifting his finger for Jeb Cane driving by in his brand-new pickup. "I lied."

"What gets into you men? He's jealous of you. You're jealous of him. I—"

"*He's* jealous of me?"

"Yes."

"He's jealous of *me?*"

"You're gonna wear that hat for a week, ain't cha?"

"Damn right!" Tony said. His voice sounded right, but his face looked all wrong.

Afraid that their relationship might be damaged, Ariana scrambled to find words of assurance. "You don't love me like that anymore."

"That don't matter, Ari. You just have a way of working under a man's skin. Like a chigger. So easy to get in, you don't even notice. But hell to get out. Even painful. And when you're gone, you leave these little marks..."

"Tony..."

"Don't worry about me. I'll get over it. Over you. It's not like I'm not seeing anybody. Or a few somebodies, actually." He laughed, then continued. "It's not even like I got designs on you. I don't. I'm just a man. Protective of a woman I love. I just want what's right for you."

"Thank you, Tony." His words settled into her soul. She wanted what was right for her, too.

Maybe she *could* marry Brax.

She should at least tell him that much.

Highway 30 stretched in a long dusty line in front of them. Their way was clear. And so was Ariana's heart. Funny how on a day celebrating independence, all Ariana thought about was how much she depended on the man she loved. And she couldn't wait to tell him.

With a quick kiss, Ariana dashed out of the truck and ran into the house. Her heart sounded like horse hooves pounding on the packed earth. If only she could run as fast.

"Brax!" she called. He teased her about the way she said his name. She didn't care. She liked the feel of those two solid syllables in her mouth. And wanted to go on saying it for a long, long time.

When he wasn't in the kitchen or living room, she headed to the second floor, skipping stairs. Shouting, "Brax!"

There was no answer and no man.

Did he leave? she wondered, the thought sickening her. Not already. Not because of what she'd said.

She checked his room. When she saw that his things were still there, relief flooded her like a rush of river water.

She headed straight for the barn, jumped on Sirocco and rode for the corral.

It was not quite dark, the evening shadows playing across her piece of grass like purple robbers stealing daylight by the handfuls.

When she got to the corral she felt like her heart had been stolen. Brax wasn't there and this forced her to wonder what she would do if he was never there again. If Brax wasn't here with the calf, he could be anywhere. Anywhere in three thousand acres.

"Well, Sirocco, we may be in for a long evening." Ariana gave the stallion a reassuring pat on the neck, turned him north and flicked the reins. "H'ya!"

Ariana leaned forward, the warm evening air rushing against her face, blowing her hair back. She moved in tune with Sirocco's well-honed muscles. The strength and power of his run. Sirocco loved to be set free. To be turned loose against the land.

They rode to each barn, trotted along the fencing, checked each pen and shed. There was no sign of him. Ariana started to think that Brax had left his things behind and just taken off. Headed back to the city without another word. But that didn't seem like him.

To rest and clear her head, Ariana headed to the west edge of her property, to the original homestead. To Red. If she was lucky, Brax would be there, drinking whiskey, playing cards, hell, she'd even accept him joining Red in a cheekful of chew. As long as he was there. *Please, Jesus, let him be there.*

Not even bothering to take Sirocco to the small barn next to the homestead, she jumped down from the tired animal and dashed up to the porch. Before she could knock, Red came out in a pair of dilapidated overalls carrying a spit can.

"He ain't here," he said.

Ariana's disappointment buckled her knees and she would have gone down if it weren't for Red's still sturdy arms catching her.

"Whoa, there," he said, holding her steady. "You got

it bad. I don't think I ever seen your mama this stirred up about a fella."

"I love him, Red." Suddenly, Ariana couldn't get enough of saying that. Admitting that. Telling the world that. "I love him."

"Well, you best go get him, then. He's out in the hay field, plowin' who knows what at this hour."

Ariana kissed Red on his cheek. The whiskers of his beard nipped her lips roughly. His eyes sparkled even in the growing darkness. He looked eager to say something, like her kiss had caught him in the middle of a great speech. But he backed down and Ariana figured whatever it was, there would be time to hear it later. Right now she had to get to Brax. Tell him the sun—or something just as powerful and far away—had made her stupid and that she'd marry him anytime, anywhere.

"Okay, Sirocco," she said after watering him and giving him an armful of hay to eat. "One more run tonight."

Not surprisingly, the horse snorted and shook his head as if he understood.

Ariana grabbed the saddle horn, stuck her boot in the stirrup and swung up.

"Get up!" she said, sucking her teeth twice loudly and turning Sirocco toward the field. Chasing the last light of that day, they headed west. West to the field. West to Brax. West to the beginning of Ariana's life.

"Brax!" she yelled as she approached. The image of him working the field grew larger with every second. He was on the old tractor. The one she'd promised herself she'd replace and never did. Just couldn't bring herself to part with the first vehicle she'd ever learned to drive.

"Brax!" she called out once again. It seemed to her she'd been yelling that man's name all of her life.

He turned and watched her approach, switched off the engine. Glared at her.

He wanted to be left alone. She knew. He wanted to finish the rest of his obligation—which he probably would in a matter of days instead of weeks—and go back to being the old Brax. The one who spoke in short sentences and kept himself capped up in a tight bottle.

"Whoa, Sirocco," she said, as she brought the horse up alongside the tractor. In the short time he'd been at it, the field had been desecrated. Enough to keep the bailer busy for a week.

What? his eyes asked. *What now?*

"You don't think I'm about to let you go now that you've finally got the cowboy swagger down, do you?"

His eyes softened but he still looked hard sittin' up there by himself.

"I got work to do," he said, starting up the tractor.

"So do I," Ariana said, and without a clear thought in her head, jumped from her horse to the tractor, fumbling a moment before Brax steadied her and she sat down beside him.

"You're crazy," he said.

"That's me. Crazy Ariana MacLeod. I musta been born that way 'cause I been known for fool mistakes all my life.

"But I know this. I learn quick. And once I learn, I don't forget and I don't make the same mistake twice.

"Now, I love you, Brax Ambrose. From my boots to my hat. And I don't ever wanna think there would be a day come in this lifetime when I would be without that love or the love you got for me. So if that means we gotta get married, then we best get married, 'cause I aim ta keep you. You hear me?"

His eyes smiled first. Then his whole face. Then his arms reached out, held her. And they smiled, too. Or at least that's how they felt. All warm and cozy and reassuring. Her soul left her body and flew higher than any eagle she'd ever seen. And she knew that she'd been set free. Free of the past. Free of a future away from her ranch. Free of the curse. Simply, sweetly and completely free.

"What is it about you?" Brax asked, pulling Ari into his lap. She'd been riding long. Probably from the house. The dirt and sweat made her cream-colored face look sooty. Hard. But in his arms she was tender. Strokable. Her lips, his own private fountain of milk and honey. His groin tightened, just at the nearness of her. No willpower at all over the way her golden hair captivated him or the way her eyes drew him into her soul.

"I can't believe I fell for you," he said, gazing into her eyes.

She wrapped her arms around his neck, but tensed at his words. "Why?"

He smiled. "Because…your idea of traveling across country is a horseback ride. You live in the middle of the country, but you talk like you're from the south. And don't get me started about your commune with nature."

"What do you mean?"

"I mean, if nature comes into your house—mouse, raccoon, giant grasshopper, skunk—you're more likely to invite it to stay for dinner than to shoo it out."

Ari's mouth parted and shock widened her eyes.

The most beautiful woman in the world and he was holding her in his arms.

"And I love it," he said, and bent to slide his tongue into that luscious parted mouth of hers and drink his fill.

Her warm, strong arms held him tighter, pulled him closer. The hum of the engine kept them company as night fell on their long kiss, surrounding them like a comfortable friend.

Her mouth was pure sweetness. And he was thirsty. Greedy for her. Emotions and feelings he'd stuffed down, tried to keep in check, like happiness, joy, vulnerability, all the things that a man's not supposed to feel came pouring out of him and onto her lips. He couldn't hold them or anything else back anymore. He didn't want to. She had opened him as wide as her land and unchained his soul. He pushed against her lips into her mouth and found heaven.

He was selfish with her, pulling her lips into his, tasting, teasing, devouring.

He pulled her closer. Flattening her breasts with his weight. Her heart beat against his chest. It echoed his own that had beat alone for way too long.

With one hand, he reached under them and adjusted the seat. It slid back, giving them more room.

"Say something," he whispered. "Tell me how you feel."

"Excited."

He slipped his hand under her skirt, past her lace panties. Rudely. He didn't care. He wanted to know just how excited she was. He was so hard the pain of it blurred his vision. He had to squint against the agony. Did Ari ache, too? Was she wet for him?

His fingers moved across her hair, thick, curly, until they found her opening drenched with arousal. They slid in easily.

Brax groaned with Ari in relief. She was so hot and so wet to his touch, her juices coated his hand with her urgency.

"Damn, Ari. You're so wet."

"You do me so good, Brax," she panted. "I get wet as soon as I see you," she whispered.

Her words stroked his ego and his manhood at the same time. He moaned again. "I can't wait to get you to the house."

Ari sat up, light from the rising moon dancing in her eyes. "You won't have to."

Stretching one leg to the other side of his, she straddled him, a smoldering look of danger on her face.

"Uh-oh," he murmured, feigning concern, yet barely containing his anticipation. He licked his fingers as if he'd been eating fried chicken.

She took off her hat and tossed it aside. It landed in the fresh-cut hay with a thin whoosh. The smugness in her eyes told him he was in for it. His arousal tightened even harder. He didn't know he could get so hard. He bit his lip.

Her gaze bored down into him as she grabbed the edge of her blouse and tugged it out of her skirt. Gathering more fabric in her hands, she lifted the blouse over her stomach, her chest, slowly over her shoulders and finally above her head. She threw it behind him. Brax began breathing hard. He reached up to touch the black silk bra covering her creamy breasts.

She blocked his hands with her own and shook her head. "No touching," she said.

Brax bit down harder on his bottom lip and his mouth watered. How could he possibly restrain himself? Against his desire, he placed his hands at his sides and grabbed on to the leather seat. It squeaked with his tight grip.

Powerless. That's what she wanted. And that's what he was. Since the moment their lives had collided, literally.

"What you got for me?" she asked.

He gave her a crooked smile and motioned toward his back pocket. She slid her hand behind him, reached in and gave his cheek a firm squeeze before pulling out a three-pack of condoms. The pulse of her fingers sent shock waves and promises throbbing through his body. "Ari," he said.

She separated one of the condoms from the other two and placed the other two beside them. "Let's start with this one."

Brax looked down at the strain his manhood put on his jeans, then looked up at her. "Whatever you want, baby."

She didn't waste any time letting him know exactly what she wanted. She put the condom package between her teeth while she unbuckled his belt, unsnapped and unzipped his pants. He raised his hips, careful to keep his foot on the brake while she pushed his jeans down past his knees. Finally free, he wanted to touch her so badly. Instead he said, "Now what?"

Keeping her eyes on him, Ari tore open the wrapper and rolled the condom down over his throbbing manhood, her hands hot, warm and squeezing. Brax sucked in a gulp of air at the heat of her touch. He gripped the seat tighter. He wanted her bad now. Before he could tell her, she lowered her head and took him into her mouth.

He closed his eyes and opened his mouth. Deep

moans rolled out, one after the other. Each lick of her tongue struck him like lightning and like thunder moans and groans of pleasure boomed in the air.

Brax let his head drop back and let the sensations take over. He breathed hard. His muscles tensed with anticipation. Ari worked him hard, coaxing a sharp groan. His eyes snapped open. So good.

He stared down at the golden hair flowing over his lap. He raised his hands to touch it. Remembering her admonishment, he put them back down. But the feeling got too good and he couldn't help himself. His thrust his hips up and wove his fingers into her silky hair. Kept his eyes on the rise and fall of her head.

"Ah, ah, ah!" he said, approaching his peak.

Ari slowed her movements and then sat up. "Not yet," she said, her smile making her voice sassy and wicked.

She rose to her knees. "You can touch me now."

Brax tugged at the top of her skirt and panties until he'd pulled them down and helped her wriggle first one silky leg and then the other out of them.

"You're so damned sexy," he said.

"So are…" she began, then lowered herself onto him. "You."

The sensation of being connected to her was so powerful and overwhelming, Brax almost came, right that second.

She sank against him, groaning. She must have felt the same way.

"Don't move," he said, trying hard to force back the explosion boiling at the base of his arousal. It jumped and throbbed strongly inside her.

"Um," she said and licked her lips, her eyes already

drunk, misty with lust. The air was filled with her scent. Another trigger to his passion. He gritted his teeth and ground his hips.

"Ah, Brax," Ariana said, matching his movements. She slid up and down, a sweet rhythm, hot and tight against him.

He wanted to come so bad. So, so bad. *Not yet,* he repeated in his mind.

Ari rocked against his hardness, juices flowing, and he watched. He loved to watch her. Loved the way passion played with her face. Made her smile and squint. Squeeze her eyes shut and gasp.

He kept watching and she kept riding. Her hands moved across his chest and then up the sides of her own body. She was exploring her own sensuality. Ari reached behind her, unfastened her bra and shrugged out of it. She brought her hands back down to her body and played with the hard pebbles of her nipples jutted out on her round breasts.

She kept riding and cried out. It was the most erotic display Brax had ever seen. He felt like a volcano on the verge of erupting. *Not yet,* he ordered his body.

She must have sensed his battle. "Let it go, Brax," she whispered. "Feel this," she said, riding him faster and stronger. "You make me feel…ssss…ooh!"

Brax did let go…of everything. He surrendered to her hips, her lips and her love. He surrendered so completely, he didn't realize that he'd taken his foot off the brake until the tractor had traveled several yards into the hay field.

"Wait, baby," he said, slowing his thrusts and trying to maneuver his foot back to the brake.

"Don't stop. It's so good. Don't stop. Please."

When Ari circled her hips and squeezed him, he forgot all about the brake. She rode him good and they rode the land. Into the night, the bumps and ruts adding to the sensations of their movements.

She braced herself against the top of the seat and used the leverage to grind him even harder.

He grabbed her then, pulled her close. Kissed her with so much force he feared their lips might bruise from it, and laid himself open for her, God and all the heavens to see.

They shook together, climaxing one after the other. Brax held her so tight he only prayed she could breathe.

"Don't ever leave me," he whispered in her ear.

"I won't," she said. "Not ever."

Chapter 20

The next few weeks passed so quickly, Ariana would have sworn there were seven hours in each day instead of twenty-four. She and Brax spent as much time together as they did apart. It was as if he was putting in double time in the field and double time in her bed. She was the happiest she'd ever been and also the most apprehensive. She and Brax had done most of their talking in the bedroom in the last seven days, neither one of them mentioning how close they'd become, if they meant what they'd said that night or the tree they hit letting the tractor go during their lovemaking.

Even if she'd wanted to talk, she'd been busy talking to Willows about potential buyers. To give herself a distraction—and an out—just in case her relationship with Brax didn't stand the test of time beyond his court order. She'd even shown the place. Once to a young couple looking to return to their country roots after graduating from college, and then to a man, recently divorced, who had been saving his money for five years and had dreamed of owning his own ranch.

Each time she'd shown the place, she'd noticed Brax close down and grow cold. Pretty soon, she thought solemnly, he'd be back to one-word answers.

So, rather than turn back time, Ariana decided not to even bring up anything she didn't want a bad answer to.

Avoidance was a strange feeling in her bones. It felt a little like having a cold or flu. Something that made you miserable for a short while, but you eventually got over. It was a strange surly feeling and all Ariana wanted was for it to go away, just as quickly and thoroughly as it came on.

Until then, she'd have to make do with long days of herding cattle, graining horses and checking fences.

One morning, Ariana finished her fence check early—at least she thought it was early. When she came up on the south end, where she'd been earlier in the week, she discovered a break.

Out of all the chores on the ranch, mending fences was the one Ariana enjoyed passing off to Red, Tony or any extra hand working the Sugar Trail. Unfortunately, Tony was off roping for the next few days and Red had all but disappeared. Which had left her and Brax with all the work. Luckily, Selena was due back that Monday. If Red and Tony hadn't returned by then, Ariana knew her sister would pitch in. In the meantime, Ariana thought that a little fence mending would be good as Brax's final chore. She'd discuss it with him during supper.

* * *

Brax didn't understand it. It was the fourth breach in the fence that week. It was as though all of the bulls had gone crazy and wanted off the ranch. Maybe their desire to mate was overpowering them. Making them do crazy things.

Kind of like him.

For weeks, Brax's better judgment had come and gone like the hours in a day. Fading with the moon and reappearing with the first light. He and Ariana had run hot and cold like neither one of them knew exactly what to do with their overwhelming feelings. Neither wanting to make a mistake or mess things up. And that alone had put them at odds.

"It was better when we didn't care," Brax said, squeezing down on the wire cutter.

Red held the barbed wire with gloved hands and brought two busted ends together. Brax wrapped the repair wire against the broken ends and twisted them into what Red called a lazy eight.

"Better without love?" Red looked up, away from what they were doing. The sun forced light into the creases and deep wrinkles of his face. His eyes were so focused and clear. For weeks that clarity had niggled at the back of Brax's mind, the expression so familiar. Like he'd grown up with it.

"There's nothing better, nothing finer than love. And don't let anything…or anyone make you believe diff'rent."

Sincerity and concern clouded the old man's face. Red really had been in Brax's corner. Since his first workday on the ranch, when Brax hated the ranch and

Ariana wasn't too crazy about him being there. Red kept the peace and smoothed the rough edges of his stay.

"Who do *you* love, old man?" Brax asked, suddenly curious if Red's disappearances, especially over the past few days, were on account of some woman in town.

Red smiled and Brax thought he actually saw the man's red-rimmed eyes water up. Brax looked away and turned back to the broken fence almost repaired now. "Keep pulling," Brax said, stepping in so Red didn't have to answer.

Together they bound new barbed wire to the old. Even though they both wore gloves, they were careful not to cut themselves or each other in the process.

The technique had become rote. Brax had fixed so many fences, he really didn't need Red's help. But Brax liked the company. He suspected they both did.

It would be a shame to put an end to it all. Now that Brax had been over every acre, every foot, every square inch of the Sugar Trail, he knew it all by heart. He could find the pen, the windmill, the water trough, the hay field if he was blindfolded and spun like a top. But it didn't seem to matter that he and Ariana had gotten close or that he had let her know he wanted more than just three months with her.

"She just needs to know that you won't leave her, is all."

Funny. Brax thought the same about her, and he was fairly certain he'd blurted out as much in the aftermath of one of their passionate exchanges.

It was obvious. The intensity of their feelings had stunned them both. If what they'd shared in their most intimate moments was true, they'd both found something neither of them had experienced before. And because they didn't want to mess up a good thing, they were messing up a good thing.

Red was right. Love was too important to treat lightly. Brax would talk to Ariana that evening and put all his cards, and his heart, on the table.

Brax couldn't imagine what Red had just seen, but the old man was standing and staring at him so intently, Brax thought for a second he must have seen or sensed everything going on in his mind. If love made you this vulnerable, he thought, maybe he'd better be careful.

The two men walked in silence to their waiting horses. Run Amok snorted and pawed the ground at his approach. Three Socks just looked off as if he couldn't care less about being ridden.

"Even Run Amok has taken a likin' to you, son."

Brax didn't want to grin like an eleven-year-old, so he settled for a half smile. He and Run Amok had come to an understanding. Brax would feed him, water him, brush him and keep his stall clean. In exchange, Run Amok would take Brax anywhere he wanted to go without a complaint. Brax knew he was getting the better part of that deal. He gave Run Amok's mane a few long reassuring strokes, making a mental note to give him a bucket of oats when they got back to the barn.

Brax and Red swung up on their horses. "Let's go home," Brax said to the stallion, flicking his reins.

"Listen, son, you took to this place like a fly takes to…well, you know what I mean.

"I've never seen nothin' like it. Like you. And I've been round the Sugar Trail the better part of half a century. Heh. Don't that beat all ta say? But it's true. Folks come and go. Young ones. Older ones. And an awful lot in between.

"But you came and stuck. Yes, sir. Right off. I ain't seen you talk about that dang cell phone of yours in a bunch of long days. And that's all you talked about when you first showed up."

Red was right. Brax hadn't checked in with his brother or sister in quite a while. He barely remembered he had a cell phone or what it was for.

"I'm quite taken with the place, Red."

When Brax reflected on his days on the Sugar Trail, the backdrop was always big sky, rolling hills, surprisingly deep valleys and grassland as far as his eye could see. The air always smelled nature-made. No exhaust fumes, perfume, construction gasses or smokestacks. Just grass, hay, alfalfa and sweat. He was in the place where God placed his unvarnished stamp on everything. The first *real* place Brax had ever lived.

"I've come to appreciate the fact that there are no real barriers between you-all and nature. If you open the door and a possum walks in, well, he just walks in. You-all try to get him out, but if he's friendly, you cook up some vittles and ask him to stay for dinner.

"I've never been one to let grass grow under my feet, but something…"

"You don't have to say another word. It's why I never left."

Brax was living the life of rolled-up sleeves, quiet wind, red-gold sunsets and night skies choked with stars.

"So," Red asked, voice toughened with emotion, "you gonna marry her?"

Brax smiled again. He didn't have the answer to the question, but he knew there was only one way to find out.

* * *

"Weren't these things used to look out for Indians?" Brax asked, looking around from the roof. They'd spent the night making love under a black velvet canopy of stars. It was almost time to start the day.

"Yes. But in this part of the country, Native Americans and African-Americans were allies. So instead, my family used the widow's walk to watch for white people. Night Riders at first. Later on, KKK."

"And now what do you use it for?"

Ariana fingered a rut in the wood floor. The place where she always stuck her fingers. They slid naturally into the slats. Always had. She wondered whose fingers would find their way into the dark private places of her home once she sold it.

"Just to get away, I guess. Sometimes to look out at this amazing land and be thankful for it.

"Maybe in some ways, I'm still looking for the enemy. Any day, over that hill, I expect to see an ethanol plant or a Wal-Mart.

"So many of the families that I grew up with, people I've known like Chuck Zimmons, his wife, Teresa, the Peterses, Buck and his wife, Sadie, they're all dead now. Sometimes their kids take over the ranch. Sometimes they sell them to private companies.

"These hills look pretty much the same as when I was a girl, but the human landscape...that's what's changing."

She stared off toward the windmill. The wind blew the front of her hair to the back like she was flying. "Most of the folks I grew up with are dead," she said, sadness flattening her words. Making them come out as dry as the soil.

"And if you and Selena move, won't you be changing the landscape?"

Ariana didn't blink or move. "Some things can't be helped."

Brax grabbed a stray wood chip and flung it in the direction of the horizon. It disappeared into the meadow. He never saw it land. He was also thinking about things that couldn't be helped. His connection with this land. This place. He couldn't believe how much his life had changed in less than a season.

He wasn't quite a cowboy. Not yet. But he was no longer a trucker. That was certain. And as far as the city went, from Brax's perspective right now, the city—any city—was a nice place to visit, but he wouldn't want to live there ever again.

How cruel would the angels be to allow him to meet one of their own but only as a ship passing? Brax could never be as chivalrous as Nick Cage and settle for one smell of her hair. Brax wanted it all: lock, stock and turkey vultures.

He kept his eyes straight ahead. On the land. On the grassy prairie in front of him. On the pastures and hills. On the mares with their colts. He kept his eye on that and his heart on Ariana.

"What if a man came along—a good man, a man who loved you, with his whole heart, a heart he didn't even know he had until you showed him how to find it, a man who wants you and everything that is you?"

He turned to her. She turned to him.

"Including this place?" he asked.

"Well, I'll be!" Ariana said. A crooked smile turned her beautiful mouth into a line as uneven as the terrain.

"Is that a yes or a no?" he asked.

Her left eyebrow rose and she slapped a hand against a big round hip. "To what?"

He smiled. Chuckled a little bit. She was going to force his hand all the way. *No punches pulled,* she'd said.

"Hell, what do they call it round these parts? Gettin' hitched? Whadaya say? Ya wanna...get hitched?"

She kissed him on the nose and slapped him on the behind. "You know I do!"

Brax grabbed her waist and pulled. She came easily. He stuck his fingers into her thicker than thick hair and played with the silky strands. "Is that a yes or a no?"

Ariana stepped closer. Her lips found his ready and eager ones. The soft flesh of her mouth pressed into his own. Her breath mingled with his. Hot with desire. And mint. Her mouth tasted like mint and jasmine. And when she slid her tongue between his parted lips, he sucked it greedily. He pulled her body all the way to him. Muscle and muscle. They went solid together. He pulled and sucked the soft, wet flesh of her tongue. Darted his in and out of her mouth. Pulling out a moan. Tasting her soul.

He slid his tongue in and out of her mouth, mimicking the motions of his hips just a few short hours ago. And like her hips, she thrust with him. Like her core, she hung on, tightened, teased...and wouldn't let go.

"Yes," she said.

His heart felt like a sledgehammer driving golden spikes into railroad ties. He mouth went dry. He breathed heavily, forcing air in and out of his lungs for fear he'd forget how. He kept still, though. Trying to fake her out. He didn't want her to know how close to passing out he was. How so very desperate for her affection, her love, her lifetime of companionship he really was. He hadn't even thought past the idea of what would have happened if she'd said no. If she refused him, he would have crumbled. Turned to dust and scattered himself on the plains of her land, getting what he wanted anyway…to be with Ariana forever.

Brax fed Run Amok a handful of oats and smiled while his rough, warm and slobbery tongue spilled more food than it lapped up. Brax laughed. Nothing like a good dose of horse spit before supper. Now, if he could just seal this deal with Ariana, everything would be—

"Brax!" a female voice called.

Brax turned to see the fashionably dressed woman stepping out of a brand-new Porsche. "Oh, Brax!" she called and ran toward him.

"Stay here," Brax told Run Amok and walked out to meet the woman. She approached, vampish in a cayenne-red dress so tight it looked like the designer sheath was tying to squeeze her out of both ends.

She flung herself into his arms and Brax caught a glimpse of Ariana, a curious expression on her beautiful face as she watched the spectacle from the porch of the ranch house.

"I was so worried. You haven't called and I thought, I thought—"

She held him tight, pushing the side of her face into his chest. Protectively, he reached up and stroked her back for reassurance. Her body went stiff. She pulled away, turning her normally smug features into bright eyes and a wide mouth. "If you ever tell anyone I was that uncool, I'll deny it and renounce you as a brother."

"I love you too, Honey," Brax said, half laughing. "What are you doing here?"

"The unflyest, most unfunky thing I have ever done. I'm chasing after a man."

At that, Brax let go a big laugh and slung his arm around her shoulder. He walked her over to where Ariana watched them very closely from the porch and Red just stroked his cheek and stood stiff as a tree trunk.

"I'm not just a man, I'm your brother. You can be uncool with me."

She smiled a little and relaxed at that.

Honey took a slow appraising walk around him. Her examination was so thorough, Brax could swear he felt it all over his skin. "Well, just look at you—darker, dirtier, bulkier. You look like the real thing."

She crinkled her nose and waved a hand in front of her face. "You smell like it, too."

"Thanks," Brax said, taking the olfactory sign of his hard work and dedication to the ranch as a compliment.

"You must be about two shades darker. How much time do you spend outside?"

"All of it, or pretty close."

Honey snorted. "You even walk like you just got off a horse."

"I did," he said, unable to fight the smile brimming at the edges of his mouth.

She blessed him with one more eye inventory. "I believe you."

Suddenly, she pushed his arm away. "Wait. Weren't you just feeding that horse with that hand?" She eyed his guilty palm with disgust.

"What about it?"

"Please tell me I don't have horse drool all over my Vera Wang."

A quick look at her dress revealed the telltale signs of Run Amok's frothy spit. He wanted to be honest, but he couldn't freak out his sister, not in front of the woman he loved.

"Nah," he said. "All clear."

"You don't lie well at all. What kind of man are you?" Honey asked.

"A good man," Ariana finished, stepping down from the porch. She stuck out her hand and stood in front of Brax. "I'm Ari," she said.

Brax watched his sister shake hands vigorously. "I'm Honey."

"Honey!" Ari said, obviously relieved.

Brax's ego inflated to twice its size. "I've been so busy fixing fences around here, I forgot to call her."

"I just came to check up on him." She patted him on the shoulder. Her crimson manicured nails glistened like glass in the afternoon sun. "Now that I know you're okay, I'll head back."

"No," Ariana said. "You drove all this way. At least stay for supper."

"Is Tony back?" Brax asked.

"Came back this mornin'. I think he's tryin' to make up for bein' gone so long, so he's makin' all my favorites."

Ariana turned to Honey. "Will you stay?"

Honey smiled broadly. It was a family trait Brax recognized. She didn't lie well, either. "I'd love to!"

"Plaid shirt, jeans, wide leather belt. You even have the boots! Next thing you know, you'll be wearing a Stetson."

Brax didn't dare tell his sister that he already had one. He held his retort in check. He knew his sister was having a rough time. After all, he'd come all this way to console her and they hadn't spent more than a few hours together. And seeing him…settled into ranch life and happy about it had to be a shock and another reminder that she was still looking for happiness in her own life. Unfortunately, Honey hadn't done as well as a child in the system as he had. Though they never spoke of it, Brax was sure that at some point in her life, Honey had been violated in some way and her difficulty with men stemmed from that ugliness.

He prayed for her and hoped that one day, she'd be able to reconcile her life in a way that made her happy and offered her a promising future…in the way he had.

Tony filled the kitchen table to overflowing with baby carrots, tomato salad, spicy baked beans, beef brisket with Jack Daniels sauce and sourdough biscuits and molasses. For dessert he'd made sweet potato casserole. He topped it all off with fresh lemonade with lemon and grapefruit slices floating inside each glass. Yep. Tony was trying to get on Ariana's good side. And he was doing a damn good job.

The kitchen was warm from the oven and all stove eyes burning and full of the aroma of Tony's hard work. Ariana's stomach grumbled so loudly, it sounded like it was speaking English.

"Let's eat!" she said.

Red said grace and started the five of them passing pots. When every plate was full they dug in.

Tony did not disappoint. Ariana thought Tony should

set aside his taste for the rodeo and become a chef. He could be workin' in some fancy place, she thought. In the past, she knew he stuck around because of her. But lately he'd been gone more and more. She guessed because of Brax. She hoped Tony would do what made him really happy. He liked the rodeo, but something about fixin' a whole room of food put a smile as big as Route 2 on his face.

"Tony, is it?" Honey asked.

"Yes," he said, reaching for another biscuit.

"This is the best brisket I've ever tasted."

Everyone else joined in with compliments on Tony's meal. He grinned like a big kid. "Well, save room for dessert."

"I'll have room," Ariana proclaimed.

"You sure?" Honey asked, obviously noticing Ari's penchant for eating.

"Lady West can handle her food," Brax said, then winked at Ariana.

That quick gesture sent sparks flying inside her. Just a wink, she thought. *Golly. I must really be in love.* Ariana shoved a carrot into her mouth before she could say something shameful to Brax, like "I need to show you something upstairs."

Honey helped herself to more brisket. "Lady West, huh? You got a name for him?"

"Big Rig," they said in unison. Then laughed.

"So, Big Rig, how much more of your court order do you have left to serve?" Honey asked.

Even with the clinking of silverware against plates, the chewing, swallowing, the whole kitchen got quiet.

"Actually, I'm finished. I worked off my debt a week

ago. But since then, some other things have come up. Fences, siding, the roof."

My relationship with Ariana, Ariana thought and waited for him to say. When he didn't, disappointment struck her like angry lightning.

"It's been crazy around here and with Ariana's sister gone until tomorrow, I thought she could use an extra hand so I stuck around."

"Oh," came Honey's weak reply. Obviously, she didn't approve.

They spent the rest of supper listening first to Red's jokes and then Tony's rodeo stories. After Tony served dessert, he and Red made themselves noticeably absent and left Ariana, Honey and Brax in the kitchen to enjoy their sweet potato casserole and coffee.

"Tony's cute," Honey said. "He single?"

"Way too single," came Ariana's answer.

Brax perked up. "There's no such thing."

They all laughed at that.

Ariana needed that laugh. She'd spent the last hour and a half as uncomfortable as a bull at branding time. If Honey looked at her mean-eyed one more time, Ariana would have to leave the room. Otherwise, she couldn't be responsible for what her backhand would do or what her mouth would say.

This love stuff is hard, she thought. She watched the brother and sister chatting across from her, wondering how Brax would take it if she suddenly said, "Baby, I love *you,* but I wouldn't give two bad stones for your sister." Ariana was sure that wouldn't go over well at all. So she made sure that she kept food in her mouth so that she didn't say the awful things stackin' up in her head like hay bales.

"So, Lucky Wagon—"

"Lady West," Ariana corrected.

Honey smiled, or tried to. It just looked to Ariana like she had lemons growing in her cheeks. "Right. What does a city girl have to do to get a refill on her coffee?"

"Ask," Ariana said.

Brax looked even worse than his sister. His eyes said, "I'm sorry," but as long as his mouth kept quiet, Ariana didn't believe him.

Ariana stood. She was as angry as a shaken hive of bees. "I need to talk to Red about something. I'll go do that and be right back to fill up your cup…unless Brax fills it before I get back."

She hoped he understood her message. She had no mind to get Honey any more coffee. No mind at all.

"Y'all excuse me," she said and headed outside. *Where's my shotgun?* she wondered. Target practice sounded real good.

"Honey, what are you doing?" Brax said as calmly as he could. Thankful that Ariana left the room, he wanted to shake some sense into her. But he wasn't that kind of man. It had taken all of his inner strength to keep from calling her out during supper. As sharp as his sister was with her tongue, she was just as easily embarrassed. So, now that they had a private moment…

"I think the real question is *what are you doing?* Out here playing cowboy? You should see yourself. Covered from head to toe with dirt, skin burnt crispy and clothes that look like you're only half a step away from yelling, 'Yee haw!'"

Honey bunched up her face as if the whole thing turned her stomach. But Brax knew that wasn't it at all.

"Good Lord, Brax, you look…you look—"

"Happy?" he asked. The word popped out before he could stop it.

"What?" Honey said, blinking and gasping like she'd just gotten caught in a strong wind. "What?"

"I know you've been going through something. Hell, I've been through something myself lately." Brief images of Hazel and their ugly breakup appeared in his mind. They were quickly and thoroughly dissolved by visions of Ariana, the Sugar Trail and the life he'd made with both of them in such a short amount of time.

He stood up, paced away from his sister sitting in wide-eyed shock in the kitchen chair across from him. Suddenly his contentment, his excitement, wouldn't let him be still or be silent. "I'm home, Honey. From the moment I set foot on this place. Even though I fought it, I felt it. I'm home. And I'm happy."

"On a *ranch?*" she said, astonishment raising her voice an octave.

"Not just a ranch. *This* ranch."

"I thought you said she was selling the place."

He spun around to face her then. "You don't know how many times I've thought about buying it. But it's not just the ranch I want. It's her, too."

Honey laughed then. It was a tight, tension-filled sound that made Brax uneasy and concerned for his sister's happiness. "Why don't you just marry her? That way you can save your money and still get what you want."

For a fleeting second that he was ashamed of, Brax wanted to order his sister to leave. For once in Brax's one-word-answer life, he couldn't come up with even one word to respond to his sister's ridiculous notions.

Finally, the phrase that came to him was as outlandish as her proposal, but he hoped it would shut her up.

"Maybe I will, Honey. Maybe I will."

Chapter 21

When he'd gotten up that morning, he would have sworn that he'd lost his mind. There was no storm, no feuding bulls, no severe wind and from what he knew, no vindictive neighbors. But within twenty-four hours, there were two more breaks in the fence and some slats on the north barn that had managed to come loose. After the past week, Brax used his insomniac time to double-check his work and make sure the repairs that both he and Red were making took. Last night, everything was fine, except for the tension he sensed between him and Ariana. No doubt from the wreck of an evening with Honey. Brax was never so glad in his born days to see a woman leave.

Although he and Ariana got up together nights sometimes to talk, often to make love, she'd stayed asleep while he made his rounds. With flashlight in hand he'd made a sweep of nearly the entire place, and now it was as though someone had come in and deliberately caused damage.

A quick thought that went through his mind was Honey. Could she have been that upset at Brax's newfound happiness to do this? But he knew, Honey's emotions came out in words and then she would calm down and see reason. So he had patience with her and knew that she wasn't capable of vandalizing the ranch.

He'd wondered about teenagers, but he'd never gotten any indication that the people of Shoresville, Nebraska, did anything except get along well with each other and show respect to one another.

Red had become his confidant over the course of his stay. He intended to ask him about it, but when he came down for breakfast that morning, Tony informed them that Red was at his place. Said his stomach was bothering him.

That's when Brax started putting two and two together. He hadn't quite come up with four, but he was close. He headed over to Red's determined to leave with that magic number.

Run Amok and Brax smelled the ham and eggs cooking several feet before they even got to Red's door.

Bad stomach, huh?

Brax swung down, tied Run Amok to the post and went inside the house.

"Got enough for two?" he asked.

Red's place was closer to a large toolshed than a home. Brax vaguely recalled Ari mentioning that Red lived in the original homestead. He'd kept it up, but even with repairs and improvements, it still looked like a one-hundred-year-old structure complete with weathered wood from ceiling to floor, brick fireplace and low-clearance entrance. Brax ducked, then stepped inside.

Red started, dropping his spit cup on the kitchen floor. Thick brown juice sprayed into a Rorschach pattern on the wooden slats. "Big Rig! What are you doing?"

"I came to find out *you're* doing."

Worry filled Red's eyes and the answer to an unexpected question came into Brax's heart. But first things first.

Red looked down at the floor. "Making a mess. Seems like I'm good at that."

Brax leaned against the wall, staying close to the front door. He didn't trust Red. Not anymore. And until he could hear a logical explanation for what the man had been doing, Brax preferred to keep his distance.

Red found Borax and wet a towel. He knelt as best he could and cleaned up the chew juice, then washed his hands.

"I got plenty," Red said, motioning to the thick slice of ham sizzling in the cast-iron skillet.

Brax kept quiet, surprised at his reaction. Red wrecking the ranch was like injuring Brax. To avoid saying something he might have to take back later, he stayed quiet.

Red fixed a plate, sat down with it and began to cut up his meat. "I knew it was getting close to your time and all. You know, the end of your court order. I just thought it would be a good idea if you stuck around a bit longer, so I...made sure you had plenty to do."

Brax folded his arms. "For how long?"

Red stuck a square of ham in his mouth, but kept talking. "'Bout a month now. Heck, you'd finished that list of chores we put together for you so fast, I had ta do somethin'."

"Why?"

"You know why."

"Ari."

"Ari."

Red pushed a mouthful of eggs on his fork with his knife. "She liked you right off. And that ain't never happened. Now, she's had her share of fellas, ones that she—"

"Spare me."

"See? That's what I'm talkin' 'bout. That there. Well, I just couldn't let that get away from her, so I busted a few things to keep your plate full."

Brax doubted if anything in the world could have kept them apart. But the old man's actions touched him and angered him at the same time. And knowing what he knew now, they made a crazy kind of sense. "So, what are you? Uncle? Cousin?"

Red reached across the kitchen table to a glass flask that Brax knew contained whiskey and took a vigorous swallow. "Grandfather," Red said without hesitation.

Brax eyed the flask and moved toward the kitchen. "I think I'll join you."

While Red finished his breakfast, Brax served himself a helping of eggs and a swift drink of Wild Turkey and listened to a story he could barely believe.

The story started when Ariana's mother fell in love with a local man who'd come around one summer to work. The man didn't seem to be able to do a lick of work, but he sure knuckled down to catch Petra's heart.

"Nothin' wrong with love," Red said. "'Cept for one thing. Galvin was white.

"There were mixed feelings round here 'bout the two of them. Some folks liked it. They just like love no matter who's in it. Other folks, most folks, hated it and tried to stop it. And the rest didn't seem to care one way or another."

"Which category were you?" Brax asked. But he could just about guess.

"I tried like the devil to bust 'em up. Back then, I was probably what you might call a racist. I had no use for blacks—no offence, Big Rig."

"I can't help but take offence to that, Red. Racists have been the bane of my people's existence for hundreds of years."

"Well, I was the bane of Petra and Galvin's existence for a long time. Finally, my son stopped speaking to me, and my wife stopped being friendly. But I didn't care. In my head, blacks were inferior and my son was making a big mistake taking up with one."

"And then the worst thing you could imagine happened," Brax added, going for a piece of ham this time and thinking about a big sip of whiskey.

"Yeah. Galvin got Petra pregnant. I was against it—one thousand percent. I even gave Petra the name of a doctor that could 'take care of things.'" Red stopped, took a long drink from the flask without coughing. "See this scar 'cross the back of my head?"

Brax nodded.

"Petra cracked me good with that skillet right there."

"Damn," Brax said.

"Uh-huh. Too bad that didn't stop me."

"What did you do?"

"What didn't I do? That'd be a shorter list. Heh. Everything I thought was right and just at the time, but nothin' I'm proud of now."

Brax sat up, squinting. His vision had changed. Instead of a salty Willie Nelson, Red started to look like a shriveled-up grand dragon. Brax's blood boiled hot. "You light any crosses?"

Red was slow to speak. "No. But there was a barn that I—"

"Stop," Brax said. "Don't give me a reason to hate you."

Red nodded. Took another swig from the almost empty flask. "Petra was stubborn, but not as stubborn as me."

"Didn't anyone call the police?"

Red gave Brax a look that said, "Now, you ought ta know better."

"Right," Brax said, knowing the police at that time might have been as racist as Red.

"Finally, right before Ari was born, I broke him down. Petra stood fast, but Galvin wanted to take her and the baby and move away from here."

"And Petra wouldn't go."

"Hell, no. She said this was her land and wasn't no fool white man gonna move her off it." Red laughed. His eyes looked clouded. Unfocused. Brax reasoned the whiskey must have been working on him. "And I didn't, either. So Petra and Ari stayed right here."

"And Ariana has no idea who you are?"

"Nope. After everything I put her mother through, she never told her. And Petra promised to put me on the hill if I said a mumblin' word. So Ari don't know. She don't know nothin'."

Brax looked away. Pity, sorrow, anger, frustration and concern wrestled for control inside him.

"Now, I ain't much like that no more, Big Rig. I mean, I ain't perfect. I was raised wrong. And sometimes them wrong thoughts, well, they just jump up without my say-so. But if one thing in this whole world is true, it's this…I love Ariana. My…" Red's voice broke. "My granddaughter." Red lifted his chin, but his sharp eyes went to liquid. "I love her with everything I got."

Red got up. Went to the kitchen sink and stood over it. His head dropped and he looked like his spirit had dropped with it. "I done wrong by her and by her mama. The Lord will make sure I see hell for that. But I got a chance now to do right. And by Jesus, I'm gonna do it!"

He faced Brax square-on then. Determination rode a fierce horse in his eyes. "You and Ari and Selena belong together. Right here. On this land. So if I gotta lasso you to the barn or rope you to the pen, well, sir, get ready. 'Cause I'm comin' for ya!"

Brax felt like he was in a showdown. A gunfight without bullets. Just promises of justice and redemption and love all finally concurring. The old man had guts, he'd give him that. Guts and insight. Brax loved Ariana with everything he had and would do everything he had the power to do to see her happy.

"I'm not goin' nowhere," Brax said.

A thick knot twisted in Brax's stomach. He tried to imagine denying love for that long and couldn't. His chest squeezed. He didn't think the tension could get any more acute until he heard the tension in the voice behind him.

"You should have told me," Ariana said.

Red looked up from the sink and Ariana stared at Red with the same pain-drenched eyes.

It was hard to miss now. Brax could see it so clearly. The A-line nose, arrow-shaped mouth, angular jaw. The evidence was all there. Now.

"I promised your mother—"

"You would have let me go on all my life without knowing who you are?"

"Ari—" Brax started with no idea of what he could say to make the situation better. He only knew he wanted to take her pain away.

"No," she said to him. "I don't know who you are, either."

"What?"

"I heard you and Honey. 'Why don't you just marry her? That way you can save your money and still get what you want.'"

Brax stood up. He couldn't believe what he was hearing. She had to know that wasn't his plan.

His heart tightened with dread. "You can't be serious."

"No, you can't be serious. Not about me or the ranch."

Brax had never thought of his heart as delicate, but at that moment, it felt soft. Pliable. Vulnerable. "This is my home, Ari. I don't know how or why, but I'm just like that old maple out there. Planted with long roots that stretch to you *and* this land."

He took a breath and a step closer. "I've been searching for a home since I came out of my mother's womb, damn it, and I've *found* it. I've found it. Right here in

Shoresville, freakin' Nebraska!" Her eyes went liquid. And so did his insides—like his heart was crying. "You can't ask me to leave, Ari. It would break me.

"You, wha—we've had…what the hell is wrong with you?" Brax couldn't get his mouth to act right. Maybe his ears were acting up. He couldn't be hearing her ending their engagement.

"Brax, it's been fun—"

He recoiled and backed away to get a full look at the woman snapping his heart like a twig. "Fun? The dunking booth is *fun.* Bobbing for apples…that's *fun.* Not this. You're trying to rob me of my soul."

She told him she could take him. Well, she did and she had. Taken him for a long ride, just when he thought his over-the-road days were over.

"You know why Uncle Jesse got out?" he asked. "She got out because you wanted her to."

Brax bit down on his tongue, but not hard enough. He wanted to hurt her the same way she'd hurt him. But more importantly, he wanted to tell her the truth. Lay it *all* on the line.

"You don't know how to appreciate what you have. *Three thousand* acres, Ari. You could walk for days and still not come to the end of it. All this belongs to you and you can't see how fortunate you are to have it. And you're too stubborn to see that there's no difference between this land and you. You *think* you can separate yourself, but you can't. And if you ever do, you'll die. You know how I know? Because *this* is killing me. If you could see what I see. What Selena sees. What Tony, Red and everyone else sees. If you could just open your eyes to the *miracle* of this place."

He placed a finger under her chin and lifted it. "The miracle of *you,* you'd hold on so tight, nothing could get away. Not a cow. Not a legacy. Not a man."

He straightened. Mustered more strength than he felt. "Now you can't be serious about calling us off."

Brax was wrong. It didn't break him. He kept enough of himself together to pack his things and get in the car when his sister came to get him. Once again, he'd gotten comfortable. And once again, he'd had to move on. Brax vowed that day to himself and to God, it was the last time that would ever happen to him.

Chapter 22

"Fire!"

Ariana started and sat straight up in bed. She'd been having a weird dream—one where Brax hadn't been scheming and Red was not her grandfather.

But that was just a dream.

She was about to glance at her clock to see what time it was, when Tony's shouts rang out throughout the hallway.

"Fire!" he called, then knocked on the door and swung it open.

Ariana sprang out of bed, gathering her nightgown around her. "Where?" she said, terrified that her property could be destroyed.

"Bar S!"

"Oh, my God!" Ariana cried. "He can't fight a fire. He can barely keep his cattle fenced!"

Ariana snatched her nightgown off and yanked on a pair of jeans and a shirt that she'd laid out the night before. Tony was as stiff as a barn door.

"I guess the secret's out, huh?" she asked, putting on her socks. "Don't act like you've never seen those catalogs come here."

Ariana pulled on her boots and tied her hair in a knot. "Let's go!"

The two of them ran downstairs and headed out to Ariana's truck. It was so dark they could barely see the smoke, but she could smell it. The fire was close.

Despite her personal turmoil, she put it aside for the good of her neighbor.

"Think we should go get Red?" she asked.

"He's already gone. Said he'd meet us there."

Dread fell like a cold stone, hard and heavy in the pit of Ariana's stomach. She drove faster. "We better hurry."

At times like these, Ariana would often imagine the worst, all the time hoping that nothing could be that bad. When she and Tony arrived at the Bar S she realized she hadn't imagined nearly enough.

Hank's barn was engulfed in flames and the fire had snaked its way to the house and the entire base was lit up as if God had lifted Hank's house and set it down on a plate of fire.

"Lord have mercy," she said, jumping out of her pickup. The fire stabbing up from the ground floor looked like a giant hand squeezing, crunching and melting the home from the outside in. The fire surged and rolled forward like a locomotive, igniting everything in front of it, overtaking and incinerating, shrubs, barrels and bales. Young trees exploded and boiled to smoke in seconds.

She dashed up to two hands who were fighting the fire with wet gunnysacks and losing badly. "Is anyone inside?"

"Don't know," one of them said.

Tony joined in the beating. "Somebody go for the water truck."

"Pete did," the other hand answered.

Ariana's eyes scanned the area, her heart beating wildly. "Where's Red?"

Panic seized her as she imagined fire feeding on hardwood floors, rocking chairs and *Nebraska Life* magazines. Her grandfather.

Heat generated by the fire made Ariana's skin feel like she was rolling in coals. She was beginning to understand what new calves went through at branding time.

She scanned the darkness for the water truck. She saw it rattling its way up to the house. Stew was driving and Tony rushed over, grabbed the hose and aimed it at the base of the raging flames.

With adrenaline propelling her, Ariana bolted toward the burning ranch house. Smoke attacked her lungs. Sharp, choking. Constricting her chest. She covered her mouth and nose with her hand, stuffed down a coughing fit and called into the house, "Red! Hank!"

Enormous tongues of heat licked Ariana's face and arms in fierce waves, singeing the fine hairs on her skin.

Fear threatened to paralyze her. She fought against it, her will driving her on and forward. "Red!"

Ariana ran around to the side of the house less inflamed, hoping to see or hear something. Gain a way in.

The sound assaulted her ears. She would never forget it. Fire is an evil noise. The ominous crackle of destruction. The loud breath of consumption. Insatiable consumption. The hum of its blistering appetite.

Before that day, Ariana thought of fire—the natural controlled fire—that ingests the layers of dead topsoil and allows the fertile underground to become available for planting. But this fire, destroying her neighbor's house, was ruthless, selfish, unyielding.

"Where's Red?" Ariana shouted, the fire no longer the sole focus of her concern. "Red!"

A soot-covered Sue Snooden ran to her side. She was dazed and coughing. "He went in for Hank. I couldn't…I couldn't wake Hank and I couldn't carry him. Red came in and said he'd get Hank out. I haven't seen either of them since."

Ariana's blood turned to ice, despite the heat. She thought her heart stopped beating. She could no longer feel it pumping in her chest. Her feet were pumping, though. They ran straight for the front door of the ranch house.

"Ari! No! You can't get in!"

Ariana heard the words fade behind her like a light breeze in a dream. "Red! Red! Get Hank and come out! Red!"

The fire became a thing alive before her eyes. Tongues, fingers, legs that crawled and devoured. A monstrous body swelling hot. And a mouth—a merciless mouth that roared and ate ravenously. Feeding a hunger that was unending.

Before her very eyes, the roof of Hank's house rolled up like a fist and burst into a red-orange ball of flame.

Ariana ran to the front door, to the side door, to the back. Flames leaped out of every opening and burned new ones. Everywhere she ran, the monster got there before her—a swift rush of red light and sound—raging and incinerating everything it touched.

Ariana coughed and gasped as ashes rose up around her, turning her milky brown skin sooty and gray. Her chest tightened as if the flames were burning inside her, scorching her heart. She grabbed her chest. It was the only thing she could think to do and went down on her knees.

"Red!" she called.

Sue, Tony and a few other hands beat the flames with wet gunnysacks and sheer determination until another water truck arrived from town.

Tears streamed down Ariana's face and she trembled like a shaken baby while the fire turned the night sky an angry red and bent the air in long heat-laden waves.

The thoughts blared in her mind. "Red!" she screamed, panic bubbling up and stealing her reason.

Then she saw them emerging from the front door. She didn't know how he was doing it, but Red came out carrying a man nearly twice his size. Ariana ran straight to them. "Red! Hank!"

Red stepped off the porch and headed for a tree where he collapsed with Hank in his arms. It would be a full twelve hours before he regained consciousness.

"How's Hank?"

Ariana sat up. She could have slapped herself for almost falling asleep. She didn't care if she'd been up over twenty-four hours. She wanted to be there for Red when he regained consciousness.

"He's fine, Red," she said, standing up from the unyielding visitor's chair. She went to his hospital bedside and took his hand.

The bony, sun-leathered hand of an old cowboy, so light and fragile, it barely felt real.

"Good. That fool could sleep through a cyclone."

"You weren't doin' too bad yourself."

"How long was I out?" he asked. His voice sounded like smoke and a whole bunch of tired.

"Half a day," she answered honestly.

Red coughed, gasped and gagged. Ariana grabbed a towel from the side table, the one she'd used to keep his head cool, and held it to his mouth until the spell passed.

"I better go tell the nurse you're up. Tony and Selena went to go get something to eat. I'll go get them."

Red reached out with a crooked hand. Still charred from the fire. The skin was an angry red over liver spots and wrinkles. She'd never noticed how old Red's hands looked until then.

"No," he said. "This won't take long."

"But, Red, at least let me go get the nurse. She's real nice and there's probably somethin' they need to do now that your eyes are open."

"I said this won't take long."

Now his words sounded garbled and Ariana's heart clenched and twisted so hard she had trouble standing. It felt like someone had snuck up behind her and snatched the floor away.

"I'm listenin', Red."

By the time Red finished telling her his fantastic tale, she didn't know if she wanted to dance in the moonlight or help him die.

He was the cause of her parents' breakup. All this time…

"I made your mother a promise that I'd never tell you.

And I figured, after all the trouble I caused between her and your father, the least I could do was honor her request. But now…now it don't matter much no how. I 'spect I'm 'bout done for."

"No!" she said, feeling the strength slipping from his hand with every second that passed. "I just found you. I just—"

Her words choked off with sobs. God wouldn't be so cruel as to take away her grandfather just when she'd found him.

"Red—"

"Shut up!" he said. "You're just like your mother. Always want to control things. Well, there's some things you can't control. And you best learn that quick. Now, that Brax fella, you can't control him, either, or the way you two feel about each other. So stop tryin'. Just give in to it."

"Red… Grandpa…"

Oh, God. Did Red smile? She'd never seen his mouth so wide. Tears rolled down their faces at the same time. The happiness overwhelmed her.

"I messed up one couple. If I can fix another one, I aim to do it. Now, do you love that man?"

"Yes," she whispered, too choked up to speak loudly or clearly.

"Then forget that damn curse!" he said, nearly sitting up in the bed. A coughing fit broke him down and forced him back onto the bed, almost doubling him in half. Ariana patted his back gently until he recovered.

Red closed his eyes for the last time after that. Ariana took his hand and held it firmly in her own. Twenty minutes later, Red Finley, her grandfather, died.

Chapter 23

On the morning of Red's funeral, the sun broke the clouds like a rider on a bronc. The cloudless sky stayed clear, hot and very blue. About a hundred folks, more than the entire town, turned out to pay respect and remembrance to Red Finley.

Ariana stood in front of them all, telling herself it was the heat making her sweat. Not nerves. Not disappointment. Not regret. Not anger. Certainly not anger.

They all waited for her at the top of that hill, the place she'd come so often to remember family.

Well, now that family, or her memories about it, would never be the same.

How long had she been standing there? One minute? Five? Fifty? She'd been so strong when her grandmother passed. Even when her mother died, she'd given the eulogy and led the mourners in "Amazing Grace."

So, why had the end of the crotchety old man, gray, wrinkled, foulmouthed and skinny, stunned her mute?

"Ari?" Selena said, moving to her side and rubbing her arm. "You okay? You want me to do it?"

"No," she said under her breath. She didn't want her kid sister to have to do any more ranch things or any bad incidents with men things. The curse had gone on too long.

It wasn't just the sun she felt blinded by right then. Part of her life had blinded her, too. From her mother, to Red, to her sister. Even to Brax. Had she ever really seen anything clearly?

To her right, a blue jay called. Down and to her left, a cricket chirped from a place that was always pitch-black.

The big tree cast a long shadow beside her. It stretched far and deep into the valley, its uppermost branches touching the edge of the pasture. The maple had brought shade over her family's final resting place for close to one hundred years. Part of her hoped it would for another one hundred.

Mustard flies swarmed like a double helix over a dry sagebrush. The big wide leaves of a nearby oak brushed together in the cool breeze and sounded like soft running water.

Tony joined Ariana. He seemed to be holding her up. Had she fallen? she wondered. She couldn't feel her knees. She'd known that for some time. But why was Tony taking her aside when all she needed to do was to say a few words?

"Six years ago, I buried Mama," she struggled to say. She didn't want to say those words. Hadn't planned on saying them. But they're what came out when she opened her mouth.

"And now I'm burying my grandfather, who I knew…but…"

She was saying crazy things. Even seeing crazy things. Out of the corner of her eye, she would have sworn on a pile of new Bibles that she saw Brax, holding up an evergreen tree. Arms crossed, eyes large with concern.

Tony held Ariana in his arms. She didn't know he was strong enough, but he did it. He held her. What was she going to say anyway? No sooner had that thought entered her head than Ariana heard a voice. It sounded like hers, only less distraught. Just firm. Steady.

"The funniest thing I ever saw Red do was ride Three Socks after he'd been drinkin'. Red loved whiskey. But it didn't care much for him. So after the second shot or third, Red would usually be all but out cold.

"Red's mouth was as foul as you make 'em, and he was as mean as a rattlesnake, but he had the softest… softest heart of any man I knew.

"I'm going to miss him so b-bad."

Selena glanced skyward. Tears in her eyes sparkled like liquid crystals. "Red, wherever you are, I hope they serve Jack Daniels on the rocks."

Yes! Ariana thought. *That's exactly what I would have said and the way I would have said it.*

Six men from town, a couple of them good friends of Red's, picked up ropes to lower his casket into the ground. Ariana might not have a mind to talk, but she could move her arms and legs. She pushed away from Tony's caring hold.

"Let me," she said.

"And me," Selena said, heading toward the men.

"All right, make room," Tony said, joining them. And

together, Ariana, Selena and Tony joined Red's best buddies in helping Red to his final resting place.

Ariana helped lower the casket. She couldn't believe how light it was.

Chapter 24

Days passed in a blur of repairs to the Snooden home. Nearly everyone Ariana knew, and even some folks she didn't, pitched in to clean up the place and start rebuilding. Ariana came home every day smelling like smoke and soot and damp from hair to heel. Hank had recovered well and was helping out himself.

When she wasn't hauling trash or throwing out charred dry wood on the Snooden place, she was showing her property to buyers. Three new ones just this week had come by. But her stomach had done acrobatics every time she spoke to people. Finally, she gave in. That idea died when Red died. It had burned up in her just like the ranch house and exploded to cinder just like the young trees surrounding it.

It took the death of her grandfather for her to realize that her whole life and identity was on the Sugar Trail.

Her past was there and so was her future. She finished dressing that morning, sure of what she was doing for the first time since her mother passed.

She knew her destiny was on the land, and before breakfast she would tell Selena and Tony that very same thing.

She marched down the stairs and the image of Brax leaning over a steaming cup of coffee while straddling a chair in the kitchen flared up in her mind. Every morning since he'd left, she'd had that same expectancy—to come down the stairs, walk around the corner and see him, smell him, be engulfed by the heat of him. And for the past two weeks, when the image disintegrated like a dry leaf, she found herself profoundly sad and strengthless. Life on the ranch without Brax had been as hard as burying Red.

"I'm not selling," she said, even before she got downstairs good.

"Whoo-hoo!"

"Well, there is a God!"

Ariana stopped in her tracks. "Wait a minute. You didn't want me to sell?"

"Nah."

"No way!"

Ariana steadied herself by placing a hand on the kitchen counter but knew it would take more than formica to quell her surprise and get her confusion in check.

"Tony, I thought you wanted a rodeo gig. And, Selena, I thought you were looking forward to life in the city."

"What did I say months ago when you came up with this idea?" Tony asked, piling a plate high with eggs and fried potatoes.

"You said you thought I was crazy," Ariana answered, taking a seat.

He put the steaming hot plate in front of her. "Umm."

Never one to let her food get cold, Ariana picked up a fork. "What about you?"

Selena offered a half smile, but her eyes were on full twinkle. "Well, I thought moving to the city was a good idea, until I spent some time there. I like it better here. And I was gonna tell you but then…Red…"

"Got it," Ariana said.

Tony fixed a plate for himself and Selena, then joined them at the table. "Red thought you were crazy, too. But we all know you are stubborn as a day-old mule and so, to go against you, well, it just never does any good. You always do what you want anyway."

Selena looked up from her plate. "You gonna tell Willows before he sends any more folks over here to look at the place?"

"Yep," Ariana said, smiling with a forkful of food in her mouth. "I'm gonna call him right after breakfast."

Ariana picked up the phone in the barn. She'd been putting it off for too long, but it was a conversation that she had to have. She'd made a decision and it was time to live up to it. But…calling the man. That was another trouble altogether.

After waiting several seconds for a dial tone, Ariana reflexively said, "Hello?"

"Ari. Hey. The phone didn't even ring."

Ariana's heart dropped. "Willows, I, I was just about to call you."

She knew Willows was counting on the sale of her property. Folks counted on each other round there. They depended on each other. They were connected like that.

Like joints. Each one helpin' and workin' the other so that they all could function.

Willows had probably already spent the commission in his head. Bought his daughter a new dress that she'd seen in a GAP catalog or bought his son a PS3 or a new pair of boots. Ready to take his wife, Matilda, to town for a twenty-five dollar supper at a fancy restaurant. One of those places where the waiter's tip could buy a Happy Meal.

She had to tell him face-to-face.

"Ari! Thank goodness!" he said when she entered Shoresville City Hall. She'd tiptoed in quietly, careful not to disturb Judge Shane.

"Sorry I'm late, Willows. I was arguing with myself all morning on the way down here. I've got some bad news for you, friend."

He stopped in his tiny tracks, but his face looked like it kept going. Bright and shining he blurted out his words.

"Well, I've got some *good* news for you! I've sold the Sugar Trail!"

"What? No! Willows? You can't...wait a minute. I came down here this morning to tell you that—"

"Can you believe it? The fella gave us everything we asked for. Sight unseen!"

Willows tossed a worn manila folder on the table between them. The contents slid out. Bank forms. Title and deed documents, bank statements and a cashier's check for half the cost of the ranch.

"Willows. No." Ariana knew the squirrels scurrying in her gut wouldn't settle down, so instead of trying to get control of them, she pressed on. "It's not for sale.

I've changed my mind. See...that's what I wanted to tell you. Willows...I'm keeping the Sugar Trail."

The hinge on Willows's bottom jaw came loose and the unlit cigar darkening the corner of his mouth fell to the floor. "When did this happen? No, never mind. It—it can't happen. Matilda's bags are already packed. I'm taking her to Denver for a week in the big city."

"I'm sorry. I'm sorry." Ariana's hands shook a bit. The squirrels got rambunctious.

It's not too late. I haven't signed anything, Ariana repeated in her head. She felt strangely anxious. "You'll have to tell 'em the property is off the market. I mean, I had a death in the family. My whole life changed since then. So you'll have to—"

"Not me! You'll have to. This fella doesn't look like he's on good terms with the word, 'No.'"

"Why, Willows, you tuckin' tail?"

"Yes! So, after you talk to the buyer, you can call my wife and tell *her.*"

"You think that'll soften the blow?"

"No. But she won't yell at you and by the time I get home, maybe she'll forget about yellin' at me."

Ariana had an itch to rub Willows's thick coppery hair. Instead, she settled for a handshake and a hug. "Well, Willows, you write the buyer's name and number down for me, and I'll call him soon as I get back."

The man collected the papers from the desk. "No need. He's waiting in the other room."

Ariana blinked in surprise. "Waiting? Why?"

"He said he wanted to be available when I came to you with the offer. When I asked him to come in he just said he'd wait in the next room."

Why would a man wait in another room unless he had something to hide? Ariana didn't like a dishonest man. She was glad she'd changed her mind. Otherwise, the ready cash in the folder might have coaxed her into the wrong decision.

"Come on," Willows said, holding the door open. "I'll...introduce you."

A familiar cologne caught the edge of her senses. She lassoed it like a runaway bronc and held it strong. Brax? Brax was here?

Willows pushed open the door for her and she stepped inside. It *was* Brax. But at the same time, it wasn't.

The man standing at the far side of the room staring out the wide window in all black was a hundred percent cowboy and all-beef rancher. She could almost smell the land on him. He stood striking, powerful, proud and a bit arrogant—like he'd just climbed down from a long ride on a big stallion.

She was tickled to see him. She'd missed him like biscuits miss gravy. And hot toast misses butter. Like the sun misses the sky.

Like a woman misses her man.

She placed her hand against her chest to feel her heart pounding. She smiled, relieved. It hadn't beat right since he left.

"Brax," she said, drawing his name out. Two syllables. It felt so good to say it.

"Hey, baby," he said, as if she'd never acted a complete and utter fool.

She gave him a long, hot, appreciative glance. "New boots?" she said.

"New everything," he responded and gave her a

striking and prideful smile. Ariana was so happy, she thought her heart would crack.

"I'm sorry. About Red," he said.

"Me, too. And I think that somehow, I knew. You know. Deep inside. I knew who he was. But I just couldn't say it. Couldn't see it. But I see everything now."

Her feet started moving before she could think good. She took five quick steps. Brax took two long strides and they were together, embraced tight, where they belonged.

His hard, warm body up against hers felt so perfect, she didn't know how she'd existed these weeks without that feeling. She hugged him tight. He felt delicious and she felt delicious against him. All she could say was, "Um, um, um!"

"Me, too, baby. Me, too."

He pulled her into the eager circle of his arms. Held her close. His heart beat heavily against her ear. Sweet music to her own heart. His hands locked around the curve of her back, and she felt secure. Forgiven.

His embrace took in more than just her waist. It took in everything they'd been through, especially what she'd been through recently with the gift and death of her grandfather. Her change of heart about the ranch, and the rift between the two of them. Hesitation flickered inside her like a silver flame.

"You sure you wanna take up with the likes of me?"

Her question was muffled and swallowed by his chest where she hung on for dear life, even as he pulled back just a bit.

"As long as I'm moving and the world goes by in a blur, I don't have to grapple with things like the fact that I don't have any roots or anchors in my life. That I don't have a clear lifeline. But out here, where sometimes all you can do is just sit down and acknowledge that out here, there's nothing to hide you from the eyes of God, well, a smart man makes choices. And I've made one, Ariana.

"It's you."

She held him tighter, her hands shaking at his waist.

"Look at me," he instructed, his voice penetrating like strong whiskey.

She did as he insisted. His gaze bored down into her. She trembled with its intensity. "What do you think? What do you *know*?"

"Brax—"

"Ariana...what does your heart say?"

"It says I love you, Brax Ambrose. And you love me!"

"I do, you know. With every part of my heart."

Willows shuffled papers across from them. "So, does that mean the deal goes through after all?" The hope in Willows's voice was unmistakable.

This time Ari pulled back a little. "Brax, you don't have to—"

"I want to buy it. *Have* to buy it. At least half of it. That's why I brought a check for half the amount."

"But where'd you get the money? With Uncle Jesse and all, I thought you were strapped."

"I was, until I sold my half of the trucking business to my brother."

Ariana's eyes widened as he got down on one knee. "Ari, I've been a rolling stone all my life. I thought that was what I wanted. Turns out, it's not even close."

Emotions rose inside Ariana and streamed down her cheeks.

"I want *you,* Ari. In the best place we should be. Right here. With your family. With *our* family."

At those words, Ariana knew he was talking about Red.

"Continuing a legacy. Starting a *new* family."

Ariana spoke through her tears. "Wh-what about the curse?"

Six degrees of separation, Brax thought. He called a friend who called a sister who called a friend. God bless Ashley Allgood for the hookup.

"I found a shaman. He's Pawnee. He's agreed to come and bless the land. Bless us."

Brax swallowed drily and stood. It was taking too long. She should have said yes by now. It was killing him and he could barely breathe. "Ariana, what does—?"

"It says yes. My heart says yes. I say, *yes!*"

Brax could not have braced himself for the force of Ariana's kiss. It was all woman and all Ariana. Wild. Unbridled. And as unrestrained as the storm they survived. Pressing against him, her body captured and surrendered to his at the same time. And the feeling said *home.* Her soft lips sucked his. Her tongue roamed freely inside his mouth. Explored every space. Found his tongue and mated. The force of the exchange left his legs wobbly like he'd slammed back two shots of Red's rotgut, golden whiskey.

He let everything in then. All the love he thought he'd never have and the permanent place he thought he'd never find.

For the first time, since he was three years old, Brax lived and breathed and understood the word *home.*

Chapter 25

It was a great day for working. The sun came up with a good temper. No angry rays punishing Brax Ambrose's arms. A line of thick, bright white clouds marched across the sky in big, overround shapes. The wind had gone into hiding as if the earth was holding its breath. Waiting.

"I feel like I'm going to fall," Honey said. Her grip wrapped around Brax's waist so tightly, he thought her arms might lock into place. She'd never been on a horse before and her unease and nervousness showed.

They rode out to the pasture, Brax, Honey, Ariana, Selena and Tony. The newest calf to the Sugar Trail was four months old. Time for branding and vaccinating. It was a small part of his life that Brax wanted Honey to see. He wanted to share his happiness with her. Give her some hope that if he could find it, so could she.

While Honey squeezed herself against his back, Brax pulled slowly on the reins. "Easy, Run Amok," he said. The stallion changed stride at once and came to a slow walk near the calf.

Brax brought Run Amok to a halt and patted his sister's arm. "You all right?" he asked.

Honey's grip loosened. She breathed a heavy sigh. Her breath warmed a spot on his back. "Yes. But I don't think I can get down."

"I got you, remember?"

"Okay," she said, voice shaky.

For the first time, Brax's all-woman sister sounded timid. Girlish. He thought it was a good sign. She put up a strong, brave front most of the time. Except for recently when her five-year beau, Cliff Watson, called it quits. That shook her up for a while. But she seemed like she was on the mend now. Which was why it was so important for Brax to bring her to his place.

He swung down easy, keeping Run Amok steady and making sure he didn't shake Honey off balance. Ariana, Tony and Selena looked on quietly. Brax reached up, steadied his wide-eyed sister by her waist. "Come on."

She took her time and got down gingerly. Brax kept a hold of her the whole time, lowering her beside the stallion with a gentle landing on the soft dirt. "See that, back on solid ground."

"Yes," she said, checking the area where her feet landed.

Brax knew she was looking for cow patties. Wouldn't want to get any natural fertilizer on those four-hundred-dollar boots she wore. He'd told Honey to dress down, but knew that was impossible. He didn't think his sister even owned a pair of jeans, let alone a T-shirt or anything fit for a dust-and-flies kind of life. True to her nature, she'd shown up in a formfitting white blouse, not much fabric but plenty of cleavage, tight black slacks, black leather boots, pointed and spiked, and Ray-Ban sunglasses. Her wardrobe probably cost as much as one of the Sugar Trail steers.

Honey swatted away a fly. Brax smiled at the frivolity. "There are some things, you just gotta let go."

"No way I'm gonna let that thing land on me. Out here, I know exactly where it's been." She spoke to him but her eyes glared in the direction of a mound, probably only a few hours old. Funny how Brax could almost tell time by the cattle droppings and thought nothing of seeing them.

He slung an arm around Honey's shoulders. "Come on. There's someone I want you to meet."

Brax opened a gate and they all entered the pen. Then he and Honey walked out a few yards to where a few cattle had broken off to graze. A young calf was closer than the others and looked up when they approached.

Brax took his sister's arm and led her inside the fenced corral where the cattle were grazing and mooing their content. His boots crunched the soft dirt and tufts of grass. Honey's heels barely touched the ground while she tiptoed as if landmines dotted the pen instead of manure.

"How can you live like this?" she asked.

"Funny," he said. "I said the same thing to you the last time I tried to navigate all the junk piles in your house to get from the living room to the kitchen to the—"

"And the smell," she said, wrinkling her nose.

"Smells like money to me," Brax chuckled. "To each

his own, right?" he said, grateful that he'd found *his* own. Hopeful that Honey would one day find hers.

A few of the Angus stepped away, but the calf kept staring. "This is Usher."

"You're kidding?" Honey said, chuckling.

He smiled. "Selena named her."

"Her?"

"She has a thing for unusual names. Ari keeps tellin' her to name horses, not cattle, but she won't listen. Anyway, you can call me Dr. Ambrose because I delivered Usher."

"You what?"

Brax tipped his hat to get a better angle against the sun that had just that moment decided to assert its authority. "You should have seen me. Covered from fingers to shoulders with blood and—"

Honey's face puckered. "Uauh!"

"I reached in, straightened the legs, put a calf puller around her ankles and pulled her out. I've been tendin' to her ever since. Stayin' with her. Watchin' her grow."

Brax grinned inwardly at the way he so easily tossed off the *g*'s at the end of some words. The words sounded better that way. Felt better to say. "I want you to know this is my life now. I want you to be happy for me. Support me."

Honey opened her mouth to speak. Before she could, Brax wanted to get his chore over with. "You all ready?"

Tony swung down from his horse.

Ariana took the lasso from the holder and gave Sirocco a soft kick. The horse trotted forward and the cattle began to disperse. In the movement, Ariana swung the lasso and whipped it toward Usher, catching her hind legs.

While Selena stayed on her horse and herded the rest of the cattle away, Ariana swung down from Sirocco and helped Tony move the calf toward Brax.

"Stay here," Brax said.

He went back to Run Amok, took a syringe as big as a caulking gun out of his pouch and walked to where Ariana and Tony worked to pull down the agitated animal.

The three of them finally got the calf on its side. It took all their strength to hold down the struggling clamor of jagged hooves and wailing calf.

Brax placed his left knee on the calf's neck for leverage and his other knee on the ground. Quickly, he popped the needle into Usher's neck right behind her ear and pushed the plunger down.

The calf squalled in protest, but the vaccination was over before it could become fully distressed.

Brax, Ariana and Tony got up together and backed away quickly.

The calf scrambled to its feet disgruntled and headed straight for the safety of the herd. Brax removed the tan leather work gloves he'd been wearing, brushed the soft earth from where it clung to the knees of his jeans and joined his sister at the edge of the corral.

He motioned to his new family. A quick nod meant *thanks.* "Give us a minute," he said.

Ariana nodded back, tossed him the sexiest smile on planet Earth and headed off to the house on Sirocco followed by Selena and Tony.

Brax escorted his sister out of the pen and closed the gate behind them. While she continued to check her designer boots for cattle duty, Brax propped a boot against the bottom rung of the gate and leaned against it. He stared out at the animals grazing, the land rolling and vast ahead of them, and wondered, when did the sky get *so* big?

"I'm at peace, Honey. Finally. I'm stuck down, just like that tree on the hill. My sweat's here. My blood." He tossed a glance at his future wife riding back to their home. "My love is here."

Honey flicked a fly from her blue-silk-clad arm. "I get it. Heck, I've never seen you so…so…put down. And I mean that in a good way."

Brax slid his hat back. Stared up. Took all that the sun had to offer. "I brought you out here because I love you and I want you to have what I have. A good life."

Honey checked the diamonds on her fingers as if to prove they hadn't fallen off. "I have a good life."

She said the words, but they came out flat and uninspired.

"You have chaos. And you're a grown woman. I can't keep coming to your rescue every time you and Cliff hit a bump in the road and you feel like you've been abandoned." He let go a smile as big and wide as the Sugar Trail. "Just so you know, I have every intention of getting Ariana pregnant as many times as she'll let me. God willing, I have a lot of baby makin' and child rearin' ahead of me. I'll be rescuin' my own, if you get my meanin'." He smiled so hard then, his face hurt. He couldn't help it. Thinking about a life with Ariana did that to him.

Honey smiled back. "That sounds nice, Brax."

"I guess I asked you out here to invite you to be a part of my new life, but also to say that you deserve to be happy and whatever happened to you in the past, if you let it go, I think you can be."

Honey didn't say much from that moment on. Brax didn't expect her to. He knew his words needed to sit with her awhile. Marinate. He loved his sister, as if they'd grown up together and known each other all their lives. And he wanted her to understand something important: If love could save his soul, it could save hers, too.

They walked toward his horse and Brax's heart swelled with a happiness he'd never known. He was standing on his own land. On his way to the woman he loved.

For the first time in his life, Brax Ambrose, the rolling stone, had found a place to lay his hat forever.

Dear Reader,

Thank you for reading *Ever Wonderful.* I hope you had as much fun reading it as I had writing it. The story line for this novel was inspired by some research that I did on African Americans in western Nebraska. Back when the Exodusters left the south, many migrated to my neck of the woods, settling the prairie, opening doors to the west, making their mark as cowboys and cowgirls and homesteading the land. There were even a few all-black towns in Nebraska at that time. Inspired by some of the women of that time, I created Ariana's backstory and a modern legacy for her character.

For those of you who've read my most recent novels, *With Open Arms* and *Chemistry,* you'll remember Brax and know that his story has a dotted line to my Allgood Series. Thank you for all of your fabulous e-mails. Brax finally has his story. Right now, I'm hard at work on his sister Honey's story. This novel, tentatively titled, *Sweet Like Honey,* will be released sometime in '08, so please stay tuned.

In the meantime, drop me a line at mskimlouise@aol.com or visit my Web site at www.kimlouise.com and let me know what you think of *Ever Wonderful.* I did everything in my writing power to make sure that Brax's story was worth the wait.

Until next time, peace and blessings!

Kim Louise

DON'T MISS THIS SEXY NEW SERIES FROM
KIMANI ROMANCE!

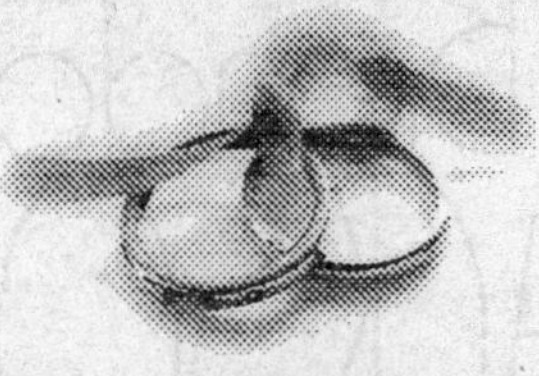

THE LOCKHARTS
THREE WEDDINGS & A REUNION

For four sassy sisters,
romance changes everything!

IN BED WITH HER BOSS by Brenda Jackson
August 2007

THE PASTOR'S WOMAN by Jacquelin Thomas
September 2007

HIS HOLIDAY BRIDE by Elaine Overton
October 2007

FORBIDDEN TEMPTATION by Gwynne Forster
November 2007

KIMANI ROMANCE™

www.kimanipress.com KPBJ0280807A

From boardroom to bedroom...

Brenda JACKSON

In Bed with Her Boss

Though D'marcus Armstrong is a demanding, cranky boss, he's the star of Opal Lockhart's fantasies. But what chance does a buttoned-up, naive secretary have with this self-made millionaire? A pretty good one actually...when Opal's sisters come to the rescue with a makeover and some attitude adjustment!

THE LOCKHARTS

THREE WEDDINGS & A REUNION

Available the first week of August wherever books are sold.

KIMANI ROMANCE™

www.kimanipress.com

KPBJ0280807

Wanted: Good Christian woman

***ESSENCE* BESTSELLING AUTHOR**

Jacquelin THOMAS

The Pastor's Woman

New preacher Wade Kendrick wants a reserved, traditional woman for a wife—but he only has eyes for Pearl Lockhart, aka Ms. Wrong. Pearl aspires to gospel stardom and doesn't fit into the preacher's world. But their sexual chemistry downright sizzles. What's a sister to do?

THE LOCKHARTS

THREE WEDDINGS AND A REUNION

FOR FOUR SASSY SISTERS, ROMANCE CHANGES EVERYTHING!

Available the first week of September wherever books are sold.

KIMANI™ ROMANCE

www.kimanipress.com

KPJT0320907

Grown and sultry...

Then Comes Love

CANDICE POARCH

As a girl, Jasmine wanted Drake desperately, but Drake considered his best friend's baby sister completely off-limits. Now Jasmine is all grown up, and goes to work for Drake, and he's stunned by the explosive desire he feels for her. Even though she still has way too much attitude, Drake finds himself unable to resist the sassy, sexy beauty....

Available the first week of September wherever books are sold.

KIMANI™ ROMANCE

www.kimanipress.com

KPCP0330907

The follow-up to *Sweet Surrender* and *Here and Now...*

Straight to the Heart

Bestselling author

MICHELLE MONKOU

Fearful that her unsavory past is about to be exposed, hip-hop diva Stacy Watts dates clean-cut Omar Masterson to save her new image. But their playacting backfires when their mutual attraction starts to burn out of control! Now Stacy must fight to keep the secrets of her past from destroying her future with Omar.

Available the first week of September wherever books are sold.

KIMANI™ ROMANCE

www.kimanipress.com

KPMM0340907

He was the first man to touch her soul...

SOUL *Caress*

Favorite author

KIM SHAW

When privileged Kennedy Daniels loses her sight, hospital orderly Malik Crawford helps heal her wounds and awaken her desire. But they come from different worlds, so unless Kennedy's willing to defy her prominent family, a future between them is impossible.

Available the first week of September wherever books are sold.

KIMANI ROMANCE™

www.kimanipress.com

KPKS0350907

Essence **bestselling author**

DONNA *Hill*

She's ready for her close-up...

Moments Like This

Part of the Romance in the Spotlight series

Actress and model Dominique Laws has been living the Hollywood dream—fame, fortune, a handsome husband—but lately good roles have been scarce. Then she learns that her business-manager husband has been cheating on her personally and financially. Suddenly, she's down and out in Beverly Hills. But a chance meeting with a Denzel-fine filmmaker may offer the role of a lifetime....

Available the first week of September, wherever books are sold.

ARABESQUE®

www.kimanipress.com

KPDH0190907

Sometimes life needs a rewind button...

USA TODAY BESTSELLING AUTHOR

KAYLA Perrin

Love, Lies & Videotape

On the verge of realizing her lifelong dream of becoming an actress, Jasmine St. Clair is suddenly embroiled in a sex-tape scandal, tarnishing her good girl image. Desperate to escape the false accusations, Jasmine heads to the Caribbean and meets Darien Lamont—a sexy, mysterious American running from demons of his own.

"A fine storytelling talent."
—*The Toronto Star*

Available the first week of August wherever books are sold.

ARABESQUE®

www.kimanipress.com

KPKP0160807